"For any kid who thinks no one else gets it, this is the book you want. Hunter and Corin are two kids simultaneously leading each other to the edge and pulling each other back. Friendship, defiance, dark humor—all the tools of survival and escape are in Kyle T. Cowan's novel. *Sunshine is Forever* wryly shows that happiness isn't just in the bright spots. It's there to be found in the midst of hard times, too."

—Anthony Breznican, author of *Brutal Youth*

"There are summer camp stories and then there are *summer camp stories*. Cowan has managed to rip off the Band-Aid to show us the darker side of being a teen in today's world. At times hilarious and heartbreaking, *Sunshine is Forever* is a powerful YA debut."

—Kari Luna, award-winning author of *The Theory of Everything*

"*Sunshine is Forever* is surprisingly relatable. Keeps you on the edge of your seat! Very suspenseful."

—Amber Portwood, author of *Never Too Late*, reality star of *Teen Mom OG*

"Kyle T. Cowan's *Sunshine is Forever* bravely reveals the story we all must hear, but are all too often afraid to tell: the human experience. Using humor and pain, Cowan bares the emotional essence of his writing with such honesty, that we are moved to self-revelation in the end."

—Lew Temple, actor in *The Walking Dead*

"Kyle T. Cowan's *Sunshine is Forever* is a powerful examination of teenage angst, sort of a *One Flew Over the Cuckoo's Nest* for young Millennials. This is a tough story, but it's also one that's filled with hope. A wholly impressive debut."

—Jason Pomerance, author of *Women Like Us*

"*Sunshine is Forever* is a beautifully raw depiction of the human condition, unabashedly showing the heart's ability to not just survive, but truly thrive. Cowan teaches us that no matter the depths of our darkest depression, so long as we have an open heart of honesty, forgiveness, and self-accountability, light and love will return—for sunshine is, indeed, forever."

—Jamison Stone, author of *Rune of the Apprentice*

"The greatest strength of *Sunshine is Forever* is author Kyle T. Cowan's dedication to unflinching honesty. Every single one of his characters is raw and flawed and the more relatable for it. Through this lens, Cowan is able to capture the doubts, desires, and dizzying heights that come with youth. *Sunshine is Forever* is a tale of self-discovery that reminds us all that we are whole, ever-changing, and perfectly imperfect."

—Brooke Wylie, critic at We Write Things

KYLE T. COWAN

A NOVEL

SUNSHINE IS FOREVER

Published by Inkshares, Inc., San Francisco, California
www.inkshares.com

Edited by Matthew Harry | Philip Sciranka | Pamela McElroy

Cover design by Xavier Comas | Interior design by Kevin G. Summers

ISBN: 9781942645627
e-ISBN: 9781942645634
Library of Congress Control Number: 2017938048

First edition

Printed in the United States of America

For siblings

ONE

LIFE AND DEATH are a series of stupid miscalculations.

You'll see what I mean.

My parents love to remind me that I was their "Little Accident." Meaning that my father was either too drunk to wear a condom, or whatever birth control they were using failed. However you break it down, my birth was a stupid miscalculation.

Every choice can result in something unfortunate, and that's exactly what I'm talking about. Every time I find myself at a crossroads, I choose the wrong path. And if I'd just been doing what I was supposed to have been doing on the day when I made the biggest mistake of my life, none of this would have happened, and I'd still have . . .

Look, I'm not sure what's important to you and what's not. You probably want my name.

I'm Hunter Samuel Thompson. Not to be confused with the much more famous Hunter S. Thompson. I'd like to tell you that I'm just a normal teenager who goes to parties and enjoys them, that I don't mind leaving the house, that I don't take so much Prozac that I practically piss tranquility, and that I have friends, lots and lots of friends. But if I told you all that stuff, I'd be full of shit. Being weird is bad enough; I'd rather not be full of shit, too.

I've been to exactly one party in my entire life. I lasted until about 8:15 p.m. We played a game of "Truth or Dare"—which is just about the dumbest game ever created, right? No one actually tells the truth in that game. No one but me—another stupid miscalculation.

Evidently it's strange not to be circumcised. I don't know why I'm telling you this, after all the weird looks I got at the party—yeah, kinda like the one you're giving me right now.

You don't have to write all this down, do you?

Let me start over. The truth is that I spend most of my time sitting around—alone—munching on Cheetos and playing video games. I've always had the hairiest legs in my class, and I'm exactly five foot six and three-quarters. Yes, the three-quarters matters to me. I have striking blue eyes—or so I've been told by every old lady I've ever met—but it doesn't make much of a difference because I'm short, stocky, have somewhat of a unibrow, and I'm equipped with small hands, big feet, and tiny teeth. No, I'm not a hobbit. But I am a virgin. You might as well know that, because it's kinda important to why we're sitting here together like this. And I'm also one of the most insecure people on the planet. But you probably already figured that out for yourself.

Here's another thing you should know: like most guys my age, I used to be absolutely desperate to lose my virginity—that's the only reason I tried going to that party in the first place—that's the reason all of this happened. Sex is supposed to be the best thing in the world. Sex releases endorphins. And endorphins make us happy.

Sex seemed to be the perfect cure for my depression—the only cure.

What can I say? I'm still depressed. I've been staring at my shoe-laces ever since I learned how to tie them. My depression used to be manageable, in a load-him-up-on-happy-pills-so-he-can't-ever-keep-a-boner kind of way. But after The Incident, everything got worse, and I'm not sure if it will ever get any better.

Told you I was weird.

It used to be that when I wasn't playing video games, you could usually find me hanging out with my girlfriend, Stoner Claire. Stoner Claire didn't know she was my girlfriend. Then again, Stoner Claire didn't know a lot of things.

When I think of Stoner Claire, I think of us sitting on her bed in the afternoon, while her parents were still at work, as she rolled weed in a wide brown cigar wrapper—she called it a blunt. She would suck on the blunt slowly, holding the smoke deep in her lungs, closing her eyes. She wouldn't move or speak as she puffed it from her lips like a car with a busted radiator on the side of the road. When she opened her eyes, I always wanted her to see something different—someone more attractive. But she would just pass the weed to me and whisper "maaaaan" under her breath, real slow like that, in appreciation of something I didn't understand until I began to smoke it, too.

We weren't exactly *in love*. But like most awkward kids who are lonely and want a girlfriend, I would have done anything to get Stoner Claire to like me—to have sex with me. So I turned into a total stoner to try to gain her acceptance. I'd smoke weed five times a day, and I started to really like it. I even named my bong—Lola. But drugs are what got me into even more trouble. So, after The Incident, I quit doing them altogether.

Okay, sorry, I'm rambling, I know. But I promise, all of this led to what happened. See, to tell this story, I have to go back to three days *after* the worst day of my life—after The Incident—when Dick was driving us home in his black BMW. I was sitting in the back, and Patricia had taken the front passenger seat. Dick is my dad. Yes, that's his real name, and yes, he looks exactly like a penis, especially when he yawns. Either way, stop picturing it. And Patricia is my harpy of a mother—more on her later.

So, we were all in the car and Harpy Patricia kept sniffling to make me feel even guiltier, as if I didn't already feel bad enough. She wore this loose black dress that she hadn't worn since my first Communion—she used to try to force us to go to church on Sundays, but like most battles, she eventually lost that one, too. Her roots were coming through at the base of her dyed hair, even though, like most rich housewives, her hairdresser was her best friend.

Dick had been so busy at the hospital that he didn't even have time to get his wrinkled black suit dry-cleaned. He was too lazy to dye his gray hairs, or have anyone else do it for him. He was even too preoccupied to shave. He looked like a homeless person who'd found a funeral director's suit in a dumpster. In case you don't know, sur-geons are way too busy for almost everything, including their fami-lies. But they always find time to tell you that they're surgeons, and to talk about how important they are.

I stared out the window as the hills streaked by, thinking about how the gloomy day reflected my mood. I felt like my brain had turned off, like the world was passing me by. I wanted it that way. The Incident had turned all the people in my life into emotional wrecking balls. They had all taken their swings at me. I could see them coming but couldn't get out of their way. And they kept at it until there wasn't much left of me to wreck.

We spent the entire car ride back from the countryside in silence and sniffles. I had planned on saying something, but I had no idea what. I didn't even know if I *could* say anything. My vocal cords were tied in a knot. And it felt like there was a noose tied around my stomach.

The tall buildings of the city came into view at dusk. The sky turned purple and the metropolis ignited into a thousand stars—which would have been a beautiful sight to a normal person.

But I'm not normal.

We sped across the bridge, over the expanse of the deep blue lake. The rivets in the road caused the car to bounce in a perpet-ual rhythm.

My house is located in a quiet neighborhood just outside the city—it snows a lot in the winter and rains just as much in the sum-mer. We live in a big house—the type fit for a person of Surgeon Dick's stature. The house is excessive—it has gigantic windows, a four-car garage, multiple peaked roofs, and a brick exterior. To put it into perspective, on the very rare occasion I invite people over to my place, they often tell me it feels like they're entering a castle.

Too bad this castle is always completely empty.

When we got home, Harpy Patricia went straight for the master bedroom, and Surgeon Dick went straight for the liquor cabinet. I sat at the kitchen table with my back to the swimming pool to eat a bowl of Corn Flakes. My dad brought his whiskey to the kitchen and sat across from me at the table. The golden flakes rang through the air as they crashed into the empty bowl. The milk splashed like rain. And with each crunch, I broke through the deafening silence.

My dad just sat there, sipping his glass of whiskey, staring out at the pool through the sliding glass doors. Then he turned to glare at me. I avoided eye contact, because I knew the guilt would return if I looked into his eyes.

After a bit, Surgeon Dick asked, "What?"

"I didn't say anything."

"Oh, you don't have anything to say?" Surgeon Dick asked.

I couldn't think of a single thing to say that he would want to hear as he stared into my eyes as if he were searching for my soul. I wanted to tell him it wasn't my fault. That Harpy Patricia shouldn't have left me alone that day. That if Surgeon Dick didn't work so much, none of this would have ever happened. But instead, I bit my tongue. And Surgeon Dick winced at his whiskey.

My stomach was on the floor at this point, hanging from the noose. I had lost my appetite. So I got up, rinsed out my dish, and escaped to my bedroom.

I could stare at a ceiling fan for hours.

That night was no different. I'd been lying on my back for hours, gripping my limp dick, watching as the fan slowly twirled around and around. I'd been trying to jack off, because that sort of thing is supposed to make you feel better. I'm not sure if my dick was so limp because of my medication, or because of how guilty I felt after The Incident. Either way, I was tired of failing at something that every other sixteen-year-old guy does five times a day—even on a day like that day. I closed my laptop and buttoned my pants.

Then, as Dick got ready for bed, my parents started to have the same fight they'd had every night since The Incident.

Harpy Patricia bawled, "I can barely look at him. After what he did!"

It wasn't my fault.

Surgeon Dick protested, "He's our son. What do you expect me to do with him? Toss him out on the street? Patricia, he's our son."

Ughhhhhhhhhh. Just kill me. Please, if I'm this terrible, just kill me.

My heart started to race. And I could feel my face getting hot. I wanted my parents out of my life. Surgeon Dick should have wrapped his tool on the night of my conception. They should have just aborted me.

Harpy Patricia snapped, "I wish he was gone."

Wish granted.

I picked up my phone to text Stoner Claire.

You awake?

Then I placed the phone facedown on my chest and waited for a response.

The fight continued. . . .

Surgeon Dick argued, "You don't mean that."

Yes, she does.

I felt like a piece of shit. I *was* a literal piece of shit. I was a waste of space in this family. Thankfully, my parents were always there to remind me of these things.

Harpy Patricia asserted, "I swear to God, I do."

Told you.

I knew that they'd be better off without me—I knew that I'd be better off without them.

My phone beeped on my chest. I picked it up to see that I had received a text message back from Claire.

Yeah. Why?????

K.

I jumped up from my bed and made for the window. It screeched through the dead air as I forced it open.

Surgeon Dick declared, "I can't talk to you when you're like this."

And that was my cue to jump out the window.

Don't worry—I didn't try to kill myself—my bedroom is on the first floor.

It was foggy that night. I needed to clear my head. I felt like I could breathe again as I walked under the beams of the streetlights that were visible in the mist. And it took less than five minutes to get over to the adjacent neighborhood where Claire lived.

I stepped off the sidewalk and onto Claire's lawn. My one pair of dress shoes sank into the muck as I trekked across the squishy grass. My heartbeat started to race as I stared at Claire's two-story Victorian house. It was after ten on a Sunday night, so the house was completely dark, but I didn't care. I had to talk to someone who cared about me. I picked up a pebble and tossed it at her window. The breeze picked up as I waited for her light to come on. It didn't, so I picked up another pebble and tossed it. Nothing.

I'm not joking. I literally threw two pebbles before I remembered that I don't live in an eighties movie. I pulled out my cell phone and dialed Claire. My heartbeat raced even faster.

What if she rejects me?

The phone buzzed three times before she picked up.

Claire's voice croaked, "What?"

"I'm outside" was all I said before I hung up and pocketed my phone.

Claire's lights flashed on, turning her house into a beacon on the dark street. She peered through the glass, and my stomach lurched as I held up one of my hands to wave hello. When she opened her window, smoke gusted from her room, forming a cloud that rose in the cool air.

Stoner Claire took pride in always being high, even before bed—her parents were completely oblivious to everything, even the smell of weed constantly radiating out of her bedroom. Her bloodshot eyes made her look like the undead. Her pale cheeks glowed like moonlight, and her frizzy brown hair exploded from her head. She definitely wasn't the model type, but neither am I.

"What, man?"

I didn't like her tone. I suddenly realized that she wasn't going to give me what I needed, but, desperately, I asked anyway. "Can I come up?"

"Not tonight, Hunter."

She was treating me just like my parents did. Maybe Claire hated me, too.

I felt like an ant being slowly crushed under a foot.

"Actually, not ever again. I can't even look at you, man," she added.

Splat!

Claire didn't understand. How could she? She wasn't there on that day. She didn't have to live with Surgeon Dick and Harpy Patricia. I wasn't the monster she thought I was, but I had no way of convincing her of that fact. I knew, at that moment, I was destined to be alone—and a virgin—forever. And that was the worst realization of my life.

And then she continued, as if she hadn't already said enough. "I don't know how you can come here on a day like today and act like nothing happened."

She took a slow rip from her bong so her words had time to really sink in. I could hear the bubbles popping in the glass base as my mind blew up with despair. I tried to think of a reply as I watched her suck in the smoke, the red ember in the bowl glowing brighter.

I wanted to tell her that I needed her. That even if she didn't love me back, I just needed someone to show me that I mattered.

Claire exhaled the hit as she waited for me to say something. It became clear to her that I didn't have a response. "I don't know what else to say. I'm sorry. Go home, man. Get some sleep."

And with that, she closed the window on our relationship forever. She turned off the light and left me in the darkness on the lawn.

I ran home, grabbed my keys from my bedroom, and got into my car. My parents were already asleep, and I knew there was absolutely no way they would hear me leaving—the garage is on the opposite side of the house. I started the engine and floored it.

I wasn't sure where I was going or what I was doing. It started to rain, and the droplets left trails across the windshield as I sped down the highway. I waited for a cop to pull me over, for someone to stop me from what I was about to do, as I exited the highway and ran a stop sign. I don't believe in God, but that would have been a good time for him to swoop in and save me from myself. But there was no flash of light from the sky. And no police lights from behind as I wove through traffic toward the exit. There was just me and my choices.

I pulled into the parking lot of a ShopMart and drove behind the building where the loading docks were.

This was it—the end.

The idling car's engine purred as I stared at the cinder block wall. I expected the tears to come. I wanted to cry, to feel sad, to feel angry, to feel *something*, but I didn't feel anything. Nothing mattered. I didn't matter. My parents didn't matter. What happened didn't matter.

They were right about me—I knew that I was a terrible person. It felt like thousands of pins were prickling every inch of my skin as I came to terms with what I was about to do. My mouth felt chalky, but I didn't want water. I didn't want, or need, anything anymore.

We come into life alone. And we die alone.

At that moment, I was more alone than I had ever been.

I pressed the pedal to the floor, slammed the car into drive, and peeled out toward the wall. The last thing I remember was the sound of metal slamming into concrete, and the airbag going for a knockout punch.

Another stupid miscalculation—I should've disabled it.

After that, everything went black.

TWO

THANKS TO THREE stupid miscalculations, I'm still alive.

In case you didn't catch that: I became suicidal after The Incident, ever since I lost everything—ever since a noose tied itself around my stomach, tightening its grip every single day. No, I don't want you to feel sorry for me. At the time, I didn't want to talk about my feelings, and no, I definitely wasn't okay. The truth is that I might never be okay.

After the first attempt, I woke up in a hospital bed with a ton of stitches and bandages wrapped around my head. The peach-colored wallpaper was peeling. The air smelled like moldy cheese. And the plastic cover on the mattress farted every time I moved.

I could hear Surgeon Dick's muffled voice as he fought with Harpy Patricia on the phone in the bathroom. He had the door closed, but his hushed words still echoed through the vents.

"Patricia," he pleaded, "don't be so cold. Please, show some empathy." Surgeon Dick paused as Harpy Patricia belittled him on the other side of the phone. "Do you want to lose him? Do you?"

She did—I promise you—she wanted me dead.

Friends and family of people who commit suicide consider it their own personal loss because humans quantify their existence by the number of friends they have, how big their family is, and how many material items they've accumulated. Humans calculate how successful or important they are based on those questions. An attempted suicide is a bruise to a family's permanent record. And a successful suicide—well, that's something that people will always whisper about around a family but never actually question the family about directly.

Surgeon Dick didn't really care about me. He cared about how it would look to the rest of the world if he lost me after The Incident. I was his failure, and the world would know it.

I felt totally worthless—I couldn't even commit suicide without causing a fight. My skin went so cold, I thought I would never know what it felt like to be warm again.

Surgeon Dick exited the bathroom with his head hanging toward his fat gut. He noticed that my eyes were open. "You're awake?"

Yeah. Unfortunately.

Surgeon Dick fidgeted. "You couldn't hear all that with your mother, could you?"

I'm not deaf.

Surgeon Dick's cell phone lit up like a game show buzzer to save me from having to listen to another explanation of why my parents hated me so much.

"Sorry, I really have to take this. It's important."

As if I cared.

But I did care. I wasn't a priority in my parents' lives. And that caused me to feel the worst pain of all. My brain throbbed as if it were pressing against my skull. I forced myself not to show that I was bothered. I was tired of constantly fighting a battle that couldn't be won—my parents weren't ever going to love me again.

But things still got worse.

That was only the first time I tried to kill myself. I'll spare you the gruesome details of my next two attempts, but let's just say that they involved short-circuiting the entire electrical system in the house by dropping ten appliances into a bathtub full of water at once—sounds foolproof, but clearly it wasn't—and digging a razor blade through the tendons in my wrists.

One thing I will say for Surgeon Dick is that he kept me company at the hospital every time. Even if he was on the phone, or asleep, he still showed up, and that's way more than Harpy Patricia or my therapist ever did. They never came to visit me in the hospital once. Not a single time.

Not all mothers are motherly, and not all therapists actually care.

Being on suicide watch doesn't help you feel better. It just makes you feel pathetic. A nurse comes in every hour to check on you. They strap you to the bed so you can't hurt yourself again, and someone has to come in to help you go to the bathroom—as if trying to kill yourself suddenly turns you into an invalid.

At the end of your watch, the doctor always comes in, holding the same file with your name on it. My file was bright red, and it was filled with at least thirty pieces of paper explaining my psycho diagnosis.

I guess you'll probably add your own report to that file when we're done.

The doctors always ask the same yes-or-no questions. "Do you feel safe in your home? Do you often feel sad? Are you taking your medication? Are you attending all of your sessions?"

Yes, I took my happy pill, but it couldn't turn back time. Of course I felt and still feel sad; that's why I kept trying to kill myself. And there is a difference between feeling safe in your home and feeling loved or even welcomed. And yes, I was going to therapy, but I hadn't said a word to my therapist since The Incident—honestly, I think she preferred it that way. I don't think she had a clue what to do with me after everything that had happened.

The last time the doctor asked those questions, I didn't even bother to answer. At that point in my life, it felt like my thoughts were drowning in a flood of emotions under a rain of neglect that I'd been feeling ever since the day I was born. I remember Surgeon Dick sleeping in a nearby chair as the doctor scolded me for trying to end my life.

"This is a serious situation, Hunter. You could really hurt yourself."

That was the point.

The doctor continued to speak, while Surgeon Dick continued to sleep. "We're recommending that your *father* . . ." The doctor really put emphasis on the word *father* so that Surgeon Dick would wake up.

It didn't work.

The doctor sighed and looked to one of the nurses to rouse Surgeon Dick. She awkwardly moved forward and gently nudged him.

That didn't work, either.

I shouted, "Dick! Get up!"

Surgeon Dick lurched to life. "I'm here. What's—" He stopped midsentence when he noticed us staring at him. He looked at his phone and asked Siri, "How long was I out?"

My whole life.

The doctor cleared his throat. "As I was saying, Dr. Thompson, I'm not sure we are getting through to your son with our usual approach. Therapy doesn't seem to be working for him. Although he's taking his medicine, that doesn't seem to help, either . . . ."

I really was taking my happy pill at the time of all of my suicide attempts.

". . . which is why I'm going to advocate something unusual. Dr. Thompson, I'm recommending that you put your son under the care of specialists for the summer."

Specialists?

"Here's a brochure," offered the doctor, handing me a glossy foldout titled CAMP SUNSHINE—THE HAPPIEST PLACE ON EARTH!

There were testimonials inside:

Camp Sunshine changed my life. I've made friendships that will last a lifetime.

Thank you, Camp Sunshine, for helping me see tomorrow.

I no longer want to die. Thanks, Camp Sunshine!

And in case those testimonials didn't convince you, the brochure also had "fun facts" about Camp Sunshine.

Fun fact #1: Camp Sunshine is the sunniest place on earth. That's because sunshine comes from the inside!

That was, like, two facts, but whatever.

Fun fact #2: It has been clinically shown that sunshine helps cure depression.

I imagined a bunch of depressed lab rats under tanning lamps.

Fun fact #3: Our sunshine experts know how to make your child happy.

Here's a fun fact for you: The edges on the Camp Sunshine brochure might have been just sharp enough to kill myself!

Fast-forward to a few weeks later: I found myself standing in Camp Sunshine's dirt parking lot—covered in sweat from the massive amounts of humidity—with a duffel bag at my feet.

As you already know, Camp Sunshine is a camp for depressed teens. I like to call it *Camp Suicide*. It's in the middle of Podunk, nowhere. Seriously, if you pull out a map of the United States, and point to a place where you would never want to go, that's where I was. The camp was in the center of a dense forest with barbed-wire fencing surrounding the perimeter. An archway over the gate to the entrance of the camp was painted like a rainbow.

Yes, a rainbow.

I waved good-bye. "See ya around, Surgeon Dick."

He was preoccupied, scrolling through the messages on his cell phone. "What?"

I sighed. He couldn't even take the time to *act* like he cared that his son was basically about to be institutionalized. Surgeon Dick cared more about a screen than his offspring.

"I said I'd see you around."

Surgeon Dick pocketed his phone. "You sure you don't have anything else you want to say to me?"

He always asked if I had something else I wanted to say to him. By then it should have been evident that I really didn't have much to say to my parents or my therapist, because they didn't have anything to say to me. I didn't respond—he didn't deserve a response.

Surgeon Dick smiled. I guess he was happy that I was finally going to be someone else's problem. "I really hope this helps you," he wished.

I shrugged. "Sure you do."

On cue, Surgeon Dick's phone started ringing again. He pulled it out of his pocket to glance at the screen. "It's the hospital; I have to take this. You're supposed to go straight to the dorm. You'll be okay from here, right?"

I was pretty sure the staff at Camp Suicide would probably frown upon him just deserting me in the parking lot.

"You should answer it," I said. "Someone might need you."

"Right," Surgeon Dick said as he opened the driver's door to his black BMW. I heard him say, "Hello," before the door slammed shut.

The BMW left a trail of dust as Surgeon Dick drove away. I picked up my bag and walked up the dirt path, through the gate, under the rainbow arch, and toward a bunch of log cabins.

And that's how my stupid miscalculations landed me in therapeutic prison.

THREE

I WISH I COULD say that Camp Suicide welcomed me with open arms.

By the time I stepped up the creaky wooden stairs of the boys' dorm, I was drenched in sweat from the humidity. I opened the flimsy screen door. The first thing I noticed was the thick steel door propped all the way against the wall. The door had keycard readers on both the inside and outside, next to the doorknobs. In other words, a person couldn't enter or leave the room without a magnetic key when the door was sealed. Comforting, I know. And there was this carved wooden sign engraved with the dorm's name—Ray—hanging just above the door.

The room smelled like my high school's locker room—wet dog and body spray. Bright sunlight pooled through five windows onto the dusty floor, as if that alone were supposed to make us feel happy. There were eight twin beds pushed up against the outer walls—five guys were already sitting on the ones closest to me. And there was a La-Z-Boy chair at the far end of the dorm, facing the door.

"Hunter S. Thompson! Welcome to Camp Sunshine! I'm C. Dermont, one of the counselors here in Ray!"

I heard C. Dermont's bubbly voice before I even saw his face. He appeared from the far corner of the room and bounced toward me as if he were in an animated film. He had very dark skin, moles on his cheeks, he was balding, and his hairy gut hung out from under a shirt that was at least two sizes too small for him.

C. Dermont reached out with his hand to say hello. "I've been waiting to meet the famous filmmaker."

I noticed the keycard attached to his belt loop, dangling out from under his stomach, before I reached out to grip his hand. "Author."

I've done my research on Hunter S. Thompson.

C. Dermont looked completely confused. "Author?"

"Hunter S. Thompson was an author and journalist whose works included *Fear and Loathing in Las Vegas* and *The Rum Diary*. Not a filmmaker. Annnnnd I've heard that joke about a thousand times."

I hated that joke more than I hated the smell of hard-boiled eggs.

C. Dermont didn't miss a beat. "Make that one thousand and one. I'll be checking you into our establishment today. Welcome to the sunniest place on earth! Or at least the sunniest place in Iowa."

Fun fact: If you pull out a map of the United States, and point to a place where you would never want to go, you'll probably end up in Sweaty Balls, Iowa.

"Prison?" I retorted.

"Camp Sunshine!" C. Dermont exclaimed.

I raised my eyebrows. "Yep. A prison."

C. Dermont smiled as he talked to me like I was a five-year-old. "No, a rehabilitation center for teens. We don't use the 'P-word' here at Camp Sunshine."

His stupid smile made me want to punch him in the face. I didn't want to be at Camp Suicide. No one in his or her right mind would choose to go to Camp Suicide.

C. Dermont continued, "We do great things here at Camp Sunshine."

He paused. I guess he was waiting for me to express my enthusiasm for being shipped off to the middle of a forest in Sweaty Balls Iowa.

"So why the rainbow over the entrance?" I asked. "Why not call it *Camp Rainbow* instead?"

"Because you can't have a rainbow without sunshine!" I didn't think it was possible, but C. Dermont's grin expanded.

I groaned. "Please just kill me now."

C. Dermont tittered nervously. "Oh, we don't say the 'K-word,' either." He paused. "Hunter the Author, grab your bag and follow me, my friend."

I mumbled just loud enough for him to hear, "I'm not your friend."

I really wasn't.

Reluctantly, I picked up my bag and followed C. Dermont down the center aisle between the beds.

C. Dermont continued to get me acclimated. "All right, so you'll be in bed six at the very end of the row, right next to me. Quint is in bed one."

I glanced at bed one, where a short, curly-haired sixteen-year-old boy sat on the edge of his bed playing a Nintendo DS with the sound off.

At least that one plays video games.

"Ash is in bed two."

Ash looked like he was older than the rest of us. He had acne-riddled skin and a medium build, and he was bouncing a racquetball against the ceiling.

"In bed three is Barry—I mean, *Blaze*."

Barry, who liked to go by Blaze, was around fifteen years old, tall, and kind of fat, and he stared at the wall in a subdued daze. I later found out that he got his name because he started smoking weed when he was eleven—his brain was already pretty fried.

None of the boys greeted or even made eye contact with me as I passed by, which immediately confirmed that this was absolutely going to blow.

"In four is Finley."

Finley was also sixteen. He was as thin as a twig, tall, and probably the most on-edge human being on the surface of the planet. He flinched as I passed by.

"In five is Wyatt."

Wyatt was around fourteen years old. He had tan skin, was short, and his face reminded me of a squirrel's.

C. Dermont stopped in front of my bed and spoke to me in a low whisper, as if he were telling me a secret. "Don't worry, the kids will introduce themselves again on their own."

Great. I was so freaking worried.

Then he laughed as if he had made a joke. Let me tell you something—C. Dermont was one of those guys who laughed at almost every single thing he said. He thought he was hilarious.

Fun fact: He was hilarious—just not in the way he intended.

"I'm Jim. I'm here to look out for your well-being."

Jim—the security guard—had appeared out of thin air and was now inches away from my neck. Seriously, he was always there, even when you thought he wasn't. He had this massive scar on the side of his cheek that ran down to his chin—some say he got it in Navy SEAL training; others say he was on a SWAT Team. Just kidding. No one ever said any of those things about Jim. The truth was that Jim was one of those power-hungry, washed-up, loser security guards who got off by flexing his muscles with what little power he actually had. He was in his late twenties, with short hair and a ripped body.

Jim ate his protein.

He twirled his keycard on its lanyard like it was a baton.

C. Dermont cleared his throat. "Right, so, now that you've met Jim, first things first. Empty out your bag on your bed."

How could have I confused this place with a prison?

I reluctantly picked up my bag and dumped my clothes, shoes, and toiletries on the surface of my bed. Jim snapped on a pair of latex gloves—like he was about to inject an enema into my ass—and pushed C. Dermont aside.

Jim never smiled—probably because he always had a massive dip in his mouth. He was the polar opposite of C. Dermont. He began, "Anything sharp in here or on your person?"

I didn't respond. The truth was that I didn't think a guy like Jim deserved a response. I hated authority figures. I hated this place. And I absolutely, positively, hated Jim.

Jim threatened me, "Listen, kid, this can go one of two ways. You can either obey me, or I put you in Mental."

Douche.

I glanced at C. Dermont, waiting for him to tell Jim to cool his jets. He didn't. Instead, he chuckled as he urged me, "It's best to respond."

Jim assured me, "It's my job to keep you kids safe."

I glared at both of them. "No."

Jim proceeded to lift a pocketknife from the pile of clothes. He held it up as if it were a dirty diaper. "Then what's this?" he asked.

I had completely forgotten about the pocketknife Surgeon Dick had given me before I left that morning. I know, you're probably questioning as to why the father of a suicidal teen would give a pocketknife to his son. Surgeon Dick may have gone to Harvard. He may have been one of the best neurosurgeons in the county. But just like Harpy Patricia, he had the parenting skills of Attila the Hun.

Jim continued to interrogate me. "You a liar, kid? You think you can get away with something?"

I hated being accused of lying. I quickly responded, "Surgeon Dick—my dad—gave it to me. I forgot it was in there."

I really did.

Jim raised both his eyebrows. "Sure you did. No razors in here? For shaving?"

The air suddenly escaped from my lungs. One of my stupid miscalculations came flashing back. I remembered breaking the plastic away from my razor, and digging the blade into my wrist. I cut horizontally instead of vertically—idiot. My eyes drifted to the floor.

"I don't have any razors," I said.

Jim stashed the pocketknife into a gallon-sized zip-lock bag before he sifted through the rest of my stuff. He picked up a pair of my plaid boxers, and C. Dermont awkwardly joked, "I'm more of a briefs man myself."

Think of the most uncomfortable experience of your life, then pretend like you had to experience it again, but without any sort of privacy or dignity—that's how I felt.

Jim confiscated my cell phone—not that I had anyone to call or text anyway—and my medication. He allowed me to keep my Nintendo DS and my game cartridges.

"At least you let me keep my video games," I said, relieved.

"Don't abuse that privilege. You're only allowed on your gaming device during downtime or Recreation," Jim explained.

There were thousands of spoken and unspoken rules at Camp Suicide—it would have been impossible to remember them all.

Jim glanced down at my shoes. "I'll need the laces."

How the hell would I kill myself with shoelaces?

I stared into his eyes. "Seriously?"

Jim nodded and gulped down some dip spit—I guess he thought he was too much of a badass to spit into a bottle like a normal person.

"You're the worst," I snapped.

"I'm good with that assessment," Jim noted.

And he really was—Jim was the type of person who liked to be hated. It made him feel powerful.

I sighed and bent down to untie my shoes. Jim reached out with his hand to receive the laces, and I dramatically yanked them from each shoe and tossed them onto the bed. Jim grabbed them and added them to the zip-lock bag.

"Great, now spread your legs and extend your arms."

Wait, what?

"Jim is going to pat you down," said C. Dermont as he stepped back. "It's just procedure."

I submitted. They would never convince me that this place wasn't a prison. Jim ran his hands up my legs all the way to my crotch—up to that point, that was the most action my little guy had ever gotten.

"Lift your shirt," he ordered.

I hesitated—now all of the guys were watching me. They were going to see my fat, hairy stomach. I felt totally embarrassed as I reluctantly lifted my shirt. I could feel the guys judging my looks—I'm not exactly *Biggest Loser* fat, but I'm stockier than most guys my age. Being stocky sucks because no matter how much weight I lose, I know I'll never look skinny.

"I'll need to take your belt as well," Jim said.

"My pants will fall down," I protested.

By this point, Jim was annoyed. "I guess a night in Mental sounds good to you." He sprayed some of his nasty dip juice in my face as he threatened me.

I sulked as I removed my belt and handed it over. I felt my pants sag down below the elastic of my boxers.

"That should do it," Jim said as he secured the belt in my zip-lock bag.

He scrawled my name across the surface of the plastic with a Sharpie, and tossed the bag on top of a small pile of other zip-lock bags, ready to be taken away.

C. Dermont's full smile returned to his face. "Make yourself at home."

And with that, I was all checked into prison.

FOUR

THE ROOM WAS so quiet that I could have heard a pin drop—that is, if pins were allowed.

C. Dermont sat in his chair staring at us, while Jim watched the room like a hawk. Anytime someone moved, everyone looked in that person's direction. The silence was totally unnerving, and it was making me have to pee.

I glanced at the clock ticking on the wall: 4:39 p.m.

I picked up the contents of my bag and stuffed everything into the small wooden drawer next to my bed. I never bothered to fold my clothes at home, either. It seemed pointless to me—you're just going to unfold them when you put them on.

I sat down on top of my bed. The wooden frame moaned like a wailing infant, and I noticed that everyone in the room was staring at me. I guess I'd made a lot of noise stashing all of my clothes into the drawer.

Oops.

I glanced at each of the boys. Squirrelly Wyatt looked like a wannabe gangster. Flinching Finley looked scared shitless of Squirrelly Wyatt. Blaze looked like, well, exactly like his nickname. And Annoying Ash looked like he played sports all day and drank a cup of milk before bed each night.

You probably guessed that I don't play sports.

My eyes stopped on Quint—the least intimidating boy there. He played video games; we had that in common at least. As long as he didn't play something lame like *Camouflage*, I knew that we would probably get along.

I could feel my bladder pressing against my abdomen. I wasn't sure if I was supposed to ask to go to the bathroom, or if there was some kind of specific protocol for that sort of thing. I decided to just try to wait it out. I thought maybe the feeling would dissipate once I calmed down.

My eyes returned to the clock: 4:40 p.m.

Time was moving in slow motion. Sitting in silence with two grown men watching your every move is one of the most unsettling experiences—the true definition of *cabin fever*. I tapped my foot on the floor until 4:41 p.m., and that was all I could stand. I had to go—right away.

I bounced up from the bed and over to C. Dermont.

Jim tensed as if I were about to commit a murder—he needed the Prozac more than I did.

The words spewed out of my mouth way faster than I intended; I was feeling pretty tongue-tied and nervous. "I have to go."

C. Dermont blankly stared at me, unsure how to respond.

Jim jumped at the opportunity to assert his authority. "Go? Go where?"

I shook my head and took a deep breath. This wasn't going well. Why did everyone always assume that I was up to no good? Had they all read my file?

My face got hot as I said, "I have to take a leak."

C. Dermont scolded Jim with a laugh. "Camp Sunshine isn't the 'P-word,' remember, Jim? Of course Hunter can use the restroom."

Jim flexed himself back into the corner and watched me.

C. Dermont turned back to me, explaining, "Jim used to be a corrections officer."

That explained everything.

"Of course he did." I laughed—even though it was really more scary than funny if you actually think about it. "So, where's the bathroom?"

C. Dermont bubbled up. "Here at Camp Sunshine, we call buildings by their names! So I'd prefer it if you'd ask, 'Can I go to the Rainmaker?' We call it the Rainmaker because—"

I stopped him there. "I get it."

C. Dermont beamed—his fat mole-infested cheeks pressed against his beady eyes. "No one at Camp Sunshine is ever allowed to be alone, even when they go to the Rainmaker. So you'll have to make a friend."

Ah, so I needed a pee buddy—that's not awkward at all.

"We are on a carefully calculated schedule to get you into a routine, and we cannot deviate from it. So, see if you can't quickly find someone to go with you."

"Um—okay," I said.

I could feel the contents of my bladder shifting as I rotated around to scan the room. I already knew who I was going to take with me—the kid with the DS. Quint was still engrossed in his game as I approached him—his big, crooked, oily nose was almost touching the screen.

"Hey," I interrupted.

Quint paused the game and looked up. "Hey."

"What are you playing?" I asked.

"It doesn't matter," he responded.

I would soon come to learn that nothing mattered to Quint. That was *his* problem.

I guess it was kind of my problem, too. Something told me we'd get along just fine.

"I'm Hunter. Wanna go pee with me?"

"Sure. I just died." Quint flipped his Nintendo DS shut.

I smiled with relief—maybe I actually had a shot at a normal life here. These guys didn't know about The Incident yet. "Cool."

I turned back to C. Dermont and exclaimed, "Found my Rainmaker Buddy!"

Yay.

C. Dermont laughed—he was seriously always laughing. "Way to go, my friend. Feels good to make another friend, doesn't it?"

Would have felt a whole lot better if Quint were a hot girl.

But yeah—it kind of felt good.

"Come right back for dinner and Campfire Orientation. Stick together."

Jim checked his military watch and added, "Hurry."

I pulled Quint out the door.

Even though the hot air immediately assaulted my senses, I felt like I could breathe again. The wind whistled through the pines, and the flowers pollinated the air. Compared to the cabin, the outside smelled like an air freshener. And the rays of sun warmed my face—no, none of that nature crap made me feel happy, but it was better than being in that room.

I stepped down from the stairs onto the dirt path that led away from the holding cell that I now called home. I searched for a sign leading the way to the Rainmaker. There were two other cabins in the distance, nestled in the trees, but they didn't look small enough to be the bathroom.

I joked, "That guy's really gonna make me want to kill myself by the end of this."

Quint didn't find my joke funny. His curly hair touched his eyebrows as he looked at me in all seriousness. "It's not like it matters."

I wasn't exactly sure what he meant by that, and I wasn't going to ask.

"This *place* is mental. Which way to the Rainmaker?" I asked.

Quint shrugged. "You actually have to go?"

"I don't lie, dude," I explained. "You'd think they'd have more signs pointing toward the different buildings here, but I guess that doesn't fit with the whole super-max prison vibe."

Quint chuckled. "Well, it's my first day here, too. I have no idea where the bathrooms are. I'm sure C. Dermont just forgot to give us directions. Should we go ask?"

"Naw, we'll find them. I don't want to interact with that guy any more than we have to."

"Agreed," Quint said as he started to push past me to lead the way.

I put out my hand to stop him. "Hold up."

And that's when I saw her. The girl who stopped my bladder. I mean, a lot of stuff can stop your heart: loud firecrackers, public speaking, bathing with electrical appliances. . . . But someone who can make you forget you have to pee is something else.

Yeah, I told you I was weird.

She looked like she didn't belong—like she had stepped out of a fairy tale. She walked with confidence. She had her bag slung over one shoulder. Her long dark-brown hair bounced off her back and down over her sapphire eyes. Her freckled cheeks shielded her rosy skin from the rest of the world. And her thin lips glistened in the sunlight. She was poised. Sexy. The type of girl I could never even imagine talking to—let alone dating.

I could feel myself getting really aroused for the first time in ages.

Maybe she could cure my depression.

My heart pounded out of my chest.

It felt good to be turned on again. It was exhilarating. I don't know why, but I immediately wanted to get to know her.

I wanted to know her name.

FIVE

"DUDE, I CAN totally see your boner," Quint said.

I quickly put my hand in my pocket and tucked my dick up under my waistband.

"You should stop drooling. It's not like you'll get the chance to use it here. Let's go find the bathrooms."

Quint dragged me along a path. Camp Sunshine was in the center of a dense forest. If you didn't know where you were going, it was easy to get lost. As we walked through the trees, I thought about the fact that I had never experienced a feeling like the one I had just felt in my entire life. Maybe that was what love at first sight felt like.

Then Quint had to go and immediately remind me that we were in prison—*what a douche.*

"I don't think we're going the right way," I pointed out. "We haven't seen any more cabins, and we've been walking for, like, five minutes."

"We probably aren't," Quint said. "But it's not like it matters. Nothing matters."

A dark silence set in as Happy Lake came into view. A ten-foot chain-link, barbed-wire-capped fence surrounded the perimeter of the small lake—I guess to prevent anyone from trying to drown in it. There were these massive gates placed about every fifty feet within the fence. The water was murky and green. And it smelled like fish as we got closer and closer.

The sight of the water made me really have to piss again—I couldn't hold it in anymore.

"Hold up," I said as I stepped off the path away from Quint.

I quickly unzipped my pants and relieved myself. I glanced over my shoulder to make sure that Quint couldn't see that I was uncircumcised, and I noticed that he had taken a seat in the sand with his shoes up against the fence.

"Where you from?" I asked.

Quint shrugged.

He was kind of being an asshole.

I was just trying to make conversation, but Quint wasn't the type of person you could immediately connect with. Quint didn't care about anything. I was getting the impression that he didn't care about relationships. People. Life. Or death. He didn't care at all.

"Okay," I said as I buttoned my pants and joined him in the sand.

Quint and I both watched our reflections dance in the ripples of the water through the chain links of the fence. Our faces were as blurry as the meds made our minds.

Quint explained, "Sorry. I just—I dunno. It just doesn't matter."

I joked, "Okay, Optimist Quint." I paused, waiting for him to say something. I don't think he found me funny. The tiny oily pimples on his cheeks glinted in the sunlight. I noticed a mosquito on his neck—suddenly, I felt like there were thousands of bugs crawling on my skin. "We should probably get back before we get devoured by mosquitoes."

I turned back to the water, where I could see a fish nibbling at something in the shallows.

"I saw the way you were looking at that girl. You a virgin?" Quint asked.

I thought of the day Stoner Claire told me she didn't have anything to say to me, and I felt like I was being choked. The noose around my stomach tightened its grip. Almost three months had passed since my first suicide attempt.

"Well, I had a girlfriend," I responded.

"Had?"

"Sort of."

Stoner Claire was as toxic as all of the smoke I had inhaled with her. I thought about how many times I had smoked weed with her. And how smoking weed had contributed to a majorly stupid miscalculation on the worst day of my life. I hated Stoner Claire. I wished I could completely erase her from my memory.

Quint understood. "Oh."

I flashed to the moment before my car slammed into a wall. I clenched my jaw—it felt like my skull was cracking open like an egg.

"Yeah," I mumbled. "It ended badly."

"But you didn't really answer the question," Quint pointed out.

I sighed. "Yeah, I'm a virgin. You?"

"Yeah, me too. I think about how it would feel all the time, though. I bet it feels amazing."

I laughed. "I thought nothing mattered."

Quint grinned. "Sex matters."

He was right. Anything that might make a depressed person feel less depressed matters a lot.

"What would you even say to her, though?" he asked.

My mind was still on Stoner Claire—I never wanted to talk to her again.

"To who?" I asked.

"Um—the girl who just gave you a massive woody."

I snapped back to present day, laughing. "Who calls it a *woody*?"

Quint shrugged.

"I dunno. I'd start with 'Hi' and go from there. I'm not exactly the expert," I admitted.

"I'm not, either," Quint said. "But I do know one thing."

"What's that?"

"Girls like that girl? They don't talk to guys like you."

Guys like me?

I mean—I agreed with him. But who was he to say?

Now I wasn't sure if I liked Quint. We'd just met, and he already thought he could read me like a book. Was I that one-dimensional? Had I become one of those transparent people who you could get to know in two seconds?

"Guys like me?" I asked.

I was slightly offended. Okay—I was extremely offended.

"Guys like *us*," Quint clarified. "Guys at Camp Sunshine."

"She's here, too."

Quint went silent. I guess he realized he was being pretty rude. Although that probably didn't matter to him, either. Remember—nothing mattered.

I tried to change the subject. "What game were you playing earlier?"

"*Karid.*"

"Nice. Which brother did you choose to start out with?"

"Caden. You play?"

Karid is, and will always be, my favorite game.

I love the idea of being born with the ability to control the life force of the planet. Apocalyptic strategic resistance games are the shit.

"Of course, dude—but I chose to be Nick."

"That's cool, I guess. But he's not as strong as Caden. Although Jacob is by far the coolest character in the game. He's the leader of the Solatists. I wish you could be him in the first game of the series." Quint's eyes lit up like he'd had a sudden realization. "How many hours a week do you spend playing video games?" he asked.

"Countless." I smiled.

I absolutely love playing video games—that's probably one of the reasons I'm so stocky.

"So, point proven," Quint said. "Guys like *us*."

Quint was trying to be a good friend by preventing me from getting hurt, but we had barely known each other twenty minutes. We weren't exactly best buds yet. In fact, at this point, he kind of annoyed me—a lot.

Quint urged, "Do yourself a favor and just forget about her."

"I didn't really ask for your love advice, okay?"

"She'll just make you even more depressed. Trust me."

I couldn't believe this guy. I felt my frustration boiling up into my head. He didn't know that girl, or me. He didn't know my situation. He didn't know what did, or did not, make me depressed. I got angry as I stared at the lake.

I flashed back to The Incident. I could see a teddy bear floating. I could hear Lola shatter. All my stupid miscalculations came flooding in, reminding me of how much I hated myself. I wondered if Quint deserved to be here just as much as I did.

I glared at him, and I'm sure my voice showed my annoyance. "So, how'd you end up here?"

Quint made eye contact with me—completely appalled.

Fun fact: You apparently can't ask that at Camp Sunshine.

I shrugged, acting like I didn't realize that there was a problem with that question. I dunno why I asked it—maybe part of me wanted to tell Quint about The Incident so that he would have a legitimate reason to hate me. I wanted everyone to hate me as much as I hated myself.

"What?" I asked.

Quint looked like he might burst into tears, but I didn't care. I didn't ask for his advice. I didn't ask to be belittled for taking interest in the most beautiful girl I had ever laid my eyes on.

Quint cursed me as he stood up: "Fuck you."

He stormed off toward Ray, but I didn't follow him. And I definitely didn't apologize or ask his forgiveness, either.

The water lapped on the shore. It echoed in my ears. It was as haunting as a ghost. It drew me in, reminding me that I was actually a terrible person. That I didn't deserve that girl. Or any sort of human connection. I didn't deserve to lose my virginity. And I definitely didn't deserve to have any friends.

I intentionally pushed everyone away. Every time I was around someone new, I felt like they would hate me once they got to know me, and every time I was alone, I immediately started thinking about The Incident.

At my lowest point in life, I was as high as a kite. I saw a teddy bear floating in the water. Lola slipped from my hand and hit the deck in slow motion—

"You know, I don't think you're supposed to be alone."

Her voice broke me out of my trance.

SIX

"ISN'T THAT ONE of the first rules they tell you when you get here?"

I looked back to see the girl standing behind me. The light reflected off the water and into her sparkling eyes.

I quickly tried to hide my pain—I didn't want her to know that I was a train wreck.

"Okay, you *definitely* shouldn't be alone," she said. "You should probably get back to Ray so you can talk about your feelings."

Damn, she saw.

I didn't want to talk about my feelings. I wanted to talk to her. I could hear my heartbeat pounding in my ears; my pits started to drip with sweat. Everything about her made me feel nervous and exhilarated.

"You're alone, too." My voice cracked.

"Yeah, but I like to think I'm above those outlandish rules, it being my third time here and all," she said.

Third time?

I knew that she probably had something seriously wrong with her, but I didn't care. I wasn't about to judge her like the world judged me. She seemed nice. And confident.

"Plus, I'm not the one staring into the abyss, wallowing in self-pity."

I retorted, "I'm pretty sure Camp Suicide is exactly the place where I should be wallowing."

She smiled. "Camp Suicide—I like that—but I can assure you that you are not the first camper to call it that. Camp Sunshine has seen many a witty depressed teen in its day."

I frowned. I thought I was being clever. But I guess I'm not as clever as I like to think I am.

Her teeth glistened. "I'm Corin. Corin Snow Young, for short."

She had an awesome name.

"I'm Hunter."

"Hunter who?" she asked.

"Hunter Samuel Thompson."

"No shit. You're *the* Hunter S. Thompson?"

For some reason, the joke was a lot funnier when she made it, even if I had heard it exactly one thousand and two times. My face went flush, my boner returned, and I nervously laughed.

I'd never had so many boners in a row—not since I started taking my happy pill. This was quickly going to become an issue, considering there wasn't exactly an easy way to take care of the problem in a place like Camp Suicide—and by take care, I mean jack off—which meant that I was destined to get hornier and hornier until I exploded.

Too much information?

"In the flesh," I responded.

"I've never met anyone famous. We don't have many famous people back in Bettendorf," Corin said.

"Bettendorf?" I asked.

It sounded made up, like something out of a video game.

"You've never been to Bettendorf? I'm flabbergasted by this." Corin grinned. "What about you? Where are you from?"

"I'm from Minneapolis."

"Ah, a city boy."

I couldn't help but smile. Even though I barely knew her, she made me feel wanted—like I mattered.

"Paisley's probably done peeing by now, so I should probably get back to her. I just wanted to stop by Happy Lake to see if they drained it after what happened last year, but it's still here in all its pathetic glory. The fence is a new, foreboding addition, though."

"What happened last year?" I asked.

Corin ignored my question—which should have troubled me, but it didn't.

"They're serious about the schedule, so you should probably stop swooning and get back before you get scolded on your first day in prison."

See? I wasn't the only one who thought this place resembled a prison.

Wait—did she say "swooning"?

"I'm not swooning," I said.

Corin chuckled. "Please." She raised an eyebrow at my crotch, so I pulled my shirt down over my boner. "You're just as typical as the rest of them."

Now I felt like a complete jerk, and thankfully, that was enough for my arousal to diminish. It's not like guys can control when their dicks get hard (or don't).

"Best get back before you get into even more trouble," she said before she took off toward the dorms.

I reluctantly rose and made my way back through the woods toward Ray. When I got there, I stomped up the stairs to face the repercussions that awaited me. As soon as I opened the door to the dorm, I noticed that C. Dermont was comforting Quint. All the other boys' eyes simultaneously locked on me as C. Dermont lurched into action. He bounded across the floor and got in my face. His smile was gone.

"Where have you been?" C. Dermont asked. "You aren't supposed to be alone, or leave your buddy alone."

C. Dermont waved his chubby finger in my face. I wasn't in the mood to be attacked by this overweight lunatic.

"Fucking relax," I said. "Technically, he's the one who left me! I was just down at the lake for a—"

Jim burst through the screen door and cut me off. "No! You listen to me, kid, and you listen good."

I could feel the anger rising up from my gut and into my head. My blood began to boil. I was already mad at Quint, and I felt unwanted by Corin. I wasn't about to take any more crap from anyone.

Jim was out of breath—I guess he'd been looking for me. He glared at me with malice, like I was the worst person on earth. I couldn't help but feel like I *was* the worst person on earth, which made me even madder.

He barked, "We have rules here for a reason, rules that you cannot disregard. You can't be alone, and neither can Quint. What if something happened? What if Quint decided to hurt himself because of what you said? Words have consequences, Hunter. You want to force me to be a hard-ass? Fine, I'll be a hard-ass. You can try to get into my head all you want, kid, but I promise that I'll always be one step ahead of you."

Jim the security guard just got a new name—Asshole Jim.

C. Dermont tried to diffuse the tension before I said something I'd regret. "Jim, cool—"

Too late. I was furious, and I hated authority way too much to let this jackass walk all over me.

"He's a freak!" I exclaimed, pointing at Quint. "I was just trying to get to know him!"

C. Dermont frowned. "We don't use words like that here, my friend."

I snapped, "I'm not your friend."

And I never would be. I hated how happy and bubbly C. Dermont was all the time—he was a freak, too, just like Quint. It was like he was trying to shove his happiness down my throat.

"How about an apology?" C. Dermont urged.

"I didn't *do* anything. He's the one who stormed off. *He* abandoned *me* just because I asked him—"

Asshole Jim grabbed me, kicked my knee, and slammed me down to the wooden floor. I felt like I'd been punched in the stomach—like my lungs were deflated balloons. I tried to get up, but he placed his knee on the center of my back, forced my wrists together, and handcuffed them.

I wanted to scream, but I couldn't breathe.

"Do not resist!" shouted Asshole Jim.

I wasn't resisting, genius. I was just trying to breathe.

C. Dermont and the rest of the boys watched in horror. "Jim, go easy. It's the first—"

"Shut up and let me do my job."

C. Dermont stepped away.

I felt powerless. Completely out of control. Like anything I did would result in these people's distrust. They could take away my dignity, and my privacy, but they couldn't force me to apologize—I didn't do anything wrong. I wasn't about to let them win.

Asshole Jim forced me to my feet and shoved me toward the door.

I would soon come to realize that there was no way to win at Camp Suicide.

I could only survive.

SEVEN

NEEDLESS TO SAY, I missed Campfire Orientation.

Asshole Jim dragged me to Mental—the worst place at Camp Suicide. It's located in a corridor of the therapy cabin—aka Sunshine or the Shrinker. The cubic room Asshole Jim tossed me into was no bigger than a small closet. It smelled disgusting. Piss-and-vomit-stained white pads covered the walls and floor. And I was to be kept locked in a straitjacket.

I learned that I was powerless at Camp Suicide. To survive, I would have to obey at least some of the rules. Sitting alone in Mental forced me to think about my stupid miscalculations, and those were thoughts I tried to avoid at all costs.

I kept hearing my bong shatter. I kept seeing the teddy bear.

I was angry and frustrated. I fumed as I rocked back and forth. I'm sure I looked insane, which wasn't exactly helping my situation. I felt pitiful. Weak. And worthless.

I heard a buzz and the locks clicked. The massive padded door swung open, and bright light flooded into the room. A slightly out-of-shape woman with plump cheeks, perfectly white teeth, and silver hair stared into my defeated eyes. She looked at me with this ridiculously stern expression while she tapped her clipboard.

She didn't say anything at first. She just stood there, towering over me like a silent giant. I glanced up the hall, where Asshole Jim was waiting at the entrance to the cabin in the bright florescent lights.

Windows lined the left wall, and there were two closed doors on the right, with keycard readers above the knobs. There was a black placard with printed white text on each of the doors—one read OFFICE, and the other read SUNSHINE ROOM.

The woman finally decided to speak. She was one of those women who kept her tone high-pitched and pleasant sounding, even though she was scolding me. "I'm Counselor Winter, the owner and founder of Camp Sunshine. We've decided to put you in Mental for the night. You're clearly having a manic episode. We're afraid that you're considering taking a drastic action, and we need to protect you."

Let's get something straight. At no point between the time I arrived at Camp Suicide and the time I ended up in Mental did I think about offing myself. This was absolutely insane. I was set up and I assumed everyone knew it.

I responded, "I'm not suicidal. At least, not at this moment. And I'm pretty sure my parents wouldn't approve of you restraining me in a straitjacket."

"Actually, your parents signed off for us to use any means at our disposal to protect you. I can show you the forms if you'd like to see them," Counselor Winter explained—her fake tone didn't fool me for a second. This woman was evil.

Of course my parents signed torture forms.

I shook my head. "It's fine."

Counselor Winter jotted a few notes down on her clipboard. "You're at Camp Sunshine for a reason. We're here to help you get better."

I fought the urge to get up and tackle her. I hated this woman. I hated all of them.

I had to try to say something that would get me out of that room.

"Being in this room is making me suicidal," I retorted.

She jotted down a few more notes before looking up at me. "That's what the straitjacket is for. Your protection."

I clenched my jaw—those words almost caused me to detonate a rage bomb. I couldn't believe my ears. I knew there was nothing I could say or do to make her understand what had actually happened. That Quint had mocked me for expressing interest in Corin. That I didn't respect C. Dermont or Asshole Jim. And that there was no reasonable explanation as to why they would keep me in Mental.

Putting me in Mental was nothing more than an effort to put me in my place.

Counselor Winter continued with a fake smile, "You have to obey the rules, Hunter. What we're doing here is for your own good. We know what's best for you."

I made eye contact with her. She knew everything. She was part of this farce. My skin was on fire.

"I shouldn't be in here."

"If you don't obey the rules, you'll keep ending up in Mental." She smiled at me again in the fakest way. "Is there anything you'd like to talk about? Or ask me?"

I couldn't trust any of the counselors at Camp Suicide. They were all in cahoots, working to punish us for our depression, all in an effort to make us submit to their rules.

I averted my eyes to the floor.

Counselor Winter kept staring at me—I wanted to gouge out her eyes. I wanted her to leave me in peace. I wanted to get out of Mental. I wanted all of this to end.

"Take your time," she said.

I was helpless, and I knew that there was nothing I could say or do to change the situation I was in. I was locked in a tomb and eventually I was going to run out of air.

After about ten more minutes of torture, she rose. "Well, let me know when you're ready to apologize." She smiled, again, before she exited the room.

I spent the rest of the night plotting what to do next. I would never obey the rules, and I would do anything to get out of that place.

Anything.

Even lie.

But when morning came, I remembered that the alternative was being stuck at home with Surgeon Dick and Harpy Patricia. I had nowhere to escape to. No home. No place to go.

I was stuck in a rat maze with no exit.

EIGHT

THE NEXT MORNING, Asshole Jim and another counselor arrived to retrieve me from Mental.

The padded door buzzed and swung open. By this point, my brain was so tired that I had become a zombie. I had to pee so freaking badly that I thought I might piss myself at any moment. I looked like a complete wreck, but it didn't faze them at all. They must have been used to abusing kids to the point of unresponsiveness.

The counselor's accent was one that I had never heard before, and his breath smelled like spearmint. "Hi, Hunter. I'm Counselor Kirk. Are you ready to apologize?"

I thought that Counselor Kirk was probably in his early thirties. He had his hair cut in a hipster sort of way, with the sides buzzed and the top long. He had a defined jawline and eyes that were both brown and green at the same time.

I slowly nodded.

Asshole Jim moved over with his lanyard of keys and keycard to unlock me from the straitjacket. Once it was removed, I tried to stand, but it felt like there were thousands of pins digging into the soles of my feet. I almost fell over, but Counselor Kirk caught me.

"Go easy," he advised. "Your body is still waking up."

The blood surged into my muscles—I was starting to get dizzy. My head floated on my neck.

Asshole Jim glared into my eyes. "I don't mind putting you in here again if you cause me any more trouble. I don't care if you spend the entire session in here; you won't disobey me again."

Counselor Kirk butted in, "I think he gets the picture, Jim. Why don't you give it a rest?"

Asshole Jim turned on Counselor Kirk. "Watch yourself."

"Or what?" Counselor Kirk asked. "I'll take it from here."

I couldn't help but grin as Asshole Jim stormed away.

"You okay?" Counselor Kirk asked.

"That's a stupid question," I said, my voice cracking with thirst.

"I'm sorry you had to experience that on your first day. The truth is that they always make an example out of one of the campers at the beginning of each session. You just happened to push the boundaries too far, too early. At least now you know what those boundaries are, and you can stay out of trouble," Counselor Kirk explained.

Fun fact: They called us *campers* to make it sound like we were at Camp Suicide by choice.

"I didn't do anything wrong."

That was my story and I was sticking to it. I decided that I wasn't going to tell him about Corin, or the fact that they should have had signs right outside of Ray clearly marking the way to the Rainmaker. I didn't want to explain my theory of everything being one big, stupid miscalculation. I was too tired to fight anymore.

"You did do something wrong," Counselor Kirk said.

I didn't think I did.

"But you didn't deserve to end up in here overnight. I don't agree with all of the founder's tactics."

I liked Counselor Kirk. He seemed like the *only* honest counselor at Camp Suicide.

"Keep your head down for the remainder of your time here, and you might learn a thing or two."

"But there are way too many rules here to keep track of."

"Rules are good for you," Counselor Kirk said. "You may not see why yet, but I promise that there are rules out in the real world, too. Our job is to make sure you're ready to handle everything on your own."

I didn't have the energy to argue. I had to pee—plus I was tired, hungry, and thirsty. I was ready to get out of that closet. Ready to move on with my life.

"Let's get you cleaned up, and then we can get some food in you."

First, I took the longest pee ever, then I showered while Counselor Kirk sat on one of the Rainmaker benches watching me. It was one of those showers with no dividers or privacy—a tiled cubic space with a drain in the floor and three faucets sticking out from the wall near the ceiling.

The words *group* and *shower* really don't belong together.

Counselor Kirk explained that all the other campers had already taken their morning showers. That usually the counselors didn't physically monitor shower time. That this was a special circumstance. But that didn't make it any less awkward for either of us.

I knew that he could see every inch of my embarrassing body, including my uncircumcised dick and extremely hairy thighs and ass crack. He probably noticed how awkwardly proportioned my stocky upper body was compared to my legs. I was as exposed as a piece of unused film in the sunlight.

As a favor to us both, I lathered up and rinsed off as fast as I could. Counselor Kirk supervised me as I got dressed and then escorted me to Beaming Bellies—the cafeteria cabin—or as I like to call it, the Crapateria. The food was absolutely awful.

Asshole Jim and a female security guard I hadn't met yet guarded the door as I entered. The Crapateria was in a log cabin, just like all of the other buildings at Camp Suicide. There were five wooden picnic tables in the open room. Windows lined the walls all the way into the kitchen at the back. And the room always smelled like scrambled eggs—*disgusting*.

You know that feeling you get when you enter a room full of people who were just talking about you? I got that feeling as soon as I walked in. Everyone stopped his or her conversation to look at me. I could feel their eyes judging my character.

Corin sat with the other girls. A girl around fourteen years old with really long curly hair sat on one side of her, and a girl around fifteen years old wearing a shirt that read LEZ BE FRIENDS and rainbow socks sat on the other.

Three other girls sat across the table from Corin. One was around fifteen years old and had short hair, tan skin, and the single most obnoxious laugh I had ever heard in my life. Another was around sixteen years old and had purple hair. The final girl was completely ethnically ambiguous and had black hair and tan skin—the other girls were whispering and giggling to each other, but she just sat there silently.

I walked past the girls' table and then moved down the row, around the counselors' table. C. Dermont, Counselor Kirk, and two female counselors I didn't recognize all watched me as I approached the steel breakfast cart. One of the female counselors at the table was clearly an athlete. She had caramel-colored skin and a wild grin. The other wore Birkenstocks and looked like a total hippie.

I could tell the counselors were talking about me because they occasionally looked up at me while they whispered to each other. I tried not to worry about it as I made my way back past the boys' table. Quint stared down at his precut fruit, and Finley had one hand on Quint's back. Ash, Blaze, and Wyatt all glared at me as I walked past.

I accepted the fact that I was an exile as I grabbed a tray, a milk carton, cereal, and some apple slices. The plump female cook—whose name I never got—watched me. Her shoulders sank as I quickly moved past a tray of untouched quiche that she had prepared. All the food was precut, and the only utensils we were allowed to use were plastic spoons.

I turned around and noticed that all the campers and counselors had gone back to their conversations. I didn't even care that most of those conversations were about me. I was just glad that they weren't staring anymore.

I spotted an empty table under a mounted plaque engraved with the phrase SUNSHINE IS FOREVER. Next to the plaque was a photo of Counselor Winter, and under the photo was a placard that read: COUNSELOR WINTER, FOUNDER. I quickly took a seat at that table. I sat there alone and started devouring my meal with a spoon.

I glanced over at the boys' table and saw that Ash, Blaze, and Wyatt were glaring at me again. I could feel myself getting angry. I shifted so that my body and meal were directed toward the plaque.

Then Corin sat down across from me, opening us both up to even more judgment. But she didn't seem to care about the nasty looks she was getting.

"So, how about all this sunshine?" She grinned at her own joke.

I wasn't in the mood for humor, and honestly, I wasn't in the mood to talk to her. She had made my emotions bungee jump. And I wasn't about to willingly allow her to make me feel like shit again.

"I thought you didn't want anything to do with me," I said.

Corin smiled. "I believe I said that I wanted you to stop gawking at me like every other guy does. That doesn't mean I don't want you to get to know me."

What the hell was that supposed to mean?

She moved in to talk in a low voice. "I heard you asked some kid *the question*, and then you called him a freak. It's ballsy to alienate yourself like that on your first day in a place like this."

I suddenly regretted all of it. I felt guilty for being a jerk. I looked up from the floating flakes of cereal in my bowl and frowned. Corin stared into my beaten eyes. I saw on her face that she could tell that I was completely defeated.

"It was that bad, huh?" she asked.

I didn't answer her. This was her third time at Camp Suicide—she had to have known about Mental. In fact, I was a little perturbed that she didn't warn me about that hellhole before I ended up in there. In that moment, I just wanted to be left in peace, to wallow in self-hatred and pity on my own.

Corin didn't care. She kept talking, "Hunter S. Thompson, you're going to need a friend or two if you want to survive this place."

I glared into her eyes. "You're the one who acted like a total bitch. Now you want to be friends? Who says I want to survive this place?"

I'd been at Camp Suicide for maybe twenty-four hours, and my suicidal thoughts had only grown stronger. Being at the camp forced me to think about The Incident, and how I didn't deserve friends or happiness in life. I didn't deserve anything. They'd been right to slap a straitjacket on me.

"I'm going to ignore the fact that you called me a bitch, because I know you don't mean that." Corin paused for a moment to think. I could see her eyes darting from side to side as she contemplated how to phrase what she said next. "See, this is the problem," she started. "This is what they do to us. They force us to evaluate our lives, as if we can turn back time. But you and I both know that we aren't time travelers, and we can't change the past."

She was right—I knew in that moment that she was right. There was no way to convince Surgeon Dick and Harpy Patricia that I was worthy of their love. No way to fix what had happened.

"You and I are going to break free from here, I promise you that," Corin assured me.

I'd thought about escaping all night. But I knew that fantasy was actually a nightmare.

"I don't have anywhere to go. That's the problem," I said. "I think I'm just going to submit until all of this is over."

What I actually meant by *until all of this is over* was *until I can try to commit suicide again*. Dark, I know, but true.

Corin's voice rose, "No!" She collected herself and returned to whispering, "No. That's exactly what they want you to do, and that's exactly why you can't do it. You can't submit, and you can't act like any of this is getting into your head. A famous guy like you, I know you're stronger than that. Aren't you? Now smile and act like you're fine."

I froze for a moment. Corin grinned at me in this goofy way, and I couldn't help but laugh. She was making me feel better—like I mattered. Maybe she was right. Maybe the only way to defeat the counselors was by pretending that their treatment was actually working. But pretending meant lying, and I hated that prospect.

"I'm not going to lie to the counselors. I don't want to end up in that closet again."

"Lying won't get you thrown into Mental, but getting caught lying will," Corin said.

A thought popped into my head. "How come you didn't end up in Mental?"

Technically she broke the same cardinal rule that I did, and she didn't even get slapped on the wrist.

Corin smirked. "Because I'm smart enough to not get caught. Paisley—*my* Rainmaker Buddy—was doing her business while I scoped out Happy Lake. It was just an added benefit that you happened to be there."

My heart pounded in my ears . . . and other places.

"An added benefit."

Was she flirting with me? She was flirting with me, right?

I gaped at her, unable to form a coherent response. I put my hand in my lap because I could feel myself getting aroused. Suddenly, all I could think about was how it would feel to have sex with her. Would it make me happy? Could she be the cure for my depression?

Possibly.

"Are you okay?" she asked. "You're doing that thing that all guys do again. Stop looking at me that way."

I realized I was acting like a total freak. "Uh—yeah. So what—uh—happened at Happy Lake last year, anyway?"

"A suicide attempt," she said casually. Like it was nothing.

"Oh," I said.

I gulped and suddenly my heart stopped beating so fast.

"Don't look so glum about it. Every single convict here has tried to commit suicide at one point or another."

"I can't believe you've suffered through this place three times already."

Corin reached out and gripped my hand. I was aroused all over again. My hand was the warmest it had ever been.

Did she like me, too? Or was she just messing with me?

I would have done anything she asked me to do in that moment. She had complete control over me.

"We're all in this together. Okay? Like I said, you're going to need a *friend* if you want to survive."

She really put emphasis on the word *friend*. Was she friend-zoning me already?

"Just promise me something," she added.

"Anything," I said.

I really did mean almost anything.

Corin looked deep into my eyes. I could see white flecks in her sapphire irises. "You have to pretend like nothing's wrong. Don't let them win."

I scanned the room. My eyes stopped on the counselors, who were all staring at Corin's and my interaction.

I raised my eyebrows. "Easier said than done. Like I said, I don't want to lie."

For some reason, the way the counselors were looking at me made me feel uneasy. My stomach froze.

"Hunter, look at me; don't look at them."

I turned back to face my only friend at Camp Suicide.

"We'll defeat them together," she promised.

C. Dermont appeared out of thin air, holding a tray of tiny paper cups with a pill for each of the campers. "Here's your medication, Hunter." He handed one of the cups to me. Then he turned to Corin. "And here's *yours*, Corin. Maybe you should get back to the other girls."

Corin took the pill cup and rose to her feet. "Yes, sir, C. Dermont, sir."

C. Dermont watched her rejoin the rest of the girls before he turned back to me and continued, "Take your pill, Hunter, and come have a chat with me outside after I'm done handing out the medication."

I sighed. "Am I in trouble again?"

He fidgeted. "Just take your pill and join me in a second."

C. Dermont walked over to the boys' table with the tray in hand. I stared down at the tiny white pill—it definitely wasn't Prozac. I didn't even know what kind of drug it was.

I popped the pill into my mouth and swallowed it down with the rest of my milk. I rose to my feet and C. Dermont joined me at the door after he was finished handing out all the happy pills.

Corin made eye contact with me before we stepped outside, encouraging me not to forget what she'd said. But I didn't think it was a good idea to start pretending like I was happy right after I'd been released from solitary. I realized that the counselors would see right through my fake grins.

C. Dermont glared at me like I was in trouble, yet again.

NINE

C. DERMONT LOOKED at me like I'd been caught making a pact with the devil.

I stood in the dirt, boiling in the heat, waiting for him to say *something*. A fly landed on his sweaty face and danced across his moles. Eventually, he swatted it away.

It became clear to me that C. Dermont was unable to start this conversation on his own. "You going to try to make me apologize for something I didn't do again?" I asked.

C. Dermont's beady eyes glared more intensely. I hadn't thought it was possible for such a bubbly guy to get this frustrated about anything.

"I'm not going to respond to that," he said.

I waited.

Ash, Wyatt, Blaze, Quint, and Finley exited the Crapateria under the supervision of Counselor Kirk, making their way back toward Ray. The guys stared at me with hateful eyes, and I rolled my eyes back at them. C. Dermont and Counselor Kirk nodded at each other.

"What do you want?" I persisted. C. Dermont was really starting to annoy me.

The door to the Crapateria opened. Out poured the girls, followed by Corin and the two female counselors.

Corin made eye contact with me as she passed and mouthed the words *Are you okay?*

I gave her a slight nod, and she went back to pretending like she was a part of the group.

C. Dermont noticed Corin's and my interaction. "What was that, my friend?"

I snapped, "I'm not your friend."

C. Dermont nodded slowly.

I was starting to get irritated with how long this conversation was taking. C. Dermont was acting ridiculous.

Spit it out!

C. Dermont took a deep breath. "Can I ask what you were talking about with Corin?"

That question crossed the line.

I immediately felt disgusted. "Why is that any of your business?"

C. Dermont explained, "All of the conversations between the campers at Camp Sunshine are the counselors' business."

I wasn't going to accept that as an explanation. They could watch me shower. They could watch me eat. They could watch me sleep. But they couldn't get into my head. And they definitely couldn't force me to expose details of a private conversation.

I raised my eyebrows. "Great."

C. Dermont grew frustrated. "Please don't make me force it out of you. I need to know what you two were discussing."

This was weird. Why did C. Dermont care about our conversation so much? I wondered what had happened during Corin's previous two sessions at Camp Suicide. But I wasn't going to give C. Dermont what he wanted, *ever*. Not after he trapped me in Mental on my first night in prison.

"Corin was discussing all the sunshine," I retorted.

Technically it was true.

C. Dermont's expression grew grim. Something was up. There was something I didn't know about Corin's past. Something serious. I tried to force myself not to care. For all I knew, this might be a trick. C. Dermont could have been manipulating me into becoming his narc. But I could feel the noose cinching tighter around my stomach.

"This isn't funny. Listen to me carefully, my"—he caught himself this time—"camper." I need to make sure that the two of you aren't going to cause us any grief this summer."

Okay, something was *definitely* up with Corin. Or at least, they wanted me to think something was up. This entire interaction with C. Dermont was starting to throw me off.

I shrugged.

This was a completely different C. Dermont from the person I had met the day before. He wasn't bubbly, he wasn't smiling, and he wasn't cracking jokes. He was totally serious, and he wanted me to think that Corin was trouble.

But weren't we all trouble?

"You need to report any of her suspicious behavior, okay?" C. Dermont urged.

I was done. I decided that this was all a part of their manipulation tactics. Pit the campers against one another so that they don't know who else to turn to besides the counselors.

"Can I go now?"

"That's fine," C. Dermont said reluctantly.

I turned my back on him and marched toward Ray. I didn't want to believe him. I liked Corin—*a lot*. Even though I was very physically attracted to her, I promised myself that I'd prove I wasn't just like every other guy. And I wasn't about to let the counselors ruin my overall impression of her before I got to know her better.

But as I walked, the uneasy feeling in the pit of my stomach didn't go away.

TEN

WE EACH GOT a half hour of therapy every day, except for Fridays.

I've been in therapy since I was twelve, but honestly, it's never helped me much. I've never gotten along with my therapists, because I've never felt like they could relate to what I was actually going through. It's one thing to study depression, but experiencing it is a completely different ball game. At first, my parents would fight with my shrinks for telling them the truth about me. And once they accepted that I was a hopeless cause, they stopped caring if I went to therapy at all. I skipped most of my sessions and spent the majority of the ones I attended in silence.

I entered the Shrinker later that morning, which was halfway between the dorms and the Crapateria. Asshole Jim left me in the carpeted cabin corridor and went to supervise Recreation. I shuddered when I saw the metal door to Mental, which was sealed shut at the end of the hall. The doors to the Office and the Sunshine Room were both open.

I waited outside the door to the Office and watched as the hippie counselor finished jotting down a few notes in a thick green file. She sat at an elegant wooden desk. There was a large window behind her. And there were tons of bookshelves filled with files of every color. Each shelf was marked with a session date, all the way up to present day.

She glanced up from her notes. "Just give me one second."

She had long blond hair and a slender physique. She wore a beaded necklace and a white doctor's coat over a floral dress. I watched as she sealed the file and rose to place it on a shelf. As she tucked it away with the rest of the colored files, I saw Corin's name on the outside of the green folder. I wondered why her file was so much thicker than the others, and I wondered if the notes the counselor had just added to the file were about me.

She grabbed my file and told me to follow her. I recognized the red folder that the doctors always carried at the end of my hospital visits. We exited the Office and the magnetic lock beeped as she secured the door shut.

She talked as she escorted me down the hall and into the Sunshine Room. "I'm Therapist Jessica, but you can call me Therapist Jess. I'm the on-site psychologist here at Camp Sunshine."

We sat down across from each other in sticky maroon leather chairs. Therapist Jess stared at me with her hands folded on top of the bright-red folder. The sun reflected off the crisp white walls of the room. The Sunshine Room might as well have been a rainforest; there were plants everywhere. And it was so quiet that the ticking of the clock was like cannon fire.

I began to count the books on the shelves. Therapist Jess had forty-seven books about the adolescent mind, seventeen books about puberty, twenty-nine books on parenting, and fifty-one books about psychology—I'd never been so intimidated by a bookshelf.

After I was done evaluating the books, I turned back to Therapist Jess and waited for her to speak.

Nothing. Nada. Zilch.

She didn't say a word. I couldn't take it anymore. This had to be some sort of trick. I was afraid that they would throw me into Mental again if I didn't start talking.

"So, are we just going to sit in silence?" I asked.

Therapist Jess smiled at me with this wide grin. "Is that what you'd like to do?"

Camp Suicide was a place filled with more rules than I could count, but I knew that the number-one rule of therapy was that we were supposed to talk.

"Isn't it your job to direct the conversation?" I asked. "I've been to therapy before."

"Have you?" Therapist Jess kept smiling—she sounded so smug. "I can't tell you what to do, or how you should act."

She was scolding me, again.

Through the window, I could see that the rest of the guys were participating in their Recreation time under the supervision of Asshole Jim and Counselor Kirk. I noticed that Quint was sitting in the grass under a tree, playing a game on his Nintendo DS. The noose tightened its grip around my stomach. I felt bad for the way I had treated Quint, and wished that I could turn back time, so that we could actually have a shot at being friends.

I continued to gaze out the window. "I have a question."

"Okay."

"If this place isn't supposed to be a prison, then why do you make it feel like one?"

"You're talking about how alienated you feel from the rest of the group," Therapist Jess psychoanalyzed.

I rotated around and glared into her eyes. The noose around my stomach forced all my anger out of my mouth. "I'm talking literally. This place literally feels like a prison. You have a solitary confinement cell to put us in for punishment, the entire place is surrounded by a barbed-wire fence, and you have a security guard who treats us like inmates."

Therapist Jess seemed unfazed. "We are a rehabilitation center, one chosen by your parents."

I sneered. "You think my parents give a shit?"

"You're upset."

That made me furious.

"Of course I'm upset! I spent the night in a padded room!"

She paused for a moment before she continued, "We have rules in place to keep you safe. We're trying to show you that your actions have consequences."

No shit, lady.

"The key is learning to admit when you're wrong, so that you can move forward," Therapist Jess explained.

But I wasn't wrong.

She waited for me to respond. I didn't. So she continued, "Again, I can't tell you what you should do or how you should act, Hunter, but you need to follow the rules."

I needed to follow the rules, but Therapist Jess wasn't going to tell me what the rules were or how to follow them. I was just supposed to blindly figure everything out on my own. I thought that the point of therapy was to get guidance from a professional—to seek advice from someone who was smarter than you.

"Then what's the point of all of this?" I asked. "If you're not going to give me any sort of advice or honest feedback, then why the hell am I here?"

Therapist Jess shrugged. "My job is to listen, to ask questions, and to help you learn to hash things out on your own."

I wanted to avoid my demons, not face them in a head-on collision.

"That sounds like a complete and total waste of time. If I could figure things out on my own, I wouldn't be sitting in this room with you."

I had a point. I thought she would see that I had a point.

"You appear to have it all figured out. You're determined to find the negativity in every situation."

I crossed my arms. "This place is bullshit."

Therapist Jess clenched her jaw. She held back her words, and instead of scolding me, she just stared into my vindictive eyes.

I was right, and she was wrong.

ELEVEN

I'LL TELL YOU, therapy exhausted me.

After my Shrinker Session, I sat on the edge of my bed, thinking. I couldn't stop reconsidering one of the things that Therapist Jess had said to me: *"The key is learning to admit when you're wrong so that you can move forward."* I realized that I was going to detest this place even more if I didn't do something to rectify my relationship with Quint.

I glanced over at Quint's bed and noticed that he was playing his DS. It seemed like he was really into his game. I convinced myself that I needed to talk with him.

I got to my feet and started to walk toward Quint's bed. All the guys' eyes followed my every move. I felt exposed. If Quint rejected me, I would be humiliated. Again.

I stopped.

Quint was way too engrossed in his game to notice me standing there.

I lingered awkwardly for a few moments before clearing my throat and mumbling, "You doing okay?"

Quint paused his game and lifted his nose away from the device. "Are you talking to me?" he asked.

No, I'm talking to the wall.

I nodded. "Yeah."

Quint raised his eyebrows, waiting for me to say something.

Say something!

I remained silent, hoping he would respond. My stomach was in turmoil. The noose kept pulling at it like it was dangling from a leash.

After an eternity of discomfort, Quint raised his device and went back to playing his game.

This wasn't going well.

I tried again, "I asked if you were doing okay."

Without glancing up from his game, Quint responded, "It doesn't matter."

I kept standing there, making a complete idiot of myself. Watching him. Waiting for him to take the lead from me. I was acting like a weirdo. But I had to do something to make it all better.

Quint finally paused the game again. "You're a real dick."

He was right. I was a total dick to him.

My voice cracked. "I didn't mean anything yesterday."

Quint looked as if he expected me to say something, but I had no clue what he wanted me to say. I'd never been good at confrontation or at reading people. People were always acting like I should know what to say—like they wanted something from me—but I was absolutely terrible at these types of interactions.

Optimist Quint shrugged. "Whatever. It's not like it matters."

"I'm sorry," I mumbled.

That came out of nowhere.

"Huh?"

I took a huge breath. "I'm sorry."

I couldn't think of the last time I had apologized for anything.

Quint smiled. I think he could tell that I was actually trying.

I continued with my apology. "I *was* a total dick, and you didn't deserve that."

Quint laughed. "Was that so hard?"

The truth was that it was *really* hard for me to admit that I was wrong when I didn't feel like I was the only one in the wrong. I felt like I deserved an apology, too. That Quint shouldn't have bombarded me with questions about Corin. But I let it all go. I realized that I wanted Quint to be my friend. No, I *needed* Quint to be my friend.

I frowned. "Kind of."

Quint grinned. "We're cool."

"Yeah?"

A wave of relief crashed over my shoulders. My stomach immediately felt a little bit better. It felt so good to free myself of that burden.

And then Quint apologized. "Yeah. I'm sorry they put you in Mental because of me. I never intended for anything like that to happen. Who could've known this place would have a shithole like that?"

Corin knew.

"Well, you were right, anyway. That girl friend-zoned me as soon as she got the chance."

"See? She'll just make you even more depressed. That's why I was warning you."

Even if I was friend-zoned, I was still going to try to get closer to the girl who stopped my bladder. I was positive that she could change my life. I thought that she could make everything better.

I clenched my jaw. I wanted to tell him that it was okay, but it wasn't. Instead, I changed the subject. "What game you playing?" I asked.

"*Tellus*, portable. Do you play?"

"Do I play? It's a great game! Only on system, though."

"That's cool," Quint said. "I have it at home, too. First-person shooter games on portable kinda suck. Have you beaten it in champion mode?"

I raised my eyebrows.

Quint sighed. "Ah, I can't get past the part where the Humanoids figure out why the Lodaxon is there, but I guess it doesn't really matter."

"Right, I get it. We're insignificant. You play online?"

"Yup."

"Well, maybe after this is all over, I could show you a few moves in co-op mode."

Quint smiled from ear to ear. "That'd be sweet."

I smiled back. It felt good to let everything go. To clear the air and move on from what had happened. I liked Quint.

"We should stick together from here on out," I said. "This place is bad enough without us fighting with each other."

Quint nodded in agreement.

I reached out to shake his hand. Quint grabbed my hand and pulled me into a hug.

"Real bros hug," he said.

At first, I was shocked. I hadn't been hugged since The Incident. Not by Stoner Claire. Not by my parents. And definitely not by any of my former friends. It felt weird to have someone who genuinely cared about my well-being. The noose around my stomach loosened its grip even more. I laughed. I don't know why, but that was my reaction.

Quint pushed me away, and he started laughing, too.

Counselor Kirk moved to the center of the room and announced. "Well, now that that's all settled, let's make our way over to the Gleeful Stables."

Suddenly, I remembered that all the other guys had watched and overheard our entire exchange. We literally had no privacy in this place—like, *at all*. My face went completely red, and so did Quint's. But I guess it didn't really matter.

All that really mattered was that Quint and I were friends.

And I may have been wrong, but I think it mattered a lot to Optimist Quint, too.

TWELVE

THE GLEEFUL STABLES were like something out of an old Western film.

I seriously felt like I should've been wearing cowboy boots and saying *y'all* at the beginning of every sentence while chewing on a long blade of grass. The stables were on the outskirts of the seven other cabins that made up Camp Suicide. The floors were padded with hay. There were pillars between the horse corrals that were carved in spirals from floor to ceiling. And the air smelled like horse shit.

Counselor Kirk and Therapist Jess were saddling up the horses for our day trip into the wild. Asshole Jim and the girls' security guard had a conversation in a corner of the stable while they watched us like Peeping Toms.

I'd overheard Therapist Jess refer to the other security guard as Nikki, so I figured that must be her name. She worked out, smelled like skunky BO, and had a buzz cut, and her face was permanently stuck in this ridiculously stern expression. She and Jim were a match made in heaven—Mr. and Mrs. Asshole.

All twelve of us campers were spread throughout the stables, having conversations of our own. The girls pretty much stuck together while we talked among ourselves in smaller groups.

Quint and I were standing in silence as Corin stared at us like a beautiful creeper. My heart raced in my chest.

"I thought you said she friend-zoned you," Quint said.

"She did," I responded. "I don't get why she's staring at me like that."

"It's kind of creepy," Quint noted.

I shrugged.

The truth was that I liked it, a lot. Everything about Corin was magnetic. Her extremely blue eyes. Her confidence. The fact that she wanted me to get to know her better. My crush was becoming more than just a physical attraction to her. Her mysterious nature made me want to get to know her better, too.

I think I was starting to fall in love with her. Is that crazy?

It was definitely crazy.

Ash noticed that Corin was acting weird, and decided to be a loudmouth about it. "Dude, Ash wants to know, what is up with that girl?"

Annoying Ash liked to refer to himself in the third person—he thought his opinion was *that* important.

I wanted to make fun of how ridiculous it was that he did that, but I kept my mouth shut, because, you know, Mental. . . .

I shrugged again. I was totally confused at this point. She'd acted like she didn't want anything to do with any guy. But now, she was staring at me with heart eyes. I wasn't about to complain. But in some ways it made me feel awkward and uncomfortable.

Was she just toying with me? Or was she actually starting to like me back? Was I making a stupid miscalculation?

Ash smirked. "I'm not gonna lie. Ash is kinda jealous, and also a little impressed."

I played it cool. "Only a little?"

He laughed. "Yep. But Ash knows you won't actually make a move."

I guess Ash had forgotten we were in prison.

"This isn't really the place to make any sort of move," I responded.

"See? Ash is right." Ash's expression flattened. "Seriously, though—there are rumors about her. You know that, right? Ash hears she's wild . . . and a bit crazy. This is her third time here."

After my conversation with C. Dermont, and all the weird looks I got from the counselors every time I talked to Corin, I had drawn the conclusion that she had a past. It didn't bother me, though. I had a past, too. We all did. I just wanted to get her to like me. I'd never been so attracted to anyone in my life.

"Aren't we all a bit crazy?" I asked. "Isn't that why we're here?"

Ash shrugged. I guess he didn't think anything was wrong with him.

Come to think about it, I didn't think there was much wrong with me, either. There was something wrong with the rest of the world. Maybe *we* were the normal ones. We could see the hopelessness of our existence. Normal people constantly try to convince themselves that they matter. We all knew that we didn't matter. Not in the grand scheme of things.

Ash turned to Quint, who had silently been listening to our exchange. "What about you, Quint? Got your eye on anyone?"

Optimist Quint responded in his usual optimistic fashion, "It's not like it matters."

Then he walked away.

Ash raised his eyebrows at me like he didn't agree, but I knew that deep down we all agreed with Quint.

Counselor Kirk and Therapist Jess had finished saddling up the horses. They turned to us, and Counselor Kirk announced, "All right. We're all set. Boys with me, girls with Therapist Jess."

The guys and I gathered around Counselor Kirk as he directed us to our horses. As we waited, Squirrelly Wyatt turned to Annoying Ash and me to make a joke. "Looks like it's gonna be another sausage fest! If only all you pricks were gay, too. I'd be in heaven."

That was the first time Squirrelly Wyatt had ever spoken to me, and I was already completely annoyed with him. Wyatt was far from a stereotypical gay guy, so I guess he felt the need to constantly remind everyone that he liked dudes.

I glanced over at Corin as she mounted a white horse. She winked at me and my face went flush again. I felt myself getting aroused, so I turned away. My heart drummed against my rib cage.

"Hunter."

Counselor Kirk's voice was muted under my beating heart, but I turned in the direction of the sound.

Don't get a boner. Don't get a boner. Don't get a boner.

I knew that getting a hard-on in front of everyone wouldn't exactly help my situation. I had to play it cool. I had to think about wrinkly ball sacks, Harpy Patricia in the shower—anything but Corin.

Counselor Kirk gestured toward a nearby horse. "You'll be riding Eclipse."

I found myself face-to-face with one of the biggest, most intimidating horses I had ever seen—my arousal diminished in a heartbeat. Eclipse had a mane of shiny black hair, a long snout, and massive hooves. I stared into his marble eyes, and then he licked my face. The wet drool dripped down from my chin, and everyone erupted in a fit of laughter.

Phew.

Once we got out on the trail, the forest was brimming with foliage, wild turkeys ran everywhere, and a cloud of dirt followed us as we made our way up the mountainside. I tightly gripped the reins as I rode Eclipse, bouncing up and down on the Western saddle while the wind blew wisps of nature into the air. The sun beat against my face, and the humidity was making me sweat balls, but for some reason, I couldn't stop smiling.

Blaze rode his horse directly in front of me. His was a white horse that was spotted like a Dalmatian. She was beautiful and ladylike. Without warning, she ripped a nasty sulfuric fart. The smell of rotten eggs assaulted my senses.

I quickly tucked my nose into the collar of my shirt. "Oh my God, dude. What did your horse eat?"

Blaze glanced back at me with the same blank expression he always had. "Huh?"

Ash chimed in, "She isn't being very ladylike. Ash thought girls didn't fart."

We all laughed at the age-old joke. The idea that girls didn't expel gas or waste was ludicrous, but all straight guys secretly wished it was true.

The horse farted again just to prove Blaze's point.

Blaze gave her a pat on the neck. "Good girl, Nova. Better out than in, that's what I always say."

Blaze would say that—he farted in his sleep.

The smell was nauseating. I could taste Nova's farts in my mouth. I gagged. "Seriously, though, this is totally disgusting."

Even Counselor Kirk couldn't hold back his laughter after he saw the look on my face. All the boys laughed at me as I tried to cough the nastiness out of my nose and mouth.

The wind picked up and replaced the stench with freshly pollinated air. "Ah, keep blowing, wind!" I exclaimed. "Blow your luscious, fresh scents into my face."

Maybe it was the new pill I took that morning; maybe it was the fact that I finally had a real guy friend and the noose around my stomach felt a little looser; maybe it was because Corin was finally giving me the time of day. Whatever it was, I was genuinely feeling good.

Funny how happiness hits us when we least expect it.

THIRTEEN

I STOOD in the center of a vast, flat meadow staring down into a pot full of gooey brown beans.

I dug a spoon into the gunk and began to stir, while Quint adjusted the stove to give the coils a bit more heat. We weren't allowed to use a gas stove, because we might have tried to blow ourselves up. I use the term *stove* loosely, because it was actually more like a hot plate that barely got hot enough to warm the food at all. The scent of beans radiated out to blend with the smells of beef, garlic, onion, and spice.

We were on a grand, grassy plain, where Counselor Winter and her husband had constructed a nice area filled with picnic tables below a wooden overhang for us to cook under. The horses grazed in the grass and drank from the stream. The sun sank toward the horizon, and the breeze shifted to brisk gusts.

Blaze and Finley had taken charge of the guacamole. I smirked as I watched them struggle to dislodge a giant seed from the pit of an avocado with a spoon.

Remember—we weren't allowed to use any utensils besides spoons, because, you know, slashy-slashy. So all the ingredients were precut.

I don't think either of them had ever cooked in their entire lives. Between Blaze's lack of enthusiasm for anything, and Flinching Finley's skittishness, the two could have made a hilarious pair for a ridiculous cooking show. The pit finally came loose, and Finley's scrawny body jerked with so much force that I thought he might fall over.

I glanced back at Asshole Jim and Counselor Kirk as they tied our horses to a rail next to a stream. Eclipse grazed in the grass near the shore, and Nova continued to expel her excess amounts of gas into the fresh air.

Ash and Wyatt were left in charge of the beef for our tacos. The two had not stopped arguing since they'd switched on the hot plates. Apparently, Wyatt loved spicy food; he kept sneaking cayenne into the concoction when he thought Ash wasn't looking.

Ash groaned. "Dude, easy on the spices. Do you want us all to have the horse farts?"

Most people like spicy food as it goes in, but hate the feeling as it goes out—sting ring.

Wyatt felt the need to defend his actions. "Whatchu talking about, fool? What's taco meat without some cayenne and chili powder?"

"Can we really call it taco meat at this point? Ash feels like it's more like taco seasoning with a dab of beef. Seriously, dude, Ash hates spicy food."

Asshole Jim and Counselor Kirk snuck up behind us.

"Everything all right here?" Asshole Jim asked.

We all responded in unison, "We're fine!"

Counselor Kirk grabbed the cayenne out of Wyatt's hand as he tried to add more. "Wyatt, that's enough cayenne. I want to be able to taste our food."

Wyatt scoffed, "*Psh*, whatever."

Blaze and Finley had finished the guacamole, so they decided to join our conversation.

"I'm starving, man. Finish that shit up. I got the munchies bad," Blaze said.

Squirrelly Wyatt changed the subject to flex his muscles again. "A'ight, since you asswipes don't swing my way, who's the hottest bitch here? Go!"

No contest—Corin was the hottest girl at Camp Suicide.

Wyatt pointed at Flinching Finley, who was sent into a flinching frenzy from the pressure.

"Too long, next!" Wyatt exclaimed.

Finley sighed with relief.

"Harper," Ash swiftly answered.

Since I had missed orientation, I had no idea which girl was Harper. I guess I was wrong about everyone thinking Corin was the hottest girl at Camp Suicide, but that didn't really bother me.

"Like 'em young, huh?" Wyatt retorted.

Ash mocked, "She looks older than you."

"I'll take that as a compliment since most gay dudes prefer younger guys," Wyatt retorted.

I had honestly forgotten that both Asshole Jim and Counselor Kirk were watching us, when Counselor Kirk weighed in. "I'm not sure this is an appropriate conversation."

"What you want us to talk about?" Wyatt asked. "What do all guys have in common besides eating, sleeping, shitting, and being horny twenty-four-seven?"

Counselor Kirk raised both eyebrows. "I just don't think we need to be sitting here objectifying anyone."

"Maybe some of us like to be objectified," Wyatt responded.

Counselor Kirk controlled his temper. "Watch it, Wyatt."

Wyatt compensated for the awkward tension. "*Psh*, we're all horny dudes here. What about you, Hunter? Got your eye on anyone?"

I wasn't sure if I should answer truthfully in front of both Asshole Jim and Counselor Kirk after C. Dermont had confronted me, and since I don't like lying, I decided to keep my mouth shut.

Ash butted in before I could stop him. "He likes Corin."

I hate when people answer for me.

I socked Annoying Ash in the arm.

"Ow!" Ash exclaimed. "What? You do!"

And just as I feared, Counselor Kirk looked me directly in the eyes and advised, "Be careful with her, Hunter."

"You're the second counselor who's said that," I retorted.

I had seen Corin's massive green file. It didn't bother me that Corin had a history—however, it did bother me that liking her was garnering me even more attention from the counselors. It's not like I even knew if she liked me back. The counselors were making a big deal out of nothing.

Counselor Kirk continued to stare into my eyes. "Just be careful."

"It seems inappropriate that the counselors talk about the campers behind their backs," I said. "I wonder what you say to everyone about me when I'm not around."

"We just want to make sure that all of you are making smart decisions, and that you're getting along with each other. We aren't bad-mouthing anyone," Counselor Kirk assured me.

"Whatever you need to tell yourself to sleep at night," I angrily replied.

Counselor Kirk's tone shifted, "Watch it, Hunter."

All the boys observed our intense exchange as if it were a reality television show.

For once, I was thankful for Wyatt's big mouth. He broke the tension, "Man, you need to lighten up, fool."

Suddenly, we all smelled smoke, and our conversation quickly came to an end.

Counselor Kirk pointed at the skillet of meat and exclaimed, "The meat's burning!"

I didn't even think it was possible for those hot plates to get hot enough to burn the food, but I guess Quint had really cranked the heat on all the devices. Asshole Jim and Counselor Kirk quickly yanked the skillets off the coils, and dinner was served.

I thought about Corin through the entire meal. I didn't care what the counselors said or what the other campers thought. Besides the friends I was slowly beginning to make, Corin was one of the only redeeming qualities about Camp Suicide.

I wasn't about to push her away.

FOURTEEN

AFTER DINNER, all the guys sat around a campfire pit as the sky morphed into a river of pink salmon.

A few clouds billowed on the horizon, but there weren't enough of them to create a storm. Crickets chirped and lightning bugs flickered between the trees as sunset shifted into night. The smoke swirled in a pillar up toward the starry sky. The logs crackled as the flames devoured them. And the warmth of the blaze soothed our skin as we shared funny stories over the fire.

Finley finished his story: "We were playing hide-and-seek in the store, and I—I hid in the center of one of those bra rack displays. My brother found me, and—and when I tried to get away, I tipped the whole rack over, spilling the bras literally everywhere. It—it was seriously the funniest thing ever."

Flinching Finley flinched as his tale came to an end.

I glanced over to see Asshole Jim watching us from the shadows—he spat his dip juice on the ground in front of him.

Annoying Ash responded in his usual fashion, "Good story, dude. Ash especially liked the part where you talked about bras."

Everyone laughed. Flinching Finley flinched at the burst of sound.

Counselor Kirk wasn't about to let the conversation get away from him again. "All right, enough talk about being horny. Let's get down to business and talk about why we're out here."

We all sniggered as if the conversation were a joke.

Counselor Kirk took a deep breath. The discussion was about to get serious. I felt the noose tighten around my stomach again—I hated serious conversations, and I especially hated talking about my feelings in front of a group.

"I've loved horses ever since I was a kid. I knew that no matter what I did when I grew up, I wanted my job to involve them in some way. There's something simple about being out in nature, and something gratifying about taking care of an animal that you love."

Squirrelly Wyatt nudged Annoying Ash. "Yo, he's talking about bestiality, fool."

Ash laughed.

Counselor Kirk glared at them. "Enough."

Wyatt and Ash both directed their eyes to the ground.

Then Counselor Kirk scanned our faces as he said, "So, let's go around the circle. I want each of you to talk about something you enjoy, and something you aspire to be."

Quint fidgeted uneasily next to me. I stared into the flames—the smoke was like the conversation; both were desperately trying to suffocate me.

Counselor Kirk waited for one of us to talk. "Who wants to go first?" he asked.

We all continued to avoid eye contact. The noose around my stomach tightened even more. I was having trouble breathing. I just wanted to disappear.

"How about you, Wyatt? Since you've been so vocal about everything else today," Counselor Kirk said through a grin.

Wyatt uncomfortably shifted. "Um, I dunno. I wanna help people like me, I guess."

Counselor Kirk pressed the issue. "People like you?"

Wyatt exhaled. "Yeah."

I wanted Wyatt to take his time—he could have taken all the time in the world for all I cared—just as long as he saved me from having to participate in this pointless conversation.

Group therapy doesn't help people with suicidal tendencies—suicide is personal.

"What do you mean by that?" Counselor Kirk inquired. "This is a judgment-free zone."

We all knew that there was no such thing as a judgment-free zone—we weren't idiots.

"Well, I mean, I know this might come as a shock, but I'm not out to my parents," Wyatt stated.

"And why aren't you out to them?" Counselor Kirk asked.

"They're religious and Republicans," Wyatt responded. "They think I'm here because I'm *just depressed*. I can't tell them the truth."

"I see," Counselor Kirk said.

"Look, fool, I like guys, but I also like Jesus and money," Wyatt declared. "I guess I want to help other gay Republican Christians come out to their parents—our sins aren't any more evil than anyone else's."

Suddenly, it dawned on me—Wyatt probably hated himself for being gay. That's why he was so vocal about his sexuality. He was constantly trying to convince himself that he was okay with it, but secretly he wasn't. That was *his* problem.

I watched everyone exchange glances. None of us cared that Wyatt was gay. But this generation is a lot more accepting than our parents' generation. I suspected that Wyatt was afraid of how his parents would look at him after he came out of the closet. Just like I was afraid of how people would look at me after I stepped out of mine.

Closets aren't just for gay people. We all come out of a closet in one way or another at some point in our lives.

Counselor Kirk praised Wyatt for being honest about everything. "Excellent, Wyatt. I think helping the LGBTQ community would be a great thing. But I hope you realize that being gay isn't a choice or a sin."

"I realize it's not a choice, fool. I was born gay, but that doesn't make it any less of a sin. We all have demons that we have to overcome," Wyatt explained.

I could tell that Counselor Kirk didn't really know how to respond to that, so he moved on in an attempt to take the attention off Wyatt. "Finley?"

Finley blinked repeatedly. He was completely unable to answer. I couldn't help but wonder what had happened to him to make him so afraid of everything. I thought that he must have been hiding something really depressing, but I knew his secret couldn't possibly be as depressing as mine. The noose got even tighter as Counselor Kirk got closer to questioning me.

Counselor Kirk didn't know what to do besides move on. "We'll come back to you. Quint?"

Optimist Quint responded in his usual fashion. "It doesn't matter. Nothing matters."

Counselor Kirk smiled. "How did I know you were going to say that?"

Quint shrugged. He didn't care about being a part of this conversation, and neither did I. I hoped that Counselor Kirk would just leave me be.

"How about finding something in your life that you enjoy? Then something might matter to you," Counselor Kirk advised.

Quint stared at him blankly.

"Think on it, okay?" Counselor Kirk urged. Then he turned to me, and the noose got so tight that all the air was forced out of my lungs. "And what about you, Hunter? What do you want to do when you're older?"

My lungs were glued together as I thought about The Incident. My heart stuck to my chest as I thought about the fact that I didn't really see a future for myself—that I didn't want to live to be old enough to become anything.

Counselor Kirk waited for me to respond while I drowned in my thoughts.

"It can be anything," he said. "Anything at all."

Since Camp Suicide was supposed to be all about releasing our demons and being honest with others, I decided to respond.

"I'll be surprised if I'm alive."

I watched the guys sink down as if they had all been simultaneously punched in the stomach at once. I guess telling the truth was a bad idea.

Counselor Kirk seemed saddened by my candor. "Well, you will be."

He cleared his throat. He had to move on, and I knew why.

Talking about depression was depressing.

"It's getting late. We'll continue another night, but next time I want all of you to have an answer. No grim images of death, or telling me it doesn't matter. I want you to aspire to be something real and tangible. It's a good life, and the world will give you everything that you're willing to take—all you have to do is reach out and grab what you want. I promise that all of you will have goals by the end of this session. Life is better when you have something to accomplish, something to look forward to."

He paused so that we could absorb what he'd said.

I tried to think of something to look forward to, and then Corin's face popped into my mind. I felt like I could breathe again—like the noose around my stomach would finally untie if I got to know her better.

Okay—it was definitely more than just a physical attraction for me.

Counselor Kirk rose to his feet and clapped his hands. "Let's pack up."

We started to rise, but I still couldn't get Corin out of my head. I wondered what she was doing at that moment. If Therapist Jess was making them go around in a circle to talk about their futures. What would Corin's response be?

I wondered if Corin saw a future with me.

Counselor Kirk walked toward me. "Hunter, can we chat?"

I slouched toward the ground as I followed Counselor Kirk to the outskirts of the campsite. Asshole Jim passed us as he moved to supervise the rest of the guys while they packed up all the gear.

Counselor Kirk stopped and turned toward me. His expression was grim and his eyes appeared even greener in the pale moonlight.

"Hunter, are you okay?" he asked—I could smell the spearmint on his breath.

I thought the whole point of Camp Suicide's campfire sessions was to talk about our feelings. But I guess I was wrong.

I shrugged, trying to keep my cool. "I was just being honest. I don't see a future for myself."

"Are you depressed, Hunter?" Counselor Kirk inquired.

I laughed. It blew my mind that he would ask me something so ignorant.

"This is serious," Counselor Kirk assured me.

I gawked. "Of course I'm depressed—I've always been depressed. That's why I'm at Camp Suicide."

Counselor Kirk looked around as if it was the first time he had heard a camper refer to Camp Sunshine by that name. "Who calls it that?" he asked.

I raised my eyebrows. "All of us tried to commit suicide at one point or another, didn't we?"

I was starting to get frustrated with Counselor Kirk. I didn't understand why he felt the need to single me out for being honest about my feelings. I didn't understand why he was trying to make me feel ashamed that I didn't see a future for myself. The noose became a choke hold around my stomach.

Counselor Kirk stuttered, "Well . . . yes . . . but calling it that—"

I'd had enough of the conversation—my anger ripped my vocal cords to shreds. "So it's a suicide camp. Calling it something else doesn't shield us from the truth of what this place actually is. It's a place for shitty parents to send their kids so that they'll feel better about themselves. Whether or not it makes us feel any better is beside the point. How's that for honesty?"

Counselor Kirk was hit hard by my tirade—his face almost melted into tears. "Hunter, all of the counselors are here to help you get better. You have to start moving forward."

The counselors were out to get me—not help me feel better. If they actually wanted to help me get better, then they wouldn't have tossed me into Mental on my first night in prison. I was starting to hate Counselor Kirk almost as much as I loathed Asshole Jim, C. Dermont, Therapist Jess, and Counselor Winter.

I fumed, "Into your glorious future? You wanna know what pisses me off? All of this fake bullshit. The world is your oyster—all you have to do is grab your pearl. You're full of it. All of you literally have shit pouring out of your mouths. And news flash—life isn't that easy."

I turned my back on Counselor Kirk and stormed toward the rest of the guys. I heard him say my name, but I didn't turn back. He should have been more empathetic with how I honestly felt, instead of trying to force me to find meaning in something I couldn't predict.

As I walked, my mind returned to Corin.

I thought that she might be my only hope for a meaningful life—the only way to untie the noose.

FIFTEEN

THAT NIGHT, when we got back, they made us all take showers.

And something happened to remind us of why we were at Camp Suicide in the first place. . . .

Ash finished rinsing off and stepped past me. I moved to take his place under one of the showerheads. Out of respect, I tried to avoid looking below anyone else's waistline. Not because I felt awkward about seeing a bunch of other guys naked, but because I felt awkward about them seeing me. I knew that every glance was a chance to judge every inch of my body—my puffy nipples, how small my flaccid dick looked under my chubby stomach, my hairy ass, and the fact that I was uncircumcised. Group showers suuuuuuck.

I stared up into the water as it sprayed down like rain.

That's when I heard Annoying Ash confront Wyatt. "Dude, Ash wants to know what happened to your leg? That's disgusting."

I turned around and wiped my eyes so that I could see what was going on.

Wyatt quickly slipped into his jeans, but he wasn't quick enough. Ash had spotted the trail of uniform scabbed cuts on Wyatt's thighs.

The blood rushed up into my head as I remembered digging a blade deep into my own wrists. The noose around my stomach ignited into flames.

"Nothing," Wyatt lied.

The water pounded against my back. I couldn't force my eyes away from the exchange. I couldn't shake the numbness that clawed its way back into my body. I remembered watching the blood gush from my wounds, pooling around my body, staining my sheets red.

Ash rebutted, "That wasn't nothing. Ash knows what that was, dude."

Blaze joined the interrogation. He was already dressed. "I'm gonna have to take Ash's side on this one, man. I saw it, too."

Wyatt slipped into his shirt, ready to storm away. "Screw you guys, and stop referring to yourself in the third person. You sound like a jackass, fool. Worry about yourselves."

I forced myself to snap out of my trance. I couldn't go back into that state of mind. Not here. Not ever.

I glanced to my side to see that Quint and Finley were also spellbound by the conversation.

Wyatt tried to leave, but Blaze's words stopped him. "We have to tell someone, man. We all saw it."

Wyatt's chest swelled. He turned to face them again. "No, you don't."

Ash stuck up for Blaze. "We all know this place is a joke, but we can't knowingly let you do that to yourself."

Blaze agreed. "Exactly, man."

Wyatt got in Ash's face. "If you tell them, I'll kill you."

Ash and Blaze both erupted into a fit of laughter.

"Says the smallest guy here," Ash mocked.

That's when the conversation turned into a confrontation.

Wyatt balled his fist and swung it into Ash's right cheek.

Ash's body fell to the ground.

And before any of us could intervene, Wyatt was mounted on top of Ash, punching him continuously in the face.

I heard Finley scream at the top of his lungs. It was like something out of a horror movie. I turned to see him cower in the corner of the shower area with his eyes closed and his ears covered.

Quint quickly shut off the water, grabbed two towels, and rushed over to console Finley.

It was as if another person took over my body. Without thinking, I lurched into action. I wrapped myself in a towel and ran over to pull Wyatt off Ash. I tackled Wyatt to the ground, while Blaze pulled Ash to safety.

Wyatt struggled to free himself, but I held his wrists and pinned them to the floor. Squirrelly Wyatt was little, but he was strong. It was hard for me to keep him on the ground. I imagined how embarrassed Wyatt must have felt in that moment, to be singled out as a cutter in front of the entire group, and to have a half-naked guy straddling him in front of everyone.

"Get off me!" he shrieked. His spit flew up into my face.

C. Dermont, Counselor Kirk, and Asshole Jim burst into the room—I guess they'd heard the commotion.

"Boys, step back!" C. Dermont ordered.

Asshole Jim pointed at me. "Get back, now! Stop fighting!"

He sounded like he was scolding me—I didn't do anything wrong. I didn't like his tone, but I got up and backed away.

"Who started this shit?" Asshole Jim asked.

We all immediately pointed at Wyatt—no one wanted to end up in Mental.

Asshole Jim grabbed Wyatt, hoisted him to his feet, and pinned him face-first into the wall.

Wyatt continued to struggle. "Get off me!"

Asshole Jim forced Wyatt's wrists together and handcuffed them behind his back. He pushed Wyatt toward the door. "Outside!" Dip flew out of his mouth and splattered onto the ground as he shouted.

Wyatt turned around and tried to charge into Asshole Jim, but the bulky guard swiftly pushed him back toward the door.

"You need to calm down. Step outside right now before you make this any worse," he threatened.

Wyatt deteriorated into tears as he realized that he had lost the fight.

"Screw all of you," he said before he stormed out of the room.

Asshole Jim and C. Dermont glared at us as if the fight were *our* fault. Then they trailed behind Wyatt.

Counselor Kirk pointed at Ash. "You. Come with me."

Ash's tan skin was dripping with blood. His cheeks were swollen like red apples. Counselor Kirk wasn't stupid; he realized that Ash was involved, too.

Ash reluctantly followed Counselor Kirk out the door. He slammed his fist into the wall as he went.

My adrenaline still surged. I was panting. I couldn't believe what had happened. That Wyatt had taken down a guy at least two times his size. And that he was cutting.

But what was he cutting himself with?

"Holy shit, that was intense," I declared.

Finley's wails echoed through the shower room.

I turned to see Blaze and Quint trying to calm Finley down.

He pushed them away. "Get away from me!"

They backed off.

I knew that Finley just needed space in that moment—that the fight had triggered a breakdown, reminding him of all his stupid miscalculations.

"Guys, leave him alone," I advised.

Tears and snot leaked down Finley's chin. "Please. Leave me alone, please."

Blaze and Quint joined me. We finished dressing while Finley sobbed on the floor. I wished that there was something I could do for him, but I knew that his emotions had control over him.

As I slipped into my clothes, I thought about the cuts on Wyatt's thighs. I had cut myself, but I had never been a *cutter*. I don't feel pain like everyone else—probably because I've been doped up on various meds since I was twelve. The reason I had tried to kill myself so many times was because I wanted to feel something besides self-hatred. Wyatt was punishing his demons with the cuts on his thighs to keep them at bay, but he wasn't trying to kill himself.

I couldn't subdue my demons—my demons had already consumed me.

SIXTEEN

THE COUNSELORS immediately put Wyatt in Mental.

We were quarantined to our beds after the fight; I guess to make sure that no one else tried to cause any more problems. The counselors needed time to search through Wyatt's belongings. C. Dermont and Counselor Kirk confiscated a razor that they found stashed under the insole of one of Wyatt's shoes. It must not have been the first time something like that had happened at Camp Suicide. They knew exactly where to look.

All of us sat quietly on our beds—all of us except Finley. No matter how hard C. Dermont, Counselor Kirk, and Asshole Jim tried, they couldn't get him to calm down after the fight.

Later, I stared at the ceiling in the dark dormitory, listening to Finley's sniffles. His cries were a haunting reminder of why we were all there.

I found myself floating in the pool next to a mangled teddy bear. I saw Harpy Patricia arrive home with her hands full of groceries. I sank down below the surface of the water. I kept my eyes open. The chlorine burned at my irises. No matter how hard I tried—I couldn't move.

I had to push the images out of my mind—I had to think about something else.

I started to think about how our parents had tossed us aside because we didn't want to be alive anymore. I thought about the fact that we should have had the right to die if we wanted. I thought about the cuts on Wyatt's thighs, and the massive scars on my wrists.

I was miserable. I'd been miserable ever since that awful day.

My stupid miscalculations weren't going away. They were going to trouble me for the rest of my life.

That's why I wanted to end my existence.

I realized that Camp Suicide was as toxic as those memories. Depression is infectious. This place required us to rehash our pasts over and over again. I was going to die if I didn't get out of Camp Suicide soon. I didn't know how much longer I could stand it.

I closed my eyes and imagined that Finley's wails were a lullaby, gently singing me into a nightmarish sleep.

The next morning, I ate breakfast with Corin and Quint—the table under the plaque and photo of Counselor Winter. The guys, girls, and counselors all ate and conversed at their respective tables. The flies glowed in the sunshine that pooled in through the windows on the walls. And the nasty smell of eggs radiated out from the kitchen.

As I ate my cereal, Corin, Quint, and I talked about meaningless things. We talked about how nice the weather had been, how many bug bites Quint had on his neck, and whether or not the drugs we were taking actually helped. We didn't talk about what had happened the night before at all—at least, not until Wyatt returned from his stay in Mental.

All of our conversations stopped when Asshole Jim escorted Wyatt into the Crapateria. Wyatt resembled a crazy person in every sense of the word. He looked like he had been crying all night. And there was a massive bruise on his forehead as if he had repeatedly banged his head against the padded walls.

Seeing him in that state of existence scared me.

I think it scared all of us.

"What happened to him?" Corin asked. "His face looks like a plum."

I shifted my focus back to the girl across the table—the girl who stopped my bladder. I think we were finally, really starting to connect. Our conversations were effortless. Her hair looked perfect, even though we had just gotten out of bed.

"Our prison shower turned into a prison riot last night," I said.

My thoughts returned to my time in Mental. I remembered the piss-stained floor. The smell of stale vomit. The feeling of the noose suffocating my stomach. And the way the straitjacket had chafed my skin.

I couldn't ever go back to that place.

Then something happened that I didn't expect. We watched as Ash got up from his table. He walked toward Wyatt and Asshole Jim. Asshole Jim tensed up as if he were about to be attacked.

Ash extended his hand for Wyatt to shake. "Ash is sorry you ended up in Mental, dude."

Wyatt sucked in a load of wet snot. "I'm sorry, too."

"Truce?" Ash offered.

Wyatt nodded in agreement.

I honestly didn't think that Wyatt had anything to be sorry about. Ash had confronted him in the wrong way. He should have waited until they were out of the showers and away from the rest of the group. He should have privately asked Wyatt about the cuts on his thighs, instead of turning Wyatt's pain into a spectacle.

"That's good," Quint said with a smile.

I didn't think it was good at all—I was disgusted that Wyatt had been thrown into Mental.

"Is it?" I asked. "I don't really get why Squirrelly Wyatt is apologizing at all. Annoying Ash was the one who provoked the fight in the first place."

Quint disagreed. "What are you talking about? Ash was just looking out for him."

"By getting him thrown into Mental?" I gawked. "I know it was just for a night, but let's not lie to ourselves. That padded closet makes even the strongest minds suicidal. Imagine what it does to the weakest."

Quint shrugged. "Sometimes more than one person can be wrong in a situation."

Corin rejoined the conversation. "Not usually, though."

"Wyatt's been cutting himself to punish himself for being gay. They had to do something," Quint noted.

I shrugged in response. I realized that if Wyatt didn't cut himself, then eventually his pain would erupt out of him in an action way worse than a cut on his thigh.

The truth was that I didn't think the counselors had to do anything at all. Wyatt should have had the right to self-inflict pain if he wanted. We all should have had complete control over how we lived our lives—or if we even wanted to live them at all.

"We all have a right to deal with our problems in our own way," Corin asserted.

I smiled. Just another reason why Corin and I were destined to meet at this place. Corin thought exactly like I did. I hoped she was starting to like me as much as I liked her. I was setting myself up to get really hurt if she didn't.

She had to see how much we had in common.

"But not that way," Quint argued.

Corin used this opportunity to preach, "We don't have any rights or privacy at all in this place. Eventually, we all end up in Mental."

Quint nodded. "I can't argue with that."

Then Corin dropped her bombshell: "That's why we have to escape, as soon as we can."

I'd been thinking about escaping since the moment I arrived, but I knew I didn't have anywhere to go.

Quint couldn't believe his ears. "Wait. What?"

Corin tried to convince Quint that he had come up with the idea on his own. "Don't act like you haven't thought about it."

Quint paused. I watched him debate the notion in his head. I knew that part of him agreed with Corin, but I also imagined that he was afraid of getting caught.

"How would you do it, anyway?" I asked.

Corin glared at Quint. "First, I need a confirmation from our moral compass over here that he won't go blabbing."

I glanced at Quint, who was still running the scenario through his head. I realized that he wasn't exactly the type of person who would jump at the opportunity to break the rules. I wasn't normally that type of person, either. But a place like Camp Suicide called for extreme modifications to a person's character in order to survive.

"It's fine; he won't tell anyone. Will you, Quint?" I asked.

Optimist Quint frowned. "It's not like it matters."

"Seriously, though," Corin said.

Quint looked into her eyes. "I won't. I don't want anyone else to end up in Mental because of me."

"See?" I said.

Corin smiled in a conniving sort of way. "Gotcha. Well, let me put it this way. A plan has been set into motion. All you have to do is come along for the ride as soon as it's ready for action."

Corin's mysterious nature was intoxicating. I loved that she was a leader. I loved that she wanted to take me along for the ride. I would blindly follow her anywhere she wanted me to go. This was all the proof I needed that she liked me, too.

Why else would she want to take me with her?

"The sooner the better," I said. "I don't know how much longer I can stand this place."

I couldn't wait to be out of Camp Suicide. I couldn't wait to be alone with Corin. I thought about how it would feel to caress her skin. To touch her lips. To feel each other's heartbeat. I couldn't contain my arousal. Everything about this plan was exhilarating.

"I'll be the Bonnie to your Clyde," Corin said.

I didn't know who Bonnie and Clyde were, but if it meant we'd get out of this place, I didn't care.

Corin reached out and grabbed my hand. It was as if her pulse connected with mine. As if our souls attached as one.

Quint raised his eyebrows. "And that's my cue."

He got up and took his tray to the wash bins.

Corin stopped my heart. "You're different from the rest of them, Hunter S. Thompson. I can see that now."

Did that mean she liked me now? Did she want to be with me?

As I stared into her eyes, I began to think about what had happened just a few months before. I knew that if Corin found out about The Incident, she would probably hate me, too. The noose tightened its grip around my stomach, and I cringed in pain.

I pulled my hand away slowly. "You don't know me."

"I know enough," Corin assured me. "You're not a pig. You're genuine."

But I knew that wasn't true. She didn't know nearly enough about me. Once people found out about The Incident, their feelings toward me always changed.

"If you actually knew anything about me, you'd run the other way," I said.

Corin shook her head. "I doubt that."

I couldn't ever tell her about what had happened—not if I wanted her to feel the way I felt about her.

"I know it," I confidently said.

I didn't want to talk about it anymore, so I got up and took my tray over to one of the wash bins. It probably hurt Corin's feelings that I didn't explain more, but I was allowed to have secrets.

Corin had a thick green file full of secrets, too.

SEVENTEEN

THERAPIST JESS sat in the chair across from me, holding my red file, with that stupid look on her face.

You know, that look where someone stares at you like you should confess your sins, but you have no idea what they want you to say. My parents and doctors always used to give me that look when they thought I was lying about something.

Maybe that's why I hated it so much.

Most of my Shrinker Sessions were spent in silence—mainly cause I didn't want to talk—and most of the time I felt like she didn't know what to ask.

I spent my sessions staring at the artwork that had been fixed to the ceiling—she had *Starry Night* taped up next to a less famous painting of the Eiffel Tower. Or I'd categorize the books on the shelves—one day I noticed that she had a copy of *Fear and Loathing in Las Vegas*, and I wondered if she had placed it on her shelf to play with my mind—or observe the little green aphids that inhabited the multitudes of plants. And sometimes I just stared directly into Therapist Jess's face in an attempt to make her uncomfortable.

Therapy always made me feel as exposed as a naked person onstage. I suspected that Therapist Jess had already read everything about me in my red file. She thought she could heal me by giving me time to talk about The Incident on my own. And that she was doing her job by being there for me. But I didn't want to talk.

A file could never have captured the magnitude of what had happened. It could never fully dictate the level of hatred that Surgeon Dick and Harpy Patricia held for me after that day. I was as broken as my shattered bong. There was no way to heal me.

Sometimes she'd say, "Why don't you start talking and see what comes out?"

And I'd respond, "About what?"

Then she'd shrug and continue to stare at me with that stupid look as if I were defying her or something. In some ways, I wished that Therapist Jess would ask me questions like the doctors did after my suicide attempts. At least then we would have had some more trajectory. Not that I would have answered any of the questions anyway. But to me, it didn't really feel like she was trying, either.

Fun fact: Therapy was less frustrating back at home, when I could ditch out on my sessions.

EIGHTEEN

IT WAS TAKE THE CAMPERS to Happy Lake day! Guys on one shore—girls on the other.

"I'm Counselor Kylie, and this is a small sailboat!"

I stood next to Quint with the rest of the guys, while the athletic Counselor Sporty Kylie enthusiastically pointed out the features on a small sailboat. She was even more excited about everything than C. Dermont.

Counselor Kylie had led us through one of the magnetic chain-link gates that surrounded the lake, and we were standing on the shore.

Remember? The lake where I destroyed Quint with just a few simple words? Yeah—*that* Happy Lake.

I wondered why Camp Suicide had a lake at all—and more importantly, why wasn't it completely off-limits? Corin had alluded to something terrible happening at Happy Lake during the previous session. To me, this activity seemed like a drowning fest waiting to happen. I guess that's probably why they installed the fence, but they couldn't exactly suicide-proof small-boat sailing.

The water was thick like fog. There weren't any clouds in the sky. And we were forced to wear our shoes on the beach because we were going to be handling heavy equipment. My shoes were completely filled with sand, and it was getting into my socks.

I could see the girls on the opposite shore as C. Dermont guided them through a relay race that involved swimming, running, and jumping. I wondered if Corin was just as bored as I was. If she thought the activities were just as pointless as I did.

I turned my attention back to the small sailboat. I'd never seen a boat like this before, and to be honest, it was a whole lot smaller than I had expected. Only two people could ride in it at a time, and it had this striped blue sail that looked like something out of a cartoon.

Optimist Quint nudged me and said, "This is actually pretty cool."

I gave him a dose of his own medicine. "It's not like it matters."

We both laughed, catching Counselor Kylie's attention. She smiled at us before she continued with her lecture. "All right, campers! Get ready! Because by next week, all of you will be able to identify the following. . . ."

And that's when I tuned her out. It was like she was yelling all the time. She was *that* excited.

Small sailboats aren't exciting, like, at all.

I didn't care to know anything about this crap. This lesson was completely useless in the real world. I guess if I lived on an island, maybe it would have come in handy. But my family wasn't exactly the type of family who would go sailing, or invest in a small sailboat. We were more of the yacht types—hey, I said Surgeon Dick was rich.

All this therapy shit was and is expensive.

Counselor Kylie's voice faded in and out. "The hull, the deck, the bow, the stern . . ."

I could see Corin running in her teal one-piece bathing suit. She was too far away for me to make out any of her features, but I could imagine what she looked like.

I closed my eyes. Suddenly, we were on that sailboat together with the front of the boat cutting through the waves. Her swimsuit matched her sapphire eyes. Her silky brown hair blew against my bare chest. I didn't feel uncomfortable about my body at all—Corin liked me just the way I was. We stared into each other's eyes and laughed until our sides hurt. We both knew sailing was dumb, but it didn't matter—we'd try anything together.

Corin got up and spread her arms as if she were flying over the lake.

"This is amazing!" she exclaimed. "I'm flying right on the hull!"

A weird thing to say . . .

"Can you point out the hull?" Corin asked.

That was even weirder. Why did Corin care about the hull so much?

"Hunter?"

And then I remembered that I was standing on the edge of the fenced-in lake—in my lace-less shoes—with a bunch of dudes surrounding me. I snapped out of my fantasy and wiped the drool from the corner of my mouth.

Counselor Kylie asked me again, "Hunter! Can you point out the hull?"

The small sailboat might as well have been an alien. I had no idea where the hull was, and I didn't really care. I just wanted to be with Corin. I wanted my fantasy to become a reality.

I sighed. "I can't."

"How about paying attention?" she scolded.

I always found some way to get in trouble, even with the happiest counselor on the planet.

Counselor Kylie scanned the rest of the group. "Who can point out the hull?"

Flinching Finley flinched as he raised his bony hand and stepped forward. He could be such a suck-up—but he was too weak and frail to dislike.

"Good! Show Mr. Thompson," Counselor Kylie ordered.

Finley found the hull without a problem and made me look like a complete idiot. I would have felt bad for not paying attention if I actually cared about sailing. But I didn't. The only thing I could focus on was Corin.

She had my complete and undivided attention.

NINETEEN

I FOUND MYSELF thinking about The Incident less and less during the day.

Corin was a great distraction.

But every night, when I closed my eyes, it seemed like my stupid miscalculations came flooding back. The dream always started with me playing video games and smoking from Lola. The world would blur into a pool, and the smell of chlorine would permeate the air. I'd stand on the deck, staring at the teddy bear, and then I'd wake up—feeling like the noose had a death grip around my stomach.

One night, after I wiped the sweat off my brow and caught my breath again, I noticed that Counselor Kirk was watching me from the La-Z-Boy—he and C. Dermont alternated overnights with us. I quickly sat up in my bed and acted like nothing was wrong—which was hard to do, considering I woke up heaving for air.

The path lamps outside illuminated the room in a pale glow. Everything was colorless, like something out of an old movie.

Counselor Kirk pushed the La-Z-Boy across the floor until he was next to my bed. The sliding of the cushioned recliner made so much noise that I'm positive it woke up the rest of the guys.

"Can I join you?" he asked.

I didn't want him to sit, but I also didn't feel like I had much of a choice. I could still feel the sweat dripping from my pits and down along my spine. I could feel the noose around my stomach tightening its grip—tighter and tighter and tighter.

I nodded.

Counselor Kirk sat down in the La-Z-Boy and faced me. In the shadowy light, his stubble looked even thicker on his completely symmetrical face. He spoke in a low whisper, "Looks like you've got some demons."

He was right, of course, but I wasn't about to tell him that. I never talked about The Incident, and when people brought it up, I either walked away or deflected the subject.

Avoiding isn't lying.

"It was just a bad dream," I said, brushing it off.

"You have a lot of those. C. Dermont and I have noticed that you have one every night."

As if I needed to be reminded.

He had been watching me sleep. I guess it made sense—that was his job. But it still creeped me out down to my core. I didn't like the idea of someone observing me in such a vulnerable state. I liked to control the information that people had about me, and how they saw me as a person. Believe it or not, how people perceived me *actually* mattered.

I shrugged. "So?"

"So, I thought I'd tell you why I'm here. I think it might help you."

I thought that it probably wouldn't help me—not in the grand scheme of things—but I decided to hear him out.

What other choice did I have?

Counselor Kirk took a deep breath. "My sister committed suicide when I was in ninth grade. She was a year older than me."

I waited for Counselor Kirk to continue his story. It seemed like this was really hard for him. When he didn't go on, I forced myself to say, "That's sad."

The truth is that suicide isn't that sad to me—in a lot of ways, suicide is a relief. The person's family no longer has to deal with a rainstorm every day, and the person is finally free of the lightning storm that consumed their life.

Counselor Kirk exhaled. "Yeah. Sorry, this is always difficult. Listen, Hunter, the reason I'm telling you this is because I think we can relate."

I disagreed. "I've never had a family member commit suicide."

"I know, just . . . just hear me out," Counselor Kirk said. "My sister and I went to the same school. She never quite fit in with any of the groups and spent her lunches alone. I knew she was having issues, but I thought she could handle them.

"One day, David Fargot asked her on a date, and my sister decided to go. It was the first time any guy had given her any sort of attention, so she was thrilled about the prospect.

"The day before the date, I found out that the popular girls had convinced David to take my sister out to see if he could get her to give up her virginity on their first date. Those girls planned to sabotage and humiliate her by telling the whole school that my sister was a slut, and David was in on the plan," Counselor Kirk explained.

"That's terrible," I said.

It really was. The cattiness of girls in high school always amazes me. Girls constantly put each other down as if it will make them feel better about themselves. In my mind, they should spend more time lifting each other up. Isn't that what feminism is supposed to be all about? People are so freaking disappointing.

"It gets worse. My sister was so excited about the date. She had talked about it for days, and my parents were thrilled that she finally had a friend—that she was finally happy. I thought about telling them about what I'd heard at school, but I decided not to. I thought that my sister would be smarter than to lose her virginity on her first night out with a guy. I thought that she would see through those girls' plan. But I was wrong.

"The day after the date, David told the girls that their scheme had worked, and that he had broken it off with her right after. The girls proceeded to tell the entire school that my sister was a slut. Everyone called her a whore, and I think she started to believe that she was one.

"It went on for weeks, but my sister pretended like it was all fine. After about a month of torment, I walked into her bedroom one morning to grab her for school, and found her body hanging in the closet."

Counselor Kirk wiped his eyes.

I didn't know what to say. I understood that most kids my age were suicidal because they were bullied. I'd been bullied, too, but not like that. After The Incident, most of the kids at my school just avoided talking to me altogether. They tormented me with silence—like I didn't exist at all—like I didn't matter.

"I've felt the weight of that guilt ever since that awful day, and I'll never get that image out of my head. I could have prevented the whole thing by stopping her from going on that date at all, but I didn't. I just let it happen. I let them humiliate her.

"I never talked to her about it. Not once. I never asked her to share her feelings with me. I just ignored the issue like it didn't exist, and let her carry the weight of that pain all on her own. If I'd just talked to her . . ." Counselor Kirk exhaled again.

What happened to Counselor Kirk's sister was a tragedy, but it didn't compare to what had happened to me. The noose around my stomach wasn't ever going to go away. I'm sure that he felt guilty about what had happened, but it wasn't his fault she was dead. It wasn't his fault that the other girls at his sister's school were complete and total bitches.

"I used to have nightmares, too, Hunter."

"Okay," I responded.

I'm positive he didn't feel like he was drowning every time he closed his eyes. His nightmares couldn't compare to mine.

"After I started working here, after I took some accountability for what happened, the nightmares started to fade away," Counselor Kirk explained. "I know that I should've said something, that I should have stepped in to prevent what happened. I take full responsibility for my wrongs."

"But it doesn't make what happened go away," I said.

"No, it doesn't; you're right. But taking accountability is the first step toward forgiving yourself."

I realized that this was all a ploy to get me to confess. To get me to talk about what event had brought *me* down to rock bottom.

Counselor Kirk wanted me to talk about how I ended up at Camp Suicide, but he knew that he couldn't just ask *the question.*

"My nightmares will never go away," I said.

"They might."

I glared into his eyes. "They won't. Talking about what happened to me won't turn back time, just like you telling me about your sister won't bring her back. You're trying to act like it's all okay because you work at a place that imprisons people who have the same problems that she did. You're not helping me by telling your story, and you're not helping anyone by working here."

I now feel horrible that I said all that, but at the time, I felt like it was true.

Counselor Kirk didn't know what to say, or how to respond. He just rose and loudly pushed the La-Z-Boy back to its spot.

I watched him sit down and stare at me for a bit before I rolled over to face the other way.

I was a total jerk to Counselor Kirk, but I hated the way he was constantly trying to manipulate me into talking about The Incident. Talking about what happened couldn't change what happened.

I closed my eyes and fell back to sleep.

I found myself standing on the edge of the pool again.

TWENTY

IT WAS BUILD a fort day!

But seriously, the first week flew by, and it was already Friday again. Fridays were the best because they merged all six of the boys and all six of the girls into one group. And I got to hang out with Corin for the entire day.

It was a sunny day, the type of day where you actually wanted to be outside instead of cooped up in a cell. We stood in a circle around a massive tree between the Shrinker and the Crapateria. It seriously might have been the biggest tree ever. There were bugs everywhere, and it was so hot that I was sweating balls. And there was a large pile of wood and tools stacked on the ground.

Counselor Winter led the group exercise on Fridays. She usually looked as kind as she did in that photo, but I knew that warm smile was a lie—I'd met the real Counselor Winter back in Mental. I would have thought that a person who founded a prison for depressed teens would have looked more like a witch out of a fantasy film. Counselor Winter was worse than a witch, though; you didn't know she was actually evil because of how nice she sounded all the time. Her fake grins and homely stature didn't fool me for a second.

Mr. and Mrs. Asshole and C. Dermont were also there to supervise us throughout the day.

Corin stared at me from across the circle, while Counselor Witchy Winter explained the exercise. By then, I had convinced myself that Corin was starting to like me back. Why else would she stare at me all the time?

"The objective is to use the diagrams to construct the fort by sunset," Counselor Winter explained. "We're trusting you to be careful with the tools. These tools can be dangerous, but there will always be things out in the real world that you can hurt yourself with, too. Our goal is to show you that using a tool properly is much more fulfilling than self-inflicting pain."

I stared down at the two hammers, nails, and shovels. All the wood was already cut. The tools available to us weren't *that* dangerous, but they wanted us to feel like we were trustworthy.

Squirrelly Wyatt had rebounded back to his former obnoxious self. "I'm Wyatt. What do we get if we do?"

We were supposed to reintroduce ourselves when we asked a question or talked because Counselor Winter was bad with names. I'm sure she wanted to make sure that she could put faces to the multitudes of files she had undoubtedly read. Even though I know she wouldn't forget Squirrelly Wyatt and me from our visits to Mental.

Counselor Winter smiled and it almost warmed my heart—*kidding*. I never fell for Counselor Witchy Winter's warm tone or phony smiles.

"The satisfaction of a job well done and the feeling of accomplishment," she responded.

"*Psh*, I want something real," Wyatt said.

I agreed with him. These outdoor team-building activities were just distractions from our actual problems. I was getting tired of them.

Blaze was standing right next to me, and I heard him mumble to Ash, "This would be so much more fun if we were high."

Ash chuckled. "This would be so much more fun if it didn't involve labor."

I agreed with Ash, and I sort of agreed with Blaze.

The girl with tan skin, short hair, and the obnoxious laugh raised her hand. "I'm Nora. I think that the girls should not have to participate in this activity unless we want to. I don't want to break a nail, and I do not lift things."

Everyone hated Nora from the second she opened her mouth.

Nora was even more obnoxious than Annoying Ash and Squirrelly Wyatt—I didn't think that was even possible.

The girl with the purple hair snapped back, "Um, I'm Violet. I think the girls should lead this exercise, because that comment was literally the most moronic thing I've ever heard, and equal rights. Hashtag: 'nough said."

Okay, Feminist Violet was almost equally as insufferable as Nora. Violet's purple hair was just so freaking trendy, am I right? I could already tell that she was going to be one of those girls who constantly shoved her feminist views down my throat as if I single-handedly opposed the women's suffrage movement.

Even Squirrelly Wyatt was annoyed by the two of them. "Fool, you did not just hashtag the end of a sentence."

I hated hashtags, but then again, I'd deleted all my social media accounts after The Incident.

Asshole Jim stepped out of the shadows to remind us that he was still an asshole. "All of you will be participating, and how about this? Everyone who doesn't participate will go to Mental."

Nora placed a hand on her chubby hip and cocked her head back. "Serious?"

Asshole Jim glared at her. "Serious. Also, we counted every single nail, and you're only getting two hammers. We'll count all the nails in the walls at lunch and at the end of the day. Don't try to pull a fast one. I don't have a problem searching every single one of you and throwing you all in Mental if you step out of line."

I couldn't help but wonder how we would all fit in that tiny-ass room. Asshole Jim's threats didn't sound practical to me. Also, it would be pretty freaking hard to kill yourself with a hammer or a nail—just saying. His threats were baseless and annoying.

C. Dermont tried to ease the tension. These planned group activities were supposed to be fun, after all.

Fun fact: The activities were never fun.

He chuckled, causing his massive gut to bounce. "We're lucky to have Counselor Winter here today, and we should show her our appreciation for founding Camp Sunshine by completing her exercise to the best of our ability."

Yes, yes, Counselor Witchy Winter should definitely have been applauded for founding Camp Suicide.

Counselor Winter puffed up with pride. "Well said, C. Dermont." She scanned our faces. "You had better figure out how to work together."

Quint noticed that Corin was staring at me with affectionate eyes. He nudged me.

"Okay, she's officially creeping me out," Quint said.

I elbowed him to shut his face.

I liked the way Corin looked at me. A lot. But it also confused me. A lot. She had said that I wasn't a pig, that I was genuine—did that mean that she wanted me to like her? Was I supposed to be looking at her, too? Did she like me? What was going on?

Counselor Winter grinned. "I'll leave you to it," she said, handing the diagrams to Nora—as if we had elected her our leader. And then Mr. and Mrs. Asshole, C. Dermont, and Counselor Winter all stepped away.

Our small world suddenly erupted into chaos. No one wanted Nora to be our leader, and everyone began to fight with her over the diagrams.

I pushed through the scuffle toward Corin. "Okay, you can't keep staring at me like that," I told her. "You're seriously going to give Quint a heart attack."

Corin shrugged. "I can't help it," she said, as if I had cast some sort of spell over her.

My heart fluttered as she left me in the dust. I quickly tucked my boner up under my waistline. Okay, her intentions were becoming clear. Corin definitely was starting to like me back.

I had completely forgotten about the noose around my stomach. I was over the moon with arousal at this point—maybe I would lose my virginity to her.

Corin forced her way through the commotion over to Nora and snatched the diagrams right out of her grimy little hands.

"Hey!" Nora protested. "I was chosen as the official leader of this activity."

Not true, but Nora was one of those people who probably believed every lie that came out of her own loud mouth.

Corin responded with some sass, "Were you?" She turned to the rest of the group. "Nora the Narcissist thinks that we chose her to be the leader of our disjointed brigade. Show of hands, who wants Nora to be in charge of building our lovely abode?"

Not a single person raised his or her hand.

Corin turned back to Nora. "The people have spoken."

Narcissists don't make very good leaders.

Nora responded by putting her hand in Corin's face and shoving it away. Corin handled the situation with grace by taking a step back.

Feminist Violet swelled with pride. "I'm so proud of this movement."

And the girl wearing the Lez Be Friends shirt said what we were all thinking. "Sometimes you sound like a tool."

"That's cruel, Mackenzie. Take it back," Violet protested.

Friendly Mackenzie stayed silent.

The young girl with long curly hair weighed in. "I honestly just wish I could sit and read."

Corin took control of the group. "Well, Harper the Librarian, since you like reading so much, you and Quint the Optimist can be in charge of the diagrams. Paisley, Mackenzie, Blaze, and Ash, you'll be in charge of hammering and construction. Wyatt and Nora, you'll be doing the heavy lifting—"

Wyatt butted in, "You are not about to pair me with her."

Nora also couldn't keep her trap shut. "I thought I made it clear that I don't lift things."

I figured out that Ominous Paisley was the ethnically ambiguous silent observer who never talked.

Corin was ready with her response. "I'm sorry, show of hands. Who thinks Nora the Narcissist and Wyatt the Wannabe Gangster should be in charge of the heavy lifting?"

This time we all raised our hands.

Narcissist Nora and Squirrelly Wyatt glared at us as if we had turned their world upside down.

Corin's leadership abilities were probably one of her sexiest attributes. She could take control of any situation. I admired that.

I admired everything about her.

Corin continued, "The people have spoken. Violet and Finley, you'll be in charge of digging the holes for the support beams. Hunter and I will oversee the operations of our beloved construction site." She clapped her hands. "Break!"

Corin grabbed my arm and pulled me right next to her. I could smell her freshly washed hair. . . .

. . . Think about hairy buttholes . . .

It wasn't working. Corin's arm touched mine. It was like I was stuck in a wonderful dream.

Quint and Harper joined us on each side. Corin held up the diagrams so that we could assess the job that needed to be done.

I glanced over at the counselors—C. Dermont and Counselor Witchy Winter were looking directly at us and talking under their breaths. Thankfully, the looks on their faces made my arousal diminish. I suspected that C. Dermont was probably gossiping about my infatuation with Corin, and how it bothered him so much.

It's not like I could control who I liked.

The noose felt snug around my stomach. I wondered if they wanted us to be miserable so that they could keep Camp Suicide in business. Or maybe they were just jealous of how happy Corin made me feel.

I turned my attention back to the diagrams. They were just regular old blueprints. There wasn't anything complicated or special about the fort we were building. It was just a shack with four walls, a roof, and a cardboard door.

Corin explained, "We'll need to construct four walls. Nora, Wyatt, I'll need you to bring the following over to our wielders of the hammer and nails. . . ."

I stared at Corin in awe of her confidence and poise.

Could a girl like her actually be interested in a guy like me?

As I watched her give out orders and direct the group, I couldn't figure out what she was doing at Camp Suicide.

Corin finished barking out directions, and her eyes connected with mine. Suddenly, I remembered the massive green file I had seen with Corin's name on it during my first therapy session at Camp Suicide. The noose started to choke my stomach. I wondered what was written on all those pages.

What was *her* problem?

TWENTY-ONE

BY MIDDAY, we had the walls and roof of the fort nailed together.

They weren't pretty or structurally sound, but they were walls, and they were nailed together pretty darn well. We laid them out on the ground and set them into position to be raised after lunch. Asshole Jim counted every single nail that we had used on the walls and the nails that were left in the bin before he allowed us to eat. I was starving—even though I hadn't really lifted a finger.

Narcissist Nora and Squirrelly Wyatt had complained all morning, but surprisingly, they did all the heavy lifting that we asked. Every time I started to feel bad for making them do all the hard work, I reminded myself of how obnoxious they both were.

The ground was soft with moss and grass. Mr. and Mrs. Asshole, C. Dermont, and Counselor Winter sat in the shade under another tree. They were already enjoying their sack lunches of peanut butter sandwiches, juice, an apple, and string cheese. And they were just far enough away so that we could enjoy some private conversation among ourselves.

I had grabbed my brown-bagged lunch and was starting to walk toward the guys when Corin reached out to grab my arm—she looked right at the massive scars on my wrists. I felt absolutely and totally exposed. The noose tightened around my stomach so tight that I felt like I was drowning—my appetite disappeared for a moment. But

Corin didn't ask me how I got them or bring them up at all. Her eyes met mine. She didn't even blink.

"Not so fast, Hunter S. Thompson. I didn't say you could go to lunch."

The noose loosened and my stomach rumbled in response.

Corin laughed at me. "You're sitting with us today."

I clenched my fist even tighter around the brown paper bag. I glanced over at the girls, horrified at the prospect. My mouth felt like it was full of cotton. Sitting with the friends of the girl you like is about as dangerous as sitting in a pen full of rattlesnakes.

"I'm good," I said.

Corin stared at me with dejected eyes. "I thought you wanted to get to know me better."

I couldn't say no to her. She could get me to do anything she wanted.

And I literally mean anything.

I sighed. "Fine. But I'm bringing Quint." I called out to my friend. "Quint, you're sitting with me."

Quint took his nose away from his sandwich and saw Corin at my side. He shook his head. "No, I'm not."

"Yes, you are."

Quint could see that I really didn't want to enter the snake pit alone, so he reluctantly joined.

"You owe me, big-time," he mumbled in my ear.

"It's not like it matters," I mumbled back.

We both smiled.

"What's so funny?" Corin asked.

We responded in unison, "It doesn't matter."

Narcissist Nora, Reader Harper, Feminist Violet, Ominous Paisley, and Friendly Mackenzie sat under a tree, enjoying their sandwiches. Their gossip went silent as we walked up.

Corin stepped into the center of their circle. "Ladies, Hunter and Quint will be joining us for lunch today, so please, put your faces on."

Quint and I exchanged a skeptical look as the girls made room for us to join their circle. We sat down on the soft moss and began to eat our peanut butter sandwiches in unbearable silence. Corin stared at me as she munched on her sandwich, and everyone noticed.

"So are you two dating?" Violet asked—her purple hair was really shiny in the sunlight.

With the way Corin was staring at me, I would have thought that we were a married couple, which confused me even more.

Did we have a connection, or not? What the heck was going on?

In some ways, I wished she would just tell me what to do and how to act around her.

"As dating is forbidden in the land of sunshine and suicide, I would have to say that no, Mr. Thompson and I are not dating."

I continued to silently eat my sandwich. I glanced over at Quint—he looked even more confused about Corin's and my situation.

"But you like each other?" Mackenzie inquired.

Corin turned to me with affectionate eyes. "I'll defer to Hunter on that one."

Did she like me? Was I allowed to admit that I liked her?

My brain was spinning like a top. I didn't know what to do or how to respond. I took another bite of my sandwich. The snakes' eyes all simultaneously locked on me, waiting to inject me with their venom if I said the wrong thing.

Luckily, Quint came to my rescue. "His mouth's full; he can't answer."

They all started giggling.

Nora tried to regain the spotlight. "I seriously need a manicure. So gross. Nobody look at my nails."

At that moment, I connected that Nora constantly had to make everything about Narcissist Nora. That was *her* problem.

She really was a narcissist, and you couldn't tell her anything.

Corin shut her down. "God, Nora the Narcissist, can we talk about me for, like, two seconds?"

This time, we all started laughing.

Mackenzie shifted the focus back to us—she had acne on her cheeks, and her voice was deeper than I had imagined it would have been. "As far as I'm concerned, you two can have love, and you can have marriage. My girlfriend and I don't need to constantly stick labels on our relationship."

Violet smiled. "That's so beautiful."

Mackenzie's cheeks flushed. "Did I tell you we met at soccer camp?"

Corin seemed annoyed. "You've told us, and you would say that, but, Mackenzie, I assure you that Hunter and I are not in a relationship—we aren't even sure if we like each other yet. Therefore, we are just as against labels as you and your lesbian lover."

I was starting to get a headache.

"Can we stop putting me on a pedestal and talk about something else?" I asked.

Corin put it to a vote. "Mr. Thompson would like to talk about something else. All those in favor?"

Nora interjected, "Wait, I have to say something—"

And we shut her down. "NO!"

Quint laughed through a mouth full of orange juice and it came squirting out of his nose. We burst into laughter at the sight of it running down his chest. Quint had humiliated himself in front of the snakes.

He saved me from being bitten, but he couldn't save me from all my uncertainty.

Did she like me? Or not?

TWENTY-TWO

THE SKY TURNED into a bed of roses, and our bodies glistened with sweat.

Sounds sexy, I know, but it actually just stank.

We all swelled with accomplishment as we stared at the fort. Sure, it was flimsy and would never survive a storm. Sure, the wood was rotting and gray. Sure, the door to the fort was just a piece of folding cardboard. And sure, the floor was just a lot of leveled dirt. But as shitty as it was, it was ours.

Asshole Jim collected the two hammers and did a final count of the nails while Counselor Winter applauded us on a job well done.

Corin and I were standing so close that our hands were almost touching.

Our hands were almost touching!

"I feel like this is extremely anticlimactic," Corin said. "It looks like a crappy shed."

I had stopped staring at our shitty fort. My eyes were locked on Corin. The lightning bugs flew in front of her face, igniting her eyes into twinkling sapphires. "Yeah." I exhaled.

Corin turned to meet my gaze and blushed. "Okay, you can't keep staring at me like that, Hunter S. Thompson. You're seriously going to creep me out. We don't even know what this is yet!"

She winked at me.

She liked me—that was confirmation, right?

We both blushed. Every part of my body felt warm. We stank like skunks. Our faces were covered in dirt. And our hair was a disheveled mess. But we were together.

I liked her so freaking much.

Therapist Jess and Counselor Kirk arrived for the night shift. They saw our construction and beamed.

"Whoa! Look at that!" Therapist Jess exclaimed.

"Beautiful!" Counselor Kirk added.

Nora glared at both of them with a disgusted look on her face. "Okay, it's just a wooden fort. Stop acting like we constructed the Louvre."

Poor Narcissist Nora. She detested the fort because she actually had to help construct it when she would rather have been doing *anything* else. She even broke a nail, which she'd have to live with until the end of the month-long session.

Optimist Quint was also tired; the dust and dirt stuck to his curly hair. "Seriously, it's not like any of this matters," he said.

Annoying Ash mocked Narcissist Nora. "Ash is surprised you know what the Louvre is."

She placed a hand on her hip. "I live on Earth."

"Be kind to one another," Therapist Jess urged. She was wearing bell-bottoms that covered her Birkenstocks. Then, she had an idea. "How about a sleepover? Counselor Kirk?"

Counselor Kirk smiled. "I think that's an excellent idea. Showers first, and then we'll convene back at the fort for a campout."

We'd started to move toward the showers when Corin whispered in my ear, "Looks like we're gonna be sleeping together."

She was teasing me with happiness—with losing my virginity. I thought that all my dreams might eventually come true, that maybe Corin was the cure for my depression. I couldn't feel the noose around my stomach at all. My insides erupted with excitement, and every muscle in my body tensed up. I got the biggest boner ever, and I didn't even care. My face flushed as Corin joined Paisley and skipped away.

Okay, that was proof. She definitely liked me back—right?

RIGHT?

We were going to be sleeping in the same area together. On the dirt ground, and in a flimsy, shitty fort, but nonetheless, in the vicinity of each other's body heat.

Then Counselor Winter walked up to me and brought me back to reality. "Hunter, can I talk to you for a second?".

I snapped out of my euphoria as I joined her away from the rest of the group, shielded in the dense trees. The sun was so low on the horizon that the rays burned through the gaps in the forest, forcing me to squint so that I could see Counselor Winter's wrinkly face.

I was getting tired of all these private conversations with authority figures.

I saw right through Counselor Witchy Winter's fake grin. "How are you enjoying your stay so far?" she asked in her obnoxiously nice voice.

I guess Counselor Winter didn't actually see Camp Suicide for the prison that it truly was.

I laughed. "That's a serious question? Did you forget the first day?"

Counselor Winter glared at me like she would throw me in Mental if I said another wrong word.

I quickly shrugged. "It's better than being at home."

Counselor Winter smiled again and her voice got even higher in pitch. "That's great to hear." She paused, I guess to contemplate how she was going to phrase her invasive examination. "C. Dermont tells me you've gotten close with Corin Snow Young."

There it was again. I didn't understand why who I decided to associate myself with at Camp Suicide was any of the counselors' business. I thought the whole point of this prison was to make us feel like we fit in somewhere—like we mattered. I finally felt like I mattered to Corin, and that made me feel good about myself. They should have understood that.

The thought of Mental loomed over my responses.

I tried not to let my anger show. "Okay?"

Counselor Winter took a deep breath. "I need to make sure that both of you are making smart decisions," she explained. And then she dropped a bombshell through the phoniest smile ever: "Corin is a manipulator."

This had to be a trick. They were just trying to drive us apart.

"I'm not sure it's appropriate to talk about my friend like that," I said.

I was appalled. I didn't even care if my response got me thrown into Mental again.

"Whether it's appropriate or not, I have to say something about it."

I couldn't believe that the founder of Camp Suicide would talk shit behind a camper's back. I thought that the conversation was pretty immature and sank to a new low. Even for prison camp.

I snapped back, "She's not manipulating me."

Counselor Winter snapped, too, but in a polite way, "Good." She was really worried about my friendship with Corin. I could see it in her eyes. "You'll tell us if she's trying to rope you into anything out of the ordinary, won't you, Hunter?"

My stomach sank and the noose burned my insides. Corin was putting me in a tough position. A position where I would have to lie. I hate liars, but I would become a liar myself to protect Corin. The counselors were the manipulative ones. They didn't deserve to know every detail about my friendship with Corin. I deserved *some* privacy.

My voice wavered. "She's not. Can I go now?"

Counselor Winter nodded. I turned to walk away.

I finally—sort of—had confirmation that Corin liked me back, and now it was all going to shit.

How far would I go to get Corin to like me as much as I liked her?

"And, Hunter," Counselor Winter called after me.

I stopped.

"If she's playing hard to get, she's already in your head. There's a reason why we installed that fence around Happy Lake, and it's partially because of her. We don't want another incident. If something's going on, you need to come clean," Counselor Winter stated.

My stomach flipped. The noose was so taut that it felt like someone was stabbing at my abdomen.

But I didn't turn back.

TWENTY-THREE

MY HEART POUNDED in my ears.

The deed was done. I had become a liar. One lie would lead to more lies, which would eventually lead to even more lies. I had become something I hated. But it was worth it if I got to spend more time with Corin. I would have done anything for her.

Corin wasn't the one forcing me to tell all these lies—the counselors were.

Camp Suicide turned me into a liar.

The forest floor crunched under my shoes. I could feel a cloud of bugs following me as I stepped onto the dirt trail. The path lights switched on, and I could see the shadows of the guys bouncing along in the distance.

I passed the girls' dorm—Solas—and eventually, I arrived at Ray. I bounded up the wooden stairs, swung the screen door open, and noticed that the inner magnetic locking door was left ajar. Asshole Jim was looming in the shadows as I walked into the dimly lit room. I could see the scar on his face, but his eyes were like black holes. All the other guys had already grabbed their pajamas, so I was alone in the dorm with Satan watching my every move.

"Hurry!" Asshole Jim barked.

"I'm going," I said.

I rushed over to the wooden drawer next to my bed. I sifted through my tangled pile of clothes to find a fresh pair of plaid blue boxers and socks. Then I opened the middle drawer and untangled my blue pajama top and plaid bottoms.

With my fresh outfit in hand, I turned to Asshole Jim and saluted him before I quickly ran out the door.

I made a right at the bottom of the stairs, onto the path that led to the Rainmaker. The rest of the guys were dillydallying, so I easily caught up with them. They also carried their pajamas so that they could change into them after showering. I slowed down so that I could eavesdrop a bit before I rejoined the group.

"What do you think Hunter did now?" Blaze asked.

"Probably nothing, fool. The counselors have a bunch of sticks up their asses, man. I'm sick of this place."

"They're gonna lobotomize me by the end of this," I said.

Flinching Finley jumped so high that I thought he might go into orbit.

"Jeez, man! What the hell?" Squirrelly Wyatt cursed. "We were just talking about—"

"I know you were," I cut him off.

I could tell they all felt extremely awkward. I started to walk next to Ash and Quint as we made our way toward the showers. Since I'd arrived at Camp Suicide, I knew that I had been a constant topic of gossip and conversation among my peers. For the first time in my life, I mattered enough to be talked about—even if it was all bullshit.

We walked in silence for a bit. Our feet slid in the dirt. I looked up at the massive green leaves whistling in the breeze. The stars were slowly shining through the twilight.

Quint finally asked, "What did Counselor Winter want?"

I lied again: "Nothing."

Quint didn't believe me, and why should he have?

"It didn't seem like nothing. What's going on with you, dude? Don't you trust me?"

I didn't want to talk about it anymore. I was starting to hate the person I was becoming, but it didn't matter as long as I could find out if I had a real connection with Corin. I thought about her all the time. Not knowing if she liked me back was driving me nuts.

She liked me back.

Right?

I mean, she said I was genuine. That had to mean something.

Ash sensed the awkward tension between Quint and me. "Dude!" he exclaimed. "You excited to hang out with Corin all night?"

I smiled, relieved that Ash had diverted the focus of the conversation back to something positive. "Yeah, yeah."

Ash joked, "Keep it in your pants. It's not like you two will be alone."

"Seriously, Hunter," Quint agreed.

"We're gonna sleep in the same room together—on separate sides of the room, but in the same room!" I couldn't contain my excitement.

"How thrilling," Quint said.

I laughed. "Hey, I'm allowed to be excited."

Quint shrugged. "And I'm allowed not to be."

"Just as long as you keep your horn dog on a leash," Squirrelly Wyatt said. "If I were into hobbits, I'd be trolling Comic-Con, fool."

"As offensive as that statement was, I am not offended. I'm not into squirrely-looking guys, or any guys for that matter," I responded.

"Don't lie to yourself. Every guy wants to try it at some point in their life," Wyatt joked. "But you're not gonna get it with me, fool."

We slowly entered the boys' bathroom so that we could take showers. As I entered the brightly lit space, I could tell that it bothered Quint that I wouldn't tell him what the conversation with Counselor Winter was about. I knew he would let it go, though.

I realized that I had become a hypocrite. But I trusted Corin.

I assured myself that she wasn't manipulating me.

TWENTY-FOUR

THE TIME HAD COME for our sleepover!

We were all showered, changed, and fed—they really did treat us like infants. The battery-powered LED candles flickered around us in the fort as we played a game of Go Fish. We weren't allowed to play poker because Therapist Jess was worried someone might get upset—like I said, infants.

Therapist Jess and Counselor Kirk had helped us lay blankets down on the dirt floor so that we would have a comfy place to sit and sleep. The fort was pretty small, so we were squished together. The hot, humid breeze crept through the cracks in the walls. Ash and Quint were positioned on either side of me. Corin, Blaze, Nora, Harper, Finley, Violet, and Paisley connected the rest of the circle.

Mr. and Mrs. Asshole had taken a post at the door and were chatting among themselves while we entertained ourselves.

Wyatt and Mackenzie were the only ones not playing the game. They were bonding on a sleeping bag, talking about how and when Wyatt should come out to his family.

It was my turn to go. I glanced down at my two aces and looked up at Corin. "Got any aces?" I asked.

She smiled at me flirtatiously and responded, "Why yes, Mr. Thompson. Yes, I do."

Corin handed me an ace with a small folded piece of paper tucked under the card. I placed the ace with the rest of my cards and carefully held the note behind my hand. The nerves crept into my body as I opened the folded note.

I stared down at the words scribbled in Corin's elegant handwriting.

I need you tonight.

I couldn't take my eyes away from the words.

She needed me? What did that mean?

A combination of panic and exhilaration pulsed through my veins. Suddenly, I got more nervous than I had ever been. I wondered if I would get to touch her—if she would want to touch me.

I might finally lose my virginity.

"Hunter?"

Ash's voice broke me out of my trance.

I realized that everyone was staring at me, waiting to see if I was done with my turn.

"That's it for me," I croaked.

"'*That's it for me!*'" screeched Ash, imitating my voice.

Everyone laughed.

"Quint, got any twos?" he asked.

I carefully folded the note and made sure that no one besides Corin was watching me as I stashed it in my pocket. My eyes connected with hers. I nodded.

This was it. I was finally going to find out how Corin really felt about me.

Even if it meant spending another night in Mental if we got caught.

TWENTY-FIVE

MY MIND WAS RACING as I lay on the floor, waiting for Corin to make her move.

The light from the trail lamps glowed through the cracks. The walls of the fort shook like an earthquake every time the wind picked up, causing me to worry that the entire place was going to collapse over our heads and bury us alive.

I couldn't stop wondering about what Corin would say.

Would she say anything? Or would she just start kissing me as soon as we got away?

Part of me didn't want to go with her.

What if she wanted to talk with me so that she could reject me? What if I was imagining all her advances?

I wasn't. Corin liked me, and I liked her.

I was positive—I thought so anyway.

I imagined what would happen if we both got caught. How we would probably end up in Mental overnight. But at least we'd be together.

Or so I hoped.

Mr. and Mrs. Asshole patrolled our small sleeping quarters as if we were locked in a jail cell—they didn't even bother to take their filthy combat boots off, so they were dragging dirt all over the blankets. The boys were quarantined to one side of the fort and the girls were on the other. I watched the cardboard door, but closed my eyes every time the guards passed so that they wouldn't notice I was awake.

After an eternity of waiting, Corin woke up Paisley to join her on a trip to the girls' bathroom. I watched them go. This was it—the time had come. I had to prepare myself for whatever she said. I'd never been more anxious. I planned to lie and say that I had to go to the Rainmaker—I knew that it was the only lie that would work in this situation.

Ugh—I'd tell any lie for Corin.

Quint was already snoring next to me, but he was a light sleeper and easy to wake up. I shook him lightly. He jolted as if he had just been woken from the dead—his curly brown hair exploded out in a 'fro.

I laughed. "Chill, dude; it's just me. I have to take a piss."

I was getting better at calming my voice when I was being dishonest. I felt worse lying to Quint than to anyone else. I was roping him into my plan. If Corin rejected me, Quint would be left to pick up the pieces. But she wasn't going to reject me.

She wasn't.

Quint moaned. "Seriously? I'd just fallen asleep."

I pulled him up. "Come on."

"Okay, fine."

He followed me toward the door.

Asshole Jim stopped us. "Gotta wait until the girls are back."

I was sick and tired of playing by the rules. I had already been forced to become a liar because of this wretched place. I wasn't about to let Asshole Jim win.

I clutched my junk like I really had to go and responded, "Either you let me go pee or I'll go on the floor. I have to go."

Asshole Jim glared at me. "You want to end up in Mental?"

I emphasized my sincerity, "Please. I seriously have to go."

Mr. Asshole looked to Mrs. Asshole. "I'm going to accompany—"

Mrs. Asshole waved her hand. "Just let them go, Jimmy. Stop being an asshole."

I smiled. Even Mrs. Asshole thought Asshole Jim was an asshole.

Asshole Jim was beaten at his own game. He stepped to the side. "Don't say I never did anything for you."

I bowed. "Thank you."

Then I grabbed Quint's hand and pulled him out the door before Asshole Jim could change his mind.

"This better not be a repeat of day one!" he called after us.

The sky was the darkest it could possibly be. The trees hung over the path like something out of a horror movie. And a fog had crept up from Happy Lake to make the air as thick as a cloud.

I was walking fast—like, really fast. I was worried that Corin would think I'd abandoned her. Or worse, that I'd chickened out. I could hear my heart pounding in my head, and my mouth turned to cotton. I felt like I needed to drink a gallon of water.

Quint was having trouble keeping up with my brisk pace. "Dude, slow down. The Rainmaker will . . ."

Quint's words trailed off as the Rainmaker came into view. We could see Corin and Paisley standing under a lamppost waiting for us to join them outside the latrines. Paisley's thick black hair was a disheveled mess, but Corin's looked perfect. Everything about Corin was perfect. The fluorescents in the log cabin bathroom pooled out onto the ground, and the smell of shit radiated into the air.

Quint grabbed my arm and stopped me. "This isn't a good idea, man. You heard what Asshole Jim said. You're going to get us all thrown into Mental."

His voice got really nasally when he was upset.

I ripped my hand from his grasp. "Be cool. I promise I'll be fast, okay? We just want to talk."

"Talk? Stop lying to yourself. I thought you said you don't lie. We both know what you want," Quint called me out.

"What?" I asked.

"Remember on the first day, when I asked if you really had to pee, you said, 'I don't lie, dude.' What if you get hurt? What if she rejects you?"

I shrugged.

Quint looked really worried; his tiny hands were clenched into fists. "Dude, this could really mess you up. She might not even like you back. She might be playing with you."

I had already considered all these things. I tried not to care and shrugged again.

"Whatever, it's not like it matters," Optimist Quint snapped.

I think it really mattered to Quint that Corin might hurt me.

Corin smiled as we joined her and Paisley under the light. Paisley's tan skin shined in the glow and her gray eyes were like a rolling storm.

"Quint the Optimist, Mr. Thompson. Nice of you to meet us here at the stalls," Corin said.

Quint seemed like he was mad at me. Probably because he thought I was lying to myself about everything. He was just trying to look out for me, and I kept pushing him away. I guess I would have been mad at me, too. I tried not to care, but I could feel the noose around my stomach. I definitely didn't want to lose Quint as a friend.

"Two minutes," he said as he walked toward the boys' bathroom.

"I need five," I said.

"More like ten!" Corin said with a flirtatious laugh.

Quint sighed because he realized that I hadn't exactly left him with any other option but to go along with my plan. He slammed the bathroom door, disappearing inside.

Corin raised her perfectly trimmed eyebrows. "Trouble in paradise?"

I shook my head. "It's fine."

Ominous Paisley silently took her leave into the girls' bathroom as Corin grabbed my arm and pulled me back onto the trail. "Follow me."

This was it. She was taking me into the woods to kiss me—to touch me—was I about to lose my virginity?

Hopefully.

Would I even last ten minutes?

My heart was in a race with my brain. Every muscle in my body felt like it was tingling. Corin's hand felt so warm as she continued to pull me along.

"Where are we going?" I asked. My mouth was so freaking dry—I was worried that I had bad breath.

"Just trust me. I promise, you'll like it."

I suddenly trusted Corin with my whole heart. She liked me back. She wanted to be alone with me. And even though I wanted to be alone with her, too—

I was secretly starting to worry about what would happen next.

TWENTY-SIX

WE STOOD OUTSIDE of the Crapateria's cracked kitchen window like a couple of bandits.

Only we weren't bandits; we were prisoners. And if we got caught, we would end up in a place far worse than a jailhouse.

"Corin," I whispered. "What the hell are we doing?"

She batted her eyelids. "I need your help. I promise, it'll be worth your time."

"But what does that mean?" I asked.

In case you didn't catch that, I was having second thoughts.

My racing heart stuck to my chest like gum. I was so nervous that I was starting to feel like I had to pee.

"Stop letting your mind control you," she said. "You're a man, right? So man up!"

Those words punched me in the gut—she was questioning my manhood. I felt insecure about my body all of a sudden—I knew I wasn't exactly the definition of masculinity. I wrapped my arms around my chest to cover up the fact that my puffy nipples were poking through my thin pajama top.

"Corin, I just want to know if you like me. That's why I followed you. Why the hell are we here?"

Corin smirked. "You'll find out. The risk will be worth the reward. Now stop acting like a pussy."

Maybe I really wasn't man enough to be with her. Part of me wanted to abandon her, but most of me wanted to stay. I had to stay. I had to find out if she liked me or not. But what the heck was she up to? Everything about her was mysterious. And as confusing as it is, in some ways, it only made me like her more.

Luckily, there weren't many lights near the Crapateria, so at least we were hidden in the shadows. I kept glancing over my shoulder, expecting Asshole Jim to come running up to find us and take us to Mental. My nerves were pinching my brain. This was reckless for a number of reasons. We were surely going to get caught.

Corin stepped forward and forced the window open while I kept watch.

"Wait, you have to tell me what we're doing," I said, panicked.

"No, I don't."

She knocked the screen into the room and it echoed as it bounced on the floor. I squinted through the trees, but it was too dark to see a thing. The fog disrupted my vision even more. If someone was coming, we wouldn't spot them until they were already upon us.

Corin poked her head inside to make sure that it was all clear. Then she turned to me and said, "You first."

I froze. The only thought running through my head was *Hell no*.

Corin looked at me like I was a wimp. "Come on, stop acting like such a bitch. We don't have a lot of time."

But I did actually feel like a little bitch. I didn't have nearly as much courage as Corin did. I shook my head. We were in prison camp. There were probably cameras everywhere. I was positive that we were going to get caught.

"Please don't call me a little bitch," I said.

Why did I say please?

Corin sighed. "Then stop acting like a bitch. Pretty please?"

Okay—the name-calling was starting to bother me.

All my insecurities were out in the open. What made her think I was a wimp? My stocky body? The fact that I barely had any muscle tone?

UGHHHHHHHH!

I had to prove that I was a man—that I was the man of her dreams.

I presented my reservations, "I don't know. What if they have cameras in there?"

"They don't." Corin was positive.

"But how do you know they don't?"

Corin was starting to get annoyed. "They don't. Look, you said you wanted to get to know me, right? Well, for that to happen, you need to trust me."

"Trust you? You won't even tell me what we're doing here."

"I've made this run a few times already and haven't been caught yet. I'm pretty sure we won't get caught tonight if you'll just grow a pair."

"Made this run a few times?" I asked. "Look, Corin, I thought you wanted me to come with you because you wanted to be alone with me."

"I do want to be alone with you, but *for real* alone—that's why we have to prepare," Corin said.

That was all I needed to hear. She wanted to be alone with me. It was finally, definitely, positively confirmed.

Corin liked me back.

"How did you know it would be open?" I asked.

Corin shrugged, like it was nothing. "I snuck into the kitchen at dinner. I promise, they won't even know we were here."

Corin was a pro at this sort of thing.

I had no choice but to go along with her plan. If I didn't, she would think that I didn't want to get to know her, and she would probably stop liking me. For fear of being rejected, I reluctantly climbed through the window.

I would like to say that I was graceful about it, but I wasn't. I fell face-first into the tile, and my feet slammed into a bunch of pots hanging from the wall. I made a ton of noise, but it didn't faze Corin at all.

She dived through the window like a ninja and turned back to secure it shut. Corin replaced the screen like it had never been touched and stilled the pots that I had disturbed.

"How are we going to get out?" I asked.

Corin ruffled my hair and responded like I was a naïve child. "Through the front door, silly. The magnetic keycard locks will automatically secure again when we go out. No one will even know we were here."

I was impressed by how good Corin was at sneaking around, but it also worried me a little bit.

If she was this good at lying to everyone else, was she also lying to me?

No. She wasn't. She wasn't manipulating me.

I forced the thought out of my mind. I trusted Corin with my life. I liked her—more than I had ever liked anyone else—and I wasn't about to mess it up by questioning her integrity.

Corin rushed over to the pantry and opened it to reveal the rows of canned goods inside. She turned back to me. "Fill your arms with nonperishable food. I'll be right back."

Corin disappeared into the back room, and I started to collect as many cans as I could carry—but I wasn't exactly sure what they were for. I grabbed a few cans of corn and green beans. Corin reappeared with all the zip-lock bags filled with confiscated items from the campers. The bags were packed with our belts, shoelaces, and hairspray—all sorts of things that I really didn't think she needed.

"Wait, where'd you get those?" I asked.

Surely Mr. and Mrs. Asshole would notice that someone had fiddled with their confiscated goods.

Corin continued to act like all of this was normal. "I stole Nikki's keycard."

This was stupid. Surely Mrs. Asshole would notice that the keycard she used to enter every single building was missing.

"Do you want to get caught?" I asked. "What the heck do we need all this stuff for?"

"Relax, woman. It's like a hotel key. I'm sure they lose them all the time. She'll just get a new one."

"But what if they confront us about it? What if they search through your belongings and find it?"

"They won't. A security guard is never going to admit that she lost her keycard. That would make her look dumb, and it might jeopardize her job."

"Won't she have to admit that she lost it to get a new one?" I asked.

Corin shrugged. "I'm sure she has access to more keycards. I doubt she has to get permission to run security at the place where she's paid to be a security guard."

"Maybe you're right."

"I am right," Corin said confidently.

"I don't like this." I shook my head. "Plus, if you had a keycard, why didn't we just go in through the front door?"

"Because I had to make sure you could be trusted first. Plus, this felt more daring and more fun," she justified. "You need to stop worrying so much—it's not attractive. I said I'd make it worth your while, didn't I?"

She liked the adrenaline rush that came with sneaking around—even when it wasn't necessary. I think she got a kick out of making me squirm, and it was really starting to bug me. Maybe she *was* just toying with me. I hated the names she was calling me. We didn't have to sneak through the window at all; she just wanted to because it made her feel more rebellious. I started to realize that this was a major part of her personality. And I was starting to wonder more and more what was in her massive green file. I was curious if it explained why she was such a risk taker, why she cared so little about the consequences of her actions.

"Corin, this is crazy."

Corin grew even more annoyed with my caution. "Please, Hunter S. Thompson. I'm a pro. We aren't going to get caught. I'm the Bonnie to your Clyde, remember?"

"I don't even know who Bonnie and Clyde are," I said.

I really didn't. And I still don't.

(Wait, seriously? Bonnie and Clyde were robbers who ended up dead at the end of their saga? Had I known that at the time, I probably would have been pretty disturbed that Corin kept comparing our connection to theirs.)

Corin touched my arm and smiled at me. "They were lovers, stupid. And they had one of the most romantic love affairs of all time."

Confirmed: I might get laid at the end of this adventure after all.

She could make fun of me all she wanted; the prospect of sex was all the motivation I needed.

She picked up the zip-lock bag with my name on it and opened it. She sifted through my belt and shoelaces before she pulled out the pocketknife that Surgeon Dick had given to me the night before arriving to camp.

My heart stopped, but not in a good way.

Corin held it up in the air. "Ah, here we go. I knew someone would be stupid enough to bring one of these to Camp Suicide. Who knew it was you?" She smirked.

"Wait, why do you need that?" I asked.

My mind flashed back to that moment on my bed—the moment where I decided to dig a razor into each of my wrists. I felt the blade puncture through my flesh all over again. My blood went ice-cold.

Corin stared at me like I was an idiot. "To cut things." She flipped up the can opener attachment. "And to open the cans you're gathering. Relax. They won't even notice it's gone."

My mind was spinning so out of control that I was starting to get light-headed.

What if they did notice that it was gone?

It was one thing to get caught with a bunch of canned goods, but it was something completely different to get caught with a knife. And what was the point of gathering all this stuff, anyway?

Corin pocketed the knife before I could object. She sealed up all the bags and returned them to the back room.

I flashed back to the story Counselor Kirk had recounted—the one where his sister had ended up dead because he looked the other way. My heart was pounding. I wanted to say something. I wanted to tell her that this was reckless. That eventually we were going to get in trouble. But I just kept my mouth shut and let it happen. I couldn't give her another reason to question my manhood, not when I was so close to finding out how she actually felt about me.

When Corin returned, I heard the front door to the Crapateria buzz open and slam shut.

Corin grabbed me and forced me down to the floor.

"Shit," I stupidly said out loud.

Corin shook her head as if to silently tell me to *shut up*.

We heard footsteps, so we scooted up against the center island. The cold steel panel sent chills shooting down my spine. This was it. We were going to get caught before Corin got the chance to give me my reward.

Counselor Kirk's voice echoed through the darkness. "Jim? Is that you?"

The lights flipped on and I began to sweat. I panicked. I wanted to run. But there was nowhere to go.

Counselor Kirk entered the kitchen. I could hear him breathing on the other side of the division.

"How'd these get left open?"

My eyes darted over to the pantry doors that I had left ajar.

I really suck at this!

We watched as Counselor Kirk moved over to shut them. He stood, inches away from us with his back turned to our bodies. I was so petrified that I didn't want to breathe. We were going to get caught. This was it. I almost pissed myself in my final moments of freedom.

Counselor Kirk paused for a second before moving toward the back room.

"Is anyone in here?"

Corin grabbed my arm and yanked me around the counter. I blindly followed her as adrenaline surged through my body. We rushed out of the kitchen, past the serving cart, the rows of tables, and out the front door of the Crapateria.

I could see the beads of sweat on Corin's brow as she gently let the front door close.

We had barely avoided detection, but would the risk be worth the reward?

Time to find out.

TWENTY-SEVEN

I KEPT GLANCING over my shoulder to make sure that Counselor Kirk wasn't behind us.

The dancing shadows of the trees made me feel on edge. Like we were being watched. Like we were going to get caught.

We had come so close to getting trapped that I was having second thoughts about Corin. I wasn't sure how I was going to tell her, but I was tired of being kept in the dark. I was tired of the name-calling. I didn't have the genes for this kind of charade. She either liked me or she didn't. I had to ask. I had to get an answer.

I could see the faint glow of the Rainmaker's lights when Corin directed me off the trail. "Hunter, this way."

We stepped into the thick trees. I could feel the dew on the tall grass soaking into the bottoms of my pajama pants. I wanted to ask her, but I also wasn't sure if I was ready for her answer. I tried to act casual even though I was panicking. I was panicking so much that I really had to pee.

"What do you think Counselor Kirk was doing in there, anyway?"

"Probably getting a midnight snack," Corin said.

We made our way off the path, down a small hill, and into a drainage ditch that was constantly filled with about three inches of water. Corin pushed back the biggest bush in the area to reveal a massive pile of supplies. She had collected tons of canned food, bottled water, flashlights, blankets, pillows—all sorts of stuff.

"Stash all of the cans here," she directed.

I gaped in disbelief. "You collected all of this? What for?"

"Our escape, dummy. You said you wanted to be alone with me, right? That you wanted to get to know me?"

"Wait, you were serious about escaping? We don't have anywhere to go."

Suddenly, it all made sense. Corin wanted me to help her, because she really liked me, a lot. She wanted me to run away with her so that we could have all the time alone together that we wanted. I started to think about what it would feel like to cuddle. How awesome it would be to kiss the back of her neck.

"Hunter, I have it all figured out. I promise. You just have to trust me," Corin said.

"I dunno, Corin. This isn't a good idea. Can I think about it?"

"If you have to think about it, then you don't really want to get to know me. Do you?" She didn't let me respond. "I thought you were different from the other guys."

"I am different."

"Then prove it. Get to know me. Now, come on. Hurry up. We have to get back so we don't get caught."

I reluctantly piled the cans that I had collected on top of the supplies, and Corin added the cans that she had carried as well. She let the bush swing back over the goods—suddenly, I remembered the pocketknife. She hadn't added it to the pile with the rest of her collection.

"What about the pocketknife?" I asked.

Corin shrugged. "What about it?"

This was getting out of hand. I couldn't follow her blindly anymore. I wasn't even sure if I wanted to escape with her at all. This was all way too risky.

I had to say something.

"Corin—"

Corin moved in and pressed her lips up to mine. I froze for a second as I tried to collect myself. I couldn't believe that this was actually happening, that this was real life. This kiss was everything; it was worth living for. Goose bumps sprouted over every inch of my skin. I felt her tongue tickle the inside of my mouth, and my senses exploded with invigoration. I got the chills, but in a good way. She sucked in some of my breath—I sucked in some of hers. Our spirits were intertwined. Everything about the kiss felt right. The noose around my stomach was so loose by then that it was almost like it wasn't even there—Corin was definitely the missing link to a happier life.

It was the best first kiss I'd ever had.

I needed to get to know her better.

I had to.

I was falling in love.

The kiss intensified—she put her hands under my shirt and ran them up my spine. I could feel my boner pressing up against her stomach. And I could smell the flowery shampoo in her hair. She put her hands down my pants and gripped my butt—she didn't seem to care about how hairy it was. She was the center of my universe. In that moment, we were in a bubble that our evil thoughts couldn't penetrate.

This was what it felt like to be happy.

And just when I thought that the moment would last forever—Corin bit my lip as she pulled away. Even through the darkness, I could see her bashful bright-blue eyes. I knew I was blushing. That my face was completely red. But I didn't care.

"I told you I'd make it worth your while," Corin said with a smile. "Promise me you'll escape with me."

"I promise," I said without thinking.

I wanted to experience more, and I knew the only way to do that was to go along with her plan. That kiss was just a taste of what we would do once we were alone together. I felt so content in that moment—like all my troubles would evaporate. Corin made everything better. She made all my stupid miscalculations feel like an afterthought.

She was my everything.

I couldn't stop focusing on that moment as she pulled me back toward the Rainmaker. I knew that I would do anything to be with her. All my worries about escaping from camp—and my disgust with the lying and name-calling—faded with that single kiss.

I stood outside the Rainmaker with a euphoric look on my face. Corin and Paisley made their way back toward the fort. Quint appeared from inside the boys' bathroom and chuckled.

"If that grin doesn't give you away, that boner sure will," he joked. "You gotta get that thing under control."

I glanced down and tucked my dick up into my waistline. "Sorry, Optimist Quint."

"Hey, if you keep calling me that, I'm gonna start calling you Horny Hunter," Quint joked.

We both laughed.

I wasn't even remotely embarrassed about my boner. This was the first time that I had actually, genuinely, felt happy since The Incident. The first time I didn't feel hatred toward my existence. The first time I wanted a future.

We started to walk toward the fort, and Quint let out an exaggerated sigh. "Get over yourself."

But I couldn't get over that kiss. I was so satisfied in that moment. I wanted the exhilaration to last forever. I wanted to experience the moment again.

I couldn't wait to escape with Corin.

When we got back to the fort, Asshole Jim scolded us for taking too long. Quint explained that he had to take a massive dump because dinner had gotten to him, and Asshole Jim stopped asking questions.

As I lay on the blankets with Corin just a few feet away, I grinned from ear to ear. I didn't sleep a wink that night. All I could think about was the way Corin's tongue felt in my mouth, and the fuzzy feeling I got in the pit of my stomach.

It really was fuzzy!

That was the first night that I didn't have a nightmare since the worst day of my life. I imagined what it would be like to feel this way all the time. Maybe I was right—*sex could be the ultimate cure for depression*. Corin's affection was a better treatment for my sickness than any medication I had ever taken.

I experienced bliss.

I would have done anything to feel like that forever.

TWENTY-EIGHT

I GOT HIT with a dose of reality at my next Shrinker Session.

At first, we sat in silence—like we always did. I gazed outside the window. Therapist Jess watched me and took notes. The green grass looked greener that day. I was feeling better than I think I'd ever felt in my entire life. I replayed my kiss with Corin over and over again in my head.

I think because I seemed so happy, Therapist Jess thought that I was ready for a breakthrough. She stared at me for an eternity, and then she asked *the question*.

"So, why are you here?"

My mouth fell open as I turned to stare at Therapist Jess in utter disbelief. Negative thoughts consumed all my happy ones. My mind was in control. I started to focus on The Incident that had gotten me thrown into this place.

I'd taken my new dose, like I was supposed to. I also took some massive bong rips while I played video games, like I wasn't supposed to.

I passed out.

Moments later, I was standing on the pool deck with Lola gripped in my sweaty hand. I was so high that the neon colors of the pool furniture and toys were extremely bright. But there was nothing bright about that moment.

I stared at what was placed on the edge of the pool. I locked my focus because I didn't want to look up. I didn't want to see the consequences of my absentmindedness.

Then, I looked up. And Lola slowly slipped from my grasp. It crashed against the pool deck, shattering into a million pieces. I watched the glass explode like the bomb that had dropped on my life.

I sat down, with my feet in the water, watching, in a complete daze. I don't know how long I sat there.

I heard Harpy Patricia's voice echo through the house: "Hunter! How about a little help? Hunter?"

The front door slammed.

I flinched.

My head slowly shifted to the sliding glass door as Harpy Patricia stepped out of the house with her hands full of grocery bags.

"Hunter? What's—" Her voice caught in her throat—she shrieked.

She lurched into the water, but I knew that it was already too late.

My mind slowly numbed the pain as my eyes wandered over to the pool. I saw her broken face.

"Stop just sitting there! Please just—"

Her words faded into an overwhelming drone of regret. Her mouth was moving as she begged for me to do *something*. But I couldn't hear the words that were coming out of her mouth. I couldn't compel myself to move. It was as if my butt were glued to the edge of the pool.

Actuality gripped my heart. A noose wrapped itself around my stomach. I was supposed to be out with Stoner Claire. I just wanted to smoke some weed and play video games. I couldn't possibly have known how strong my new dose was, or the fact that the combination of weed and my higher level of meds would make me pass out. It wasn't my fault.

I blinked as I sat across from Therapist Jess, tears welling in my eyes. The hatred I'd had for her before was nothing compared to what I felt for her now. The noose was so tight that it was suffocating my stomach—it was suffocating me.

My voice wavered. "You can't just ask that."

Therapist Jess smiled at me warmly, as if she had done me a favor. "Hunter, I already know what happened. You can't hide from this trauma forever. You need to face it head-on so that you can find a way to move forward."

It felt like my knees were going to give. The numbness clawed its way up my body from the tips of my toes. I couldn't breathe. "You can't just ask that," I repeated.

"I can. It's my job to help you get better. Hunter, I—"

She stopped herself as I blankly stared into her eyes. I think she could see that I couldn't deal with this. That was part of *my* problem.

"You don't have to deal with everything at once," Therapist Jess said. "This is the first step of many."

But I wasn't planning on taking any more steps. She didn't understand. She wasn't there that day. She couldn't possibly know how I felt about The Incident. I would never allow myself to feel that pain again.

My eyes dried before a single tear could fall.

Asshole Jim escorted me back to Ray, and all the guys watched me walk in. I looked like I'd been beaten into submission. Like the entire world had come crashing down on my shoulders. Like the moon had stopped orbiting the earth. Like the sun had fallen out of the sky. But I didn't care about my appearance.

I didn't care about anything.

I promised myself that I'd never care about anything again.

As I sulked across the room, Annoying Ash asked, "Yo, Hunter, you have a good Shrinker Sesh?"

I would have thought that from my appearance, Annoying Ash would have put two and two together and realized that I did not at all have a good Shrinker Session. But I guess Annoying Ash wasn't smart enough to figure that one out.

Ash was so absent to the world around him that everything came as a shock to him. He couldn't handle or empathize with extreme emotions. He saw everything from the outside in. That's why he was so vocal and insensitive about everything. That was *his* problem.

Quint could tell that something was really wrong—that I needed a friend. "Hunter, are you okay?" he persisted.

Another dumb question. I probably looked like a fanatical mess. Of course I wasn't okay. Nothing about this was okay.

C. Dermont weighed in. "Boys, leave him be. He's had a rough one."

He said that with such assurance that it sounded like he must have known that Therapist Jess was going to ask *the question*. Like they had observed my happiness and conspired to bring my depression back. I didn't have the energy for conspiracy theories, though. I didn't have much energy at all.

I collapsed onto my bed. I wanted to cry, but I held the tears back with all the force I could muster. I could see the teddy bear bobbing up and down in the water.

And as I stared at the wall, I could see Patricia's shattered expression, like she was haunting me.

TWENTY-NINE

I GAZED into the flames at Campfire Confession, wishing that the fire would rescue me from hell.

It was Friday again. C. Dermont, Counselor Kirk, Counselor Kylie, and Therapist Jess all sat next to one another on the opposite side of the fire from us. The girls sat on the left and the guys sat on the right.

Therapist Jess wore these beaded bracelets that clicked on her skinny wrists as she led the discussion. "We're at the halfway point. Tonight we want to have a conversation that everyone will have to participate in."

The campfire area was placed directly in the center of the eight cabins that made up Camp Suicide. We sat on these large logs that had been laid out in a hexagon around the pit. There wasn't any wind that night. The smoke drifted in a pillar straight up into the sky. The warmth of the blaze radiated from the epicenter of the gathering. The mosquitoes devoured our skin. And the sparks swirled through the air like lanterns.

I could see the teddy bear and I could feel the noose pulling at my stomach as I stared into the flames.

"We want to talk about the *whys* of suicide," Therapist Jess explained.

We listened as she went through each diagnosed reason as to why a person would choose to hurt him- or herself. As if there were a formula to the equation. As if the reason why a person would choose to commit this act could be quantified in a few simple words.

The conversation was pointless; there wasn't a simple answer. Suicide is a culmination of thousands of bad moments built up into one single event. Suicide is a way out when it doesn't seem like any alternative exists. Suicide is the only choice when a person can't find any way to feel happy. Suicide is escape.

I understood why I was suicidal. One single horrible event had turned my life upside down. My depressed stoner world suddenly morphed into a world of self-hate. My parents detested me after that day—even though it was their fault, too. Stoner Claire turned on me because she couldn't look at me the same. My teachers stopped acknowledging me altogether. And my emotions completely abandoned me.

For me, suicide was the only way to run away from the way people saw me. An eye for an eye—or, in my case, a tragedy for a tragedy.

Therapist Jess folded her hands on her lap as she finished. "All of you possess your own *why*. Now I want to go around the circle to have each of you try to identify what your *why* was in the moment you chose pain."

The guys and girls all glanced at each other with these horrified expressions—I continued to focus on the abyss.

Surprisingly, Corin was first to step up to the plate. I guess probably because this was her third time experiencing this type of group therapy. "Because I can't control what they did to me."

I wondered who *they* were and what *they* had done. I still couldn't figure out what *her* problem was, but in that moment, I no longer cared. My connection with Corin had diminished to the back of my mind. My depression buried the happiness she'd made me feel under a layer of mind-numbing, self-hating grief.

Nora was next. "To get them to listen."

Ominous Paisley just shrugged. She still hadn't said a word the entire time we were there. I wondered if she'd ever speak again.

Mackenzie was after. "Because they can't force me to be something I'm not."

"Because I feel alone," Harper said.

"Because I don't have any friends," Violet said.

"Because none of this matters," Quint said.

"Because I went from having everything to nothing at all," Ash said.

"Because my life is a sin," Wyatt said.

"Because I can't stop. And when I can't have them, I can't feel anything unless I cause myself pain," Blazed said.

"Because of what he did to me." Flinching Finley flinched.

Then it was my turn. All their reasons were so vague and simple. My reason couldn't be quantified in just a few simple, vague words. I wanted to tell all of them off. I wanted to explain to them that their problems were nothing compared to mine.

Therapist Jess urged me to talk. "What about you, Hunter? What's your why?"

I responded in my head—*because I have shitty parents, because I passed out, because everyone blamed me for something I didn't prevent.*

I didn't respond; I just couldn't. I hated that Therapist Jess kept trying to make me talk about that horrible day. As if confessing my sins would change the outcome. I knew better.

I couldn't turn back time.

I could see the disappointed look on Patricia's face in the sea of flames.

THIRTY

AFTER A FEW more days of my wallowing, Corin and the guys were starting to really worry about me.

It was Friday again, and we were on Happy Lake's shore, constructing a raft under the supervision of Counselor Kylie and Counselor Winter. I refused to participate and had chosen to sit at the water's edge so that I could pity myself alone.

Most of the time they talked about me like I wasn't even there—like I couldn't hear them.

I listened to Corin talking to Counselor Winter as if I wasn't three feet away.

I'm not deaf.

"Counselor Winter? As fun as it is having Hunter over there being a sad clown and dampening the mood, would you mind me going over to try to lighten him up?" Corin asked. "Hunter the Author and I have kind of become friends."

I didn't want to be cheered up. I had forgotten all my happiness in my moment of self-hate. I hadn't thought about my kiss with Corin in days. I hadn't thought about our escape plan. Or the way she stopped my bladder.

But that didn't mean Corin had stopped thinking about me.

"You promise you're just friends? Nothing more?" Counselor Winter asked. "You know the terms of your treatment," she said through a smile.

That statement bothered me. What were the terms of Corin's treatment? What was in that massive green file? I was still in the dark about what Corin was actually doing in a place like Camp Suicide. She didn't appear to be suicidal to me. She didn't seem to have any of the problems that came with constant depression. I wanted to know what was in that file. I wanted to know why she was at Camp Suicide.

"Just friends," Corin lied. "I promise."

Counselor Winter continued to talk about me like I was invisible. "And you're being careful? I'm not sure the two of you socializing is a good idea."

More mystery. Why didn't she want Corin to socialize with me?

"I realize he's as fragile as a piece of glass. I promise not to shatter him," Corin assured her.

I was already shattered.

Counselor Winter searched for truth in Corin's eyes. "I was talking about you." Then Counselor Winter turned to gaze at me for a few seconds. I think she could see the hopelessness in my expression. She would have tried anything to make me feel better. She sighed and went against her better judgment. "See what you can do."

Corin slowly approached me like I were a scared animal that might run away. She placed a hand on my back, and I shuddered at her touch. She sat down and stayed silent for a few moments before she whispered in my ear, "See, this is what they do to you. They beat you down and then force you to confess. The problem is that once you do, it doesn't change anything. We aren't the problem. They are—all of the people out there who are trying to rectify problems that can't be fixed," Corin assured me.

I kept my eyes locked on the water. "You're the one who's here for your third time."

Corin's thin lips glistened as she continued to try to bring me back to her side of the picture. "Because my aunt forces me to come here every summer, because she thinks it helps. It doesn't, and as soon as we can, you and I are going to break free from here, no matter the cost, so that we can live, just the two of us, away from all of this bullshit. Forever.

"You can't be happy unless you know how to feel sad, but you also can't let yourself be sad for all of eternity. Focusing on your past will only bring back more pain. You and I both understand that. They don't."

She paused for a moment to let me absorb what she was saying. She wanted me to lie. She wanted me to pretend like it was all fine so that we could continue with our original plan. She wanted to be there for me. She wanted to understand my pain. Maybe she was the only one who could empathize with a person in my position. Maybe she was right. I needed to break free.

"I think I'm falling in love with you, Hunter S. Thompson," Corin sincerely said into my ear.

My eyes turned to meet hers. We stared at each other for a second before she rose to rejoin the exercise.

My heart started beating with the warmth of feeling again. The numbness cleared out of my body as fast as it had returned. The noose around my stomach loosened its death grip.

Corin thought she loved me.

I smiled for the first time in days and rose to my feet. My smile wasn't even a lie. I really was happy again.

I followed Corin through the open gate in the fence and joined the raft-building exercise. The guys genuinely seemed glad to have me back.

"Hunter! Get over here, man!" Ash exclaimed.

"Hunter the Author is back!" Blaze noted.

I laughed as Ash and Blaze patted me on the back, welcoming me with open arms.

Counselor Winter walked over to Corin, clearly worried about our connection. "Please be responsible this summer, Corin," I heard her say. "We don't need any repeats."

Corin assured her, "I promise. I'm getting better. I won't repeat my mistakes. And, in case you didn't notice, I'm not as useless as everyone makes me out to be."

Counselor Winter noticed that I was listening to their exchange, so I nodded like I was engrossed in a conversation with Blaze, Ash, and Quint.

Counselor Winter assured Corin, "You did a good thing."

The interactions between Corin and Counselor Winter were starting to mess with my brain.

I couldn't help it. The counselors had planted the seeds of suspicion. Seeing Corin's file made me worry that I was getting in over my head. I wanted to read what was in that file. I wanted to be able to rely on Corin, but I couldn't possibly do that until I knew her truth.

It wasn't only about sex anymore. We loved each other.

I had to man up and ask her. If she really loved me—like she said she did—then she couldn't possibly get mad at me for asking her about her past. I realized that eventually, I would have to tell her about The Incident. I just hoped that she would understand my situation. I hoped that she would see that it wasn't completely my fault.

That it was just a tragic, stupid miscalculation.

Corin was right about one thing, though: we weren't the problem—Camp Suicide was the problem. The people out in the rest of the world were the problem. My parents were the problem. The noose around my stomach was a problem.

I had to trust that Corin would tell me everything about her past when she was ready. We would know when the time was right. We knew what was best for us. We knew how to heal on our own.

But as it turns out, that was a stupid miscalculation, too.

THIRTY-ONE

"WHO LIKES DANCING?"

We were all sitting quietly, minding our own business, when Counselor Kirk decided to deliver some unexpected news.

A few days had passed since raft-building day. It was a sunny day, the kind of day that was supposed to breed cheerfulness in a place like Camp Suicide. Quint and I were sitting on his bed, participating in some local multiplayer on our DSes. Finley's gangly arms rested on his knees as he watched over our shoulders. Ash, Blaze, and Wyatt were playing a game of cards on the planks of the floor.

Quint and I both paused our game so that we could exchange looks of desperation. We realized that we were about to be forced to participate in yet another one of Camp Suicide's planned group activities.

Squirrelly Wyatt scrunched up his face in annoyance, making him look even more like a squirrel. "I'm sorry, Counselor, fool, but what teenage boy actually likes dancing?"

We stared at Counselor Kirk blankly, wondering if deep down he was just as much of an idiot as the rest of the counselors; he was supposed to be the cool one. He had a hipster haircut—hipsters were supposed to rebel against ordinary conventions, right?

Right.

Counselor Kirk faked a grin as though he'd been taking lessons from Counselor Winter. "Well, regardless of if you like it or not, we're having a dance!" He waited for us to clap in excitement. When we didn't, he awkwardly said, "Yaaaaay."

I don't exercise or watch or play sports, and I don't dance.

I loathe dancing down to my fat, Cheetos-eating core.

We kept our eyes on him but stayed absolutely silent.

I thought about how stupid it was to force a bunch of depressed teens to partake in a dance. We were at our awkward stage: I was totally self-conscious about the way I looked. I hated my stomach, my tiny hands, my round face, and the fact that I was starting to grow body hair literally everywhere. Later in life, we would go to extreme lengths to hide photos that were taken during this period of time. It's like they were setting us up to fail.

Counselor Kirk was so freaking awkward about the whole thing. When it was clear that we weren't thrilled about the prospect of a dance, he continued, "Right, so, I have your date assignments—"

Ash interjected, "You're assigning us dates?"

"So no one gets left out," Counselor Kirk explained.

But what he really meant was: *So that we can keep Corin and Hunter apart.* I realized that the counselors didn't like our connection, but it's not like the dance was going to be unsupervised.

The only thing dumber than a dance, is a dance with assigned dates.

"This is truly the lamest place on earth," Blaze said.

"The sunniest place on earth," Counselor Kirk corrected.

Flinching Finley began to continuously flinch. His delicate bones looked like they might break from his convulsions.

Quint asked the question that we already knew the answer to: "What if we don't want to go?"

Counselor Kirk ignored Quint's inquiry. We all knew that we'd be forced to participate. "Ash, you'll be with Violet. Finley and Nora. Hunter and Paisley—"

They paired me with the girl who doesn't talk—probably because I'd been conversing with Corin so much.

"Blaze and Harper. Wyatt and Mackenzie—"

Wyatt scoffed, "Of course you put the two gay kids together."

My heart lurched as I realized that Corin was paired with—

"Quint and Corin."

I exhaled, but my muscles tensed up. This was ridiculous. The counselors had chosen to pair the girl who stopped my bladder with my best friend. They were trying to cause a rift between us so that we would fight. So that Corin and I would go our separate ways. I saw right through their scheme. It wasn't going to work.

Quint already felt bad, even though he hadn't chosen his date assignment. "Why can't we choose our own dates?"

Counselor Kirk was quick with his response: "Because someone would get left out."

Quint grew frustrated and his voice got even more nasally. "But you don't know that. You're just assuming that. I don't want to go with Corin."

Counselor Kirk stared directly at me while he responded to Quint. "Well, that's your assignment for the night. You don't have a choice. I'm sorry. . . ."

He said *I'm sorry* as if he was apologizing to me. As if he was trying to communicate that he wasn't on board with the rest of the counselors' asinine plan. Counselor Kirk was trying to look out for me again. He was trying to convey that I shouldn't let this get into my head. That I shouldn't let this bother me, but it did bother me. I could feel the noose tightening its perpetual hold around my stomach.

"This is just the way it's gotta be," Counselor Kirk finished.

Quint let out the biggest sigh ever and made eye contact with me as if to apologize for something he didn't do. But I wasn't going to let it bother me.

Counselor Kirk was right.

I couldn't let a stupid dance tear us apart.

THIRTY-TWO

"I'LL JUST PRETEND I have diarrhea or something," Quint suggested.

"Gross, dude. I'm eating."

I chewed slowly. We were sitting at our usual table. There were tons of fruit flies and mosquitoes flying over our heads, dodging through the rays of sunshine pooling through the windows on the walls.

"Besides," I explained, "I know you didn't ask for her to be your date. It's fine."

I could tell this was really bothering Quint. I could see his brown eyes darting from side to side as he tried to come up with a way to not go to the dance. I think he thought he might lose me as a friend over this whole ordeal, even though I kept assuring him that he wouldn't. I was smart enough to see through the counselors' plan. I honestly preferred Corin to be paired with Quint as opposed to any of the other guys. I trusted that Quint would never try anything with Corin. He wouldn't stab me in the back.

"It doesn't feel fine," Quint said. "Seriously, if you want me to pretend like I have the shits, I will."

I stared at the brown gooey peanut butter in the center of my sandwich and almost gagged. "Still eating, and it's a creamy peanut butter sandwich. I'd prefer it if you didn't incept the image of the runs into my head."

We both laughed and the tension was broken. It was just a stupid dance. It's not like Quint was taking Corin to the prom.

Corin joined us, holding a lunch tray. "What's so funny?" she asked.

We both figured that Corin would probably find our conversation to be inappropriate, even though we thought it was hilarious.

"It's not like it matters," we quickly blurted out.

"Right." Corin realized that we were probably talking about something gross. She looked at Quint. "So I hear you and I are going to be dates. You better prove to be chivalrous, or I will expose your treachery to Hunter the Author."

Quint went totally red. "Can you not make this more awkward for me?"

Corin smiled. "It just means we'll for sure have to bring you with us."

"Bring me with you where?"

I realized that she had finally planned our moment of escape. The moment I'd been eagerly awaiting. I realize that we only had a week and a half left of the session, but we were escaping from more than just Camp Suicide—we were escaping from our lives. I couldn't wait to get out of this hellhole, even if it meant more lying. I couldn't wait to be away from Camp Suicide with Corin. I was finally going to lose my virginity—more than that, I was going to get to sleep with a girl who really mattered to me.

A girl who promised that I mattered to her, too.

"On our jailbreak," Corin responded like it was nothing.

"You're still hung up on that? You're for real?" Quint asked.

Corin blinked like Quint was an idiot. "Duh."

Quint frowned. "Yeah. I can't say I'm on board with that idea."

"You're my date. You have to be on board with it," Corin said. "Besides, do you want to be assigned dates for the rest of your life? Or are you ready to make a decision on your own?"

Quint was extremely worried about the prospect. "What if we get caught and have to live the rest of our lives in asylums? There is a lot that could go wrong with this plan. What about our medication, food, water, toilet paper?"

Little did Quint know, Corin had thought about pretty much everything. I had seen the mass of supplies that she'd gathered. We were prepared for most scenarios.

"Luckily for you, I've considered all of these things," Corin said. "And you can go without your meds. Free your mind."

Quint turned to me. "You're cool with this?"

"I am." I nodded.

My happy pill didn't seem to be helping me much, anyway. I was still on a roller coaster of the highest of highs and the lowest of lows. Plus, I didn't trust any meds—not after The Incident. I thought that Corin's love was the only medication I needed.

Corin finally revealed the plan in its entirety. "Listen: I've been stashing food, water, and supplies next to the Rainmaker since the day we arrived. I have the perfect place for us to hide, where there isn't even the slightest possibility that we will be found. I satellite-mapped the hell out of this place after last summer."

Finley joined our table after having been eavesdropping on us the entire time.

"Wait, y-you three are planning an escape?" he asked.

We all went silent. We had been caught before we had even tried to carry out the plan. Finley was going to narc on us and turn us over to the counselors.

We all quickly whispered in response, "You can't tell anyone!"

Flinching Finley flinched. "I—I'm going w-with you."

As it turns out, everyone wanted to escape just as badly as we did. I'm sure we could have gotten the entire camp on board with our plan if we had wanted. All the campers hated this place and wanted to get out alive.

Corin sighed with relief. "Fear not. I have enough supplies for all of us. Hunter, you should bring Paisley along for the ride as well. I feel like it would be a bit too much of a gang bang for me unless we had another girl there. Finley, you'll have to ditch Nora the Narcissist, because she is the absolute worst."

We had collectively decided that Narcissist Nora was even more obnoxious than Annoying Ash and Squirrelly Wyatt.

Flinching Finley flinched. "Agreed."

"So, where is this hideout?" Quint asked.

Corin smiled. "It's a surprise."

Quint shook his head. "You at least have to tell us where we're going."

Corin wasn't about to reveal her hand. Not until she was positive that we could all be trusted. "The night of the dance."

It was like she had been arranging this escape for years. Just waiting for me to come along to join her on the expedition. I was starting to get really excited. The world could throw anything at us, just as long as Corin and I could be together.

"I'm game," I said. Then I added, "What's life without a little living?"

"Y-yeah," Finley agreed.

Quint didn't want to get left behind. "It's fine. We all know I'm going."

Corin couldn't wait. "It's settled."

We were breaking out of prison on the night of the dance.

THIRTY-THREE

WHEN I WALKED into my last Shrinker Session, Therapist Jess was writing in Corin's thick green file.

"I'm just finishing something up," she said.

I watched as she scribbled on a page, wondering how many of the pages in Corin's file were dedicated to our friendship. I wanted to know what was on those pages. I fought the urge to grab the file out of Therapist Jess's hands. Corin would tell me about her past eventually. I had to have faith that the conversation would come.

Therapist Jess finished her notes and closed the fat green folder. I could see Corin's name on the cover. "I'm so sorry; my session with Ms. Young ran over. Just give me a second to return this to my office. I'll be right back."

Therapist Jess exited the room with the green file in her hand. I wondered if Corin actually talked to Therapist Jess about her past in her Shrinker Sessions. I wondered what it would feel like to tell Corin the truth about The Incident. I could feel the noose clenching around my stomach. And I suddenly became curious if discussing The Incident with Therapist Jess could loosen the noose just a little.

I was still standing when Therapist Jess came back into the room. She took a seat in her leather chair and waited for me to sit across from her. But I didn't sit down—I wanted to stand.

The words jumped out of my mouth before I knew what was happening, "You think you can help me, right? If I talk about The Incident."

It felt like all my thoughts were trying to escape from my mouth at once—like thousands of daggers were poking out of my skin from inside my throat. I swallowed deeply.

Therapist Jess moved to the edge of her seat, ready for action. "I want to hear your account, Hunter. I've read about what happened on paper, but the page can't tell me how you feel about everything. If you're willing to share, I'll be your ear to listen."

"I don't want you to just listen. I need advice," I explained.

I wanted to tell her my story so that she could understand that my case was hopeless. That there was nothing I could say or do to rectify the damage that had been done. To see that may parents completely blamed me for something that was partially their fault. And to see if she could appreciate what it felt like to have a noose constantly choking my stomach.

Therapist Jess nodded. "Okay."

My tongue was a piece of sandpaper, rubbing the inside of my mouth raw. My body didn't want me to confess—all my muscles felt like they were in pain.

I began, "So, ultimately, I'm here because I have shitty parents."

And that was my truth. Surgeon Dick and Harpy Patricia had always been absent parents.

Therapist Jess mocked me with her tone, "Is that so?"

My blood boiled at her response. "Yeah," I snapped back. "I'm here because if they get me out of sight, then they get me out of their minds. I'm here because they don't want to deal with the truth."

I took a deep breath. My words were caught. I had to force them through my body and out of my mouth. But this was the first time in my life that I had talked about The Incident out loud.

My voice shattered like glass. "My parents blame me for what happened, because they think I'd rather play video games and smoke weed than pay attention to what's going on around me. But it's not entirely my fault. How could I have possibly known that a few rips of weed on my new dose would make me pass out?"

The noose was so tight now that my abdomen was throbbing, screaming at me to *STOP TALKING!*

"The truth is that what happened was a stupid miscalculation. I was supposed to be out with my girlfriend that day, but my parents forced me to stay home. I just wanted to have a little fun. I started smoking weed and playing video games at three o'clock sharp, because that's when they were supposed to get home. It's not my fault Harpy Patricia didn't get home until after four o'clock."

The noose loosened for a split second and then tightened its grip again. I almost threw up from the torture.

"There's nothing I can say or do to make them realize that it's just as much their fault as it is mine. They'd rather place all the blame on me than accept the fact that they should have been back on time. That they should have been better parents to begin with."

Therapist Jess continued to sit with her hands folded on her lap—like she always did. I waited for her to respond. To say *something*. But she didn't have *anything* to say.

The noose was desperately trying to split my stomach in two.

"So, what should I do?" I asked her.

She responded with a question. "What do you think you should do?"

I couldn't hold back my laughter, even though it *really* hurt to laugh. It was ludicrous to me that my own therapist wouldn't even give me advice. "See? I was right. You don't have any answers, and that's why all of this is complete and utter bullshit. You can't fix a shattered pane of glass. I mean, there's no way to get them to look in the mirror. I can't make them see that it wasn't entirely my fault."

Therapist Jess was calm and collected. "Hunter, my job isn't to tell you what to do. My job is to help you seek out the answers for yourself."

I clenched my jaw so tight that I thought my teeth might split under the pressure. My point was that there *wasn't* an answer. That there was nothing that I could do to make the people in my life see that I wasn't the monster that everyone made me out to be. My parents hated me because they hated themselves. They focused all their guilt and grief on me because they didn't want to face the reality: they should have been there to prevent The Incident.

"Well, think about it. If I could do that, I wouldn't be here," I said.

"Is it your fault?" she asked.

My parents were just as much at fault as me.

"No, it wasn't my fault. My parents should have been home on time."

"Hunter, you won't even talk about it completely. You keep leaving out a key element from your story."

I froze. I couldn't talk about it completely, because if I did, I would admit the fact that a piece of the puzzle was missing—part of me was missing.

"It wasn't my fault."

"Hunter, you're not recognizing the full story; therefore, you can't see the whole picture."

I cringed—my stomach hurt so freaking badly.

"I see my stupid miscalculations every time I close my eyes," I said. "My brain's been fucked with my whole life. Ever since my parents figured out that something is wrong with me. If people hadn't been fucking with my head, then I wouldn't have passed out. I assure you. I'm not the fucking problem!"

Therapist Jess stopped responding, and we went back to staring into each other's eyes—like we always did. I realized that she didn't want to get into a heated argument with me. She wanted me to figure out the answers to my problems on my own, because she didn't know the answers to them herself.

She didn't have anything to say. I finally opened up and she just sat there like she did when I was silent. Corin was right. We needed to escape.

The noose had the tightest death grip that it had ever had on my stomach.

Fuck Therapist Jess. And fuck therapy. I tried.

I was done talking about my problems with idiots.

THIRTY-FOUR

IT WAS ALMOST dancing time!

My heart would not stop hammering as I dressed. The beat drummed in my head so hard that it was starting to make me dizzy. I'm not sure if it was pounding so fast because I was nervous about escaping from prison—especially because of how shitty my last therapy session had gone—or because I was excited that I would finally get to be alone with Corin, away from this place. I had never been this close with a girl.

I was finally going to find out if Corin could make me happy.

I reviewed the plan in my head—on Corin's cue, we would use the only excuse there was; we would pretend like we had to go to the Rainmaker. The bathrooms were literally the only place where a counselor or security guard wasn't in your face at Camp Suicide. It was the only excuse we knew that had a chance of working.

Once Quint, Finley, and I got away from the dance, it was our job to meet Corin at the bathrooms to borrow the keycard, stop by Ray to gather our gear, and then meet back at the Rainmaker.

It was a foolproof plan—it had to work.

Quint joined me as I slipped into my only pair of nice pants. He was in a dress shirt that looked gigantic on his small upper body. The mosquito bites on his neck blended in with the acne on his cheeks. "You ready for this?" he asked.

I was sweating. I was as nervous as I was excited. "Never been more ready for anything in my entire life."

Quint didn't share my enthusiasm for the adventure. I could tell he was really worried something would go wrong.

"What happens if we get caught?" he whispered.

I responded in a low voice, "What happens if we succeed? We'll never know if we don't try. It's time we started making some decisions for ourselves, right?"

It probably wasn't the answer that Quint wanted to hear. I know he wanted me to back out at the last minute to spare us both the agony of a night in Mental. He didn't actually want to go along with this plan. The only reason he was going along with it was because he wanted to keep me as a friend. We had become close. I know he would have done anything for me. I appreciated Quint—he was the best guy friend I'd ever had.

"But how are we going to get back into Ray to get all our stuff? The magnetic locks will be sealed—"

I hushed him. "Corin has a keycard."

Quint wasn't shocked by this revelation. "Of course she does." He sighed. "I guess. I mean, it's fine."

"Besides, what's the worst that could happen? We're already at Camp Suicide."

Optimist Quint raised his eyebrows as if to assert that there were places and situations worse than the one in which we currently resided—that I was lying to myself if I actually thought that this was the worst place on earth. If we got caught, there was the possibility that we would be committed to asylums.

It's not like I wasn't worried about all those possibilities, too.

I pulled a shoe box from under my bed and exposed the only other pair of sneakers that I had brought with me to Camp Suicide—minus the laces, of course.

Quint laughed. "You brought a new pair of sneakers to Camp Suicide?"

I shrugged as I slipped into my fresh kicks. "Just for special occasions."

I brought a new pair of shoes on every trip just for special occasions.

I liked shoes, a lot. Probably because shoes were the only item of clothing that didn't reveal how awkward my body was.

"That's weird, dude," Quint said.

"No, it's weird that you don't have a pair of sneakers stashed away for special occasions."

I was all dressed and ready to go. I wished that I had a mirror so that I could see how I looked. I wanted to fix my hair—good hair was a good distraction from a stocky body.

Fun fact: Mirrors were banned contraband at Camp Suicide . . . in case we broke them to . . . you know . . .

I asked Quint, "How's my hair?"

He didn't care. "It's fine."

I could feel that it wasn't fine. It wasn't sitting correctly on top of my head. "In other words, it looks like crap," I responded.

"It's fine."

I tried to fix it as best as I could. We were about to head out. "You're such a confidence booster."

But I was confident—more confident than I had ever been in my entire life. I was confident in my decision to abandon Camp Suicide. Confident in my connection with Corin. Confident that she would make me happy. Confident in my best friend—Quint. Confident that this plan would work. Confident that we could survive on our own.

I was ready for action. Ready for anything.

But at the same time, I knew that what we were doing was absolutely crazy. It was crazy to think that we could get away from this place without getting caught. Crazy to think that we could survive on our own. Crazy for me to trust Corin after I had seen her gigantic green file. Crazy to go along with her plan after I'd been warned.

If I was so confident, then why was I so nervous?

THIRTY-FIVE

IT WAS DANCING time! Guys in the corner of the room—girls on the dance floor.

Justin Bieber's "Where Are Ü Now" blared from a single speaker. You know, that song that everyone pretends to hate but secretly dances to in the car. Come on, you know you love it.

I secretly love it, too.

The counselors had pushed the tables against the wall with the "Sunshine is Forever" plaque. They had made a bowl of punch, because everyone knows it's not a dance unless there's punch. The room was brightly lit. And they had secured a miniature disco ball to the ceiling—because every dance takes place in the '70s.

C. Dermont, Counselor Kirk, Therapist Jess, Counselor Kylie, and Counselor Winter were chaperoning us from the corner of the room. Mr. and Mrs. Asshole guarded the door in case any of us tried to escape. And the girls were already having a great time.

I've never met a single girl who couldn't dance.

Sadly, that wasn't the case for the guys—we were determined to act like we were too cool for school.

The truth was that none of us knew how to dance.

Quint spoke over the noise, "Could they have picked lamer music?"

"Seriously," I agreed.

It was Guy Code to pretend like the music sucked at every dance. We acted as if *that* was the reason why we weren't dancing. As if once they turned on better music, we would be out on the dance floor.

"I wish they'd put on some JAY-Z or some shit; then I'd bust a move," Squirrelly Wyatt assured us.

Ash laughed. "You have moves? Ash doubts that."

None of us actually had any moves, but of course, Wyatt would be the one to pretend like he was a trained hip-hop dancer.

"Duh, fool. I'm a gay. All gays got moves."

"Prove it," Blaze said—he was wearing sunglasses and a shirt covered in marijuana leaves even though it was night and we were inside.

Wyatt resorted back to Guy Code. "*Psh*, if they play a better song, I will."

There are always one or two chaperones at every dance who feel obligated to get the guys onto the dance floor. At our mockery of a dance, those chaperones were none other than C. Dermont and Counselor Kirk. They sauntered up to us, with their hips swinging, as if they had swagger.

"Boys!" C. Dermont exclaimed in his usual bubbly fashion—he already had massive pit stains on his baby-blue shirt, and his hairy stomach was hanging out over his khakis.

Flinching Finley flinched. Come to think of it, the entire dance was a flinch fest for him. He had his hair slicked to the side with pomade.

"Dances are for dancing," Counselor Kirk pointed out. I could smell the spearmint on his breath, which was a welcoming scent in the midst of C. Dermont's body odor.

Quint quipped, "Thanks for informing us. We thought dances were just for looking like dumbasses."

"What, kind of like this?" asked Counselor Kirk.

Then he and C. Dermont started dancing with each other.

I'm not kidding.

They looked like absolute fools, grinding on each other and making idiots of themselves.

"Come on, guys," pleaded Counselor Kirk.

"Don't you want to look cool like us?" C. Dermont asked.

Wyatt couldn't take it anymore. "Yo, watch and learn."

Once one guy abandons Guy Code to dance, it's okay for the rest of the guys to abandon it as well.

We followed Wyatt onto the dance floor, leaving C. Dermont and Counselor Kirk to dance with each other on their own.

"What? Come on, guys. We look cool!" C. Dermont called after us.

I found Paisley and began to awkwardly sway my hips at her side. She wore this slim purple dress that went perfectly with her dark skin. Her black hair was effortlessly combed to the side. And her gray eyes twinkled in the disco ball's light. She smiled at me and began to sway her hips to the same beat, which wasn't actually to the beat of the music. I laughed, and then "Fourth f July" by Fall Out Boy came on.

The guitar blasted from the speakers—through our bodies. We all raised our hands into the air. And our souls became one. Suddenly, we were jumping up and down, completely in sync. I vigorously shook my head, making myself dizzy. The colors swirled around me as if I could see the notes of the music. The song brought something out of me that I hadn't felt before. A passion that I didn't know I had. It was like ecstasy that sent energy rolling down my spine. For the first time in my life, I experienced harmony.

Our feet caused an earthquake on the floor. The "Sunshine is Forever" plaque crashed down from the wall. It was like we were moving in slow motion, but the world was continuing around us at a normal pace. My feet tapped as the notes exploded in my ears. Strings were attached to my shoulders, bouncing with the beats. The song filled us with life. And then the music slowed into a couple's dance: Ed Sheeran's "All of the Stars."

We found our respective dates and began to gradually sway our hips to the tune. Paisley kept her face at least a foot away from my chest the entire dance, while I continuously watched Corin and Quint.

I couldn't help it.

I wondered if Quint could feel Corin's heartbeat—if it was as exhilarating for him as it would have been for me. Corin was wearing this shiny blue dress. Her slender hips were snug against the fabric. Her bangs were parallel to her perfectly trimmed eyebrows. And her glowing pale skin shone through the dim light.

I was tense with jealousy, even though Quint kept his distance from Corin for the entire song. There may as well have been a universe between her boobs and his chest. I could tell that he felt completely, absolutely, and totally awkward about the whole thing. It was the longest three minutes and fifty-four seconds of my life—I counted every single second in my head.

After the song ended, Corin approached Paisley and me. She grabbed Paisley's arm and pulled her away. "I have to tinkle."

I mumbled in her ear, "You couldn't have done this before the slow song?"

Corin smiled at me with a devious grin. "I like seeing you get jealous."

My senses perked up at once—that sentence turned me on so freaking much!

She dragged Paisley away toward Mrs. Asshole and Counselor Kylie to ask for permission to go to the girls' bathroom. I joined Quint on a search for Finley.

We found Flinching Finley flinching as he stood completely still with Narcissist Nora dancing up against him. She was wearing this puke-green dress and her hair was a disheveled mess. Finley looked petrified, like Narcissist Nora was torturing him. We pulled him away to spare him from more agony.

"You look like you have to pee," I said.

"Thank God." He sighed with relief.

Nora stopped us. "Wait! Where are you taking my date?"

She stared seductively into Finley's eyes like he was her prized possession.

"Your date really has to pee, like, right now," I told her. "Didn't you notice the way he was dancing?"

"He did look weird," Nora agreed.

Flinching Finley flinched. "I—I did not! I wasn't even moving!"

"Because you have to pee so badly. Finley, don't be embarrassed." I convincingly stared into Nora's eyes. "Finley's pee shy."

I was getting really good at lying.

Nora whined, "But what about me? I don't want to be left alone."

"You'll be fine," I assured her.

When we were far enough away from Nora, Finley spoke again. "Thank you for humiliating me."

I laughed. "Anytime."

And just as we were about to make our quick exit, Asshole Jim put out a hand to stop us. "Two at a time."

We hadn't thought about the fact that we were only allowed to go to the Rainmaker in pairs, not in groups of three. I had to come up with an explanation, and fast. But the only explanation I could come up with was one that was completely embarrassing to us all.

"Dinner gave us food poisoning," I lied—again.

Asshole Jim stared blankly into my eyes. The giant wad of dip made it look like his mouth was full of shit. "So? Two at a time. And you need to wait until Corin and Paisley get back."

I thought food poisoning would have been enough of an explanation, but it wasn't enough for Asshole Jim.

"We have the shits," I said.

"So, shit yourselves. Two at a time," Asshole Jim rebutted, splattering a bit of his nasty dip spit onto our dress clothes.

I'd had enough of Asshole Jim and his asshole tactics.

"Don't you think we already have enough problems with our self-esteem?" I angrily snapped. "Don't you think shitting ourselves would be really embarrassing? Embarrassing enough to, you know, send a kid over the edge? And who would they blame if something like that happened? Maybe the guy who made a bunch of kids shit themselves at a dance?"

Asshole Jim was a bit taken aback by my response, but he wasn't going to allow us to get off that easy. "Fine. But I'll escort you."

This wasn't going well.

Asshole Jim was going to ruin our entire plan.

Counselor Kirk stepped in. "Everything all right here?"

Asshole Jim responded as if we were up to something. "They claim that the dinner gave all three of them diarrhea. I'm going to escort them to the Rainmaker. Nikki will take charge of security while I'm away."

Counselor Kirk made a face. "Okay, too much information. Just let them go. If they aren't back in ten—"

Counselor Kirk made eye contact with me. I cringed like I was really holding it in.

"—twenty minutes, you can go searching for them. I don't think they'd lie about having the runs."

We were obviously lying, but I appreciated the fact that Counselor Kirk trusted us when no one else did.

Asshole Jim grabbed me by the arm. "No. I'll go with them."

He forced me out the door, escorting Quint, Finley, and me toward the Rainmaker.

We were all petrified. And silent.

My stomach churned, pressing up against the noose around my stomach. At this point, I was starting to feel like I might actually shit myself—I clenched my cheeks together.

Our plan was already in shambles. We were about to get in serious trouble.

THIRTY-SIX

I WAS NEVER going to be able to break free from Asshole Jim's iron grip on my arm.

This was bad. Like, really bad.

My mind moved at light speed as I tried to come up with a plan, but all I could focus on was how screwed we were going to be. My stomach acid boiled up against the noose as my brain rolled down an endless hill.

We were completely silent. Our feet dragged through the dirt as we journeyed along the trail. The trees clawed at our heads like monsters warning us about an impending doom. And the lamplights burned our eyes, blinding us as we passed through each of their rays.

I could see the Rainmaker up ahead, looming as a beacon in the distance. I wished that I could warn Corin about what was coming. I wished that I hadn't entirely ruined our plan.

We stepped up in front of the Rainmaker, but Corin and Paisley were nowhere to be found.

Asshole Jim nodded at the entrance. "Well, go if you have to go. We don't have all night."

Quint and Finley both stared at me with absolute horror on their faces as we made our way into the boys' bathroom. The fluorescent lights blinded us as we gathered on the benches outside of the group shower.

Quint whispered, "What do we do?"

I didn't have an answer. I was absolutely petrified and speechless.

Flinching Finley flinched. "Th-this was your idea. You have to do something."

Quint agreed. "Finley's right."

I racked my brain as I tried to come up with a solution.

Then we heard Asshole Jim scream in pain. "Ouch! Put that down! Now!"

And Corin: "You know I'm not going to do that. Sorry, this is about to hurt even more."

"Wai—" Asshole Jim's voice was cut off by a loud crack.

What did she do?

We all exchanged horrified looks before I led everyone back outside.

We found Corin standing over an unconscious Asshole Jim with a fire extinguisher in her hands. There was blood leaking down from a gash in his eyebrow, and he looked like he wasn't going to wake up for a while—or *at all*.

"Holy shit," Quint said.

I agreed with Quint—holy shit.

Corin glanced up at all of us and shrugged. "What?"

That's all she had to say for herself. She acted like it wasn't anything out of the ordinary. Like it was nothing. And that horrified me even more.

I quickly moved to check his pulse. "He's still alive."

"Of course he's alive," Corin said. "I'm not a murderer. He'll be fine."

Quint was absolutely horrified. "What if he doesn't wake up?"

"He will. Now grab your stuff before he does! We don't have a lot of time," Corin ordered.

But I was afraid that he wouldn't wake up, and that Asshole Jim's head wound would result in his death. At that moment, as I stared at Quint's alarmed expression and down at Asshole Jim's unconscious body, I decided that there was something else I had to grab.

I quickly yanked the lanyard out of Asshole Jim's pocket.

Corin held up her stolen keycard. "You could have just borrowed mine."

I shrugged. "I'm fine having my own." I needed to regain some control over the situation. "We have to tie him up, now."

They all looked at me as if their feet were glued to the ground.

"I'm serious. Corin, do you have any rope? We need to tie him up and lock him in one of the bathroom stalls before someone sees him like this," I explained. "Plus, this way he won't be able to follow us right away when he wakes up."

"I knew you were a genius," Corin said. Then she ran off into the trees.

"Hunter, this is bad. We shouldn't be doing this," Quint pleaded.

The noose tightened its grasp around my stomach. I glared at Quint, and he shut his mouth.

Corin was back within seconds with a bunch of neon-yellow rope in her hands.

"Where'd you get that?" Quint asked.

"Our supplies. Paisley will help me bring out the crates while you three grab your gear. Let's get this done."

I helped her roll Asshole Jim onto his stomach, and we tied his wrists behind his back and secured his ankles together. It took all five of us to drag him into the girls' bathroom. We left him sitting on the toilet with his pants down to his ankles, like he was taking a massive dump.

Asshole Jim was a piece of shit, and deep down, I think we were all glad that he was finally getting what he deserved.

"We'll be back," I said.

Quint and Finley followed me as we sprinted toward Ray.

I tried to bury my fears and regrets deep in the back of my mind. I couldn't believe that Corin would have the nerve to knock Asshole Jim unconscious. It was one thing to escape, but I hadn't agreed to be an accomplice to assault. She had made us into hardened criminals. But there was no turning back now. We were fully committed to her plan. And I was also committed to the decision I'd just made.

No matter what the cost, I was determined to find out Corin's truth.

THIRTY-SEVEN

MY ENTIRE BODY surged with adrenaline as we burst into Ray.

I ran toward my bed and pulled out my backpack.

Quint didn't like the plan. "Hunter, you know this is nuts—she's nuts. She literally knocked Asshole Jim unconscious."

I frantically began to stuff some clothes into the backpack. "Is recounting what happened really going to help?" I asked Quint. "Besides, you should be glad that asshole finally got his."

I could hear my heart pounding in my head. My ears were ringing.

"Are you sure we should be doing this? I mean, we could just turn ourselves in," Quint said.

"We aren't turning ourselves in. Do you want to spend the rest of your life in Mental?"

Quint didn't have a response. He realized that we didn't have a choice. We either had to go along with Corin's plan, or face the major repercussions of allowing her to assault Asshole Jim.

Finley was a wreck. "SO much pressure! I can't find all my underwear!"

I laughed. "How many pairs do you need?"

Flinching Finley flinched. "E-enough pairs!"

I zipped up my backpack, slung it over my shoulder, and made my way down the center aisle between the beds. I could feel the noose around my stomach pinching down.

"I'll meet you guys back at the Rainmaker. I need to grab something else," I said.

"You can't be serious. You're leaving us?" Quint sounded pissed.

The humidity was getting to me; I was starting to sweat, a lot. "I'll meet you back at the Rainmaker," I repeated as I opened the door.

I bounded down the stairs, slamming the door on Quint's skeptical face.

I sprinted down the trail. My backpack bounced against my back so hard that I thought it might break my spine. But I didn't slow down. I only had so much time. I didn't want to draw suspicion from Corin about where I was, and why I was away from Quint and Finley.

The Shrinker cabin was completely dark when I arrived. Even the lamp outside the door was black.

I tried to swallow, but my mouth was so freaking dry. I pulled out Asshole Jim's lanyard and waved his keycard over the magnetic lock. The little LED light on the surface of the pad blinked from red to green. I heard the locks open. I turned the doorknob and entered the cabin.

The door to Mental glowed in the faint moonlight at the end of the hall. A looming reminder of where I would spend the rest of my life if we got caught. I forced the fear of Mental to the back of my mind.

I was in a hurry. I had a job to do.

I waved the keycard over the magnetic pad on the door to the Office. It was hard to see inside, but it was too much of a risk to turn on the lights.

I rushed over to the shelf and found our session's folders. I slid my hand over all the files until I stopped on the thickest one. The noose was suffocating my stomach, forcing the air out of my lungs. I pulled Corin's fat green file off the shelf and held it in my sweaty hands.

My heart was clawing at my chest—I contemplated how I would have felt if Corin had stolen my file and read about The Incident. But I was different from Corin. You could tell that something was seriously off about me. I wasn't confidently doing crazy things. Still, though, I realized that if I ever wanted to have a serious connection with her, she could never find out that I had taken her file without her knowing. But I needed to know about her secrets. The only way I would ever be happy with Corin was if all her truths were forced out into the open.

I couldn't be happy in a world of lies.

I decided that I would give her the chance to tell me about her past on her own. If she wouldn't expose her truth, then I would have no choice but to look through her file. I realized that *the question* we were forbidden to ask was actually the most important question of all.

I planned to ask Corin why she was here.

My lungs finally inflated again as I shoved the file into my backpack. As I left, I made sure the doors locked behind me.

My chest was on fire and my heart felt like a scorching ember burning in my chest. I panted as I ran toward the faint glow of the Rainmaker, thinking about how Corin would feel if she caught me red-handed with her green file. I hated going behind her back, but this whole thing was absolutely crazy. Even though I hated Asshole Jim, knocking him unconscious was the final straw for me. This confident, mysterious girl was about to get a whole lot less mystifying. I was going to force her to tell me the truth, or I was going to read about it on my own.

The smell of the latrine assaulted my senses as Corin, Quint, Finley, and Paisley came into view. They were already standing outside the entrance to the Rainmaker with backpacks slung over their shoulders and five crates lined up at their feet. I could see that the crates were filled with the supplies that Corin had gathered over the past few weeks.

"You ready?" Quint asked.

Corin's looked a bit on edge. "Where were you?"

I shrugged, feeling the heaviness of the file in my backpack. "It doesn't matter."

Corin seemed bothered by my answer, but we didn't have time for an argument. "Great. Everyone grab a crate."

We all picked up a crate. The weight of the contents was so heavy that I thought I might fall over. I placed a hand under the bottom to prevent that from happening. "Where'd you get the crates, anyway?" I asked.

"I got them by being a rule breaker, Hunter the Author. I've been planning this breakout since the day I arrived at this godforsaken place. Soon, I will be a legend."

Maybe that was Corin's problem. Maybe she was one of those people so desperate not to be forgotten that she would do anything to be remembered. I could feel the influence of her thick green file in my backpack, like it was calling to me. Soon, I would know the answers.

Then she kissed me on the cheek and sent my heartbeat racing—but in a good way. The burning in my chest stopped, and the noose loosened its grip around my stomach enough for me to comfortably breathe. Corin had the ability to make me feel better in any situation; it really bothered me that I didn't fully trust her.

Finley appeared to be disgusted. "Gross," he said.

"Don't you think we should get going?" Quint asked in annoyance. "As fun as it is watching you mack on each other and all."

"Chill, Quint the Optimist. They haven't even noticed we're missing," Corin pointed out. "Grow some balls."

Then a flashlight scanned the area from a distance.

I heard Counselor Kirk's voice. "Boys! Corin! Paisley! Jim? What's going on out here?"

Our hearts stopped beating at once.

THIRTY-EIGHT

WE LOCKED OUR eyes on Corin for direction. "What do we do?" I asked.

Corin stared at us like we were idiots. We hadn't actually been caught yet. All we had to do was stay ahead of Counselor Kirk. "We run, quietly. Come on, let's move."

We hurried through the night, Corin leading the way. I tried to trust that she knew what she was doing, that she would get us out of this unscathed. But I also knew that Counselor Kirk was on our trail. As soon as he found Asshole Jim's unconscious body in the girls' bathroom and realized we weren't in the Rainmaker, he would alert the other counselors and the search would be on.

I kept glancing over my shoulder. I felt like we were being watched, like Asshole Jim was going to jump out of the trees at any moment. I was shivering and sweating at the same time. My skin felt cold and my blood turned to ice. My muscles tensed up at the same time—every step was a chore. Part of me wanted to turn back, but I forced myself to push forward.

We stayed off the trails, making our way through the dense trees, away from the lamplight. My legs were starting to itch—our feet sank into the mucky plants. I peered up at the sky and noticed that the clouds were beginning to grow thick above our heads. The stars began to disappear. I hoped that it wasn't going to start raining.

More flashlight beams illuminated the ground behind us, scanning the area at our backs. My heart was punching my ribs so hard that it felt like I had just sprinted a mile. We realized that the hunt was on—we were the prey. A cloud of mosquitoes followed us as we journeyed around the mysterious fence surrounding Happy Lake, making our way to where the dirt road connected with the rainbow entrance into prison camp.

I was consumed by my thoughts as we made our way onto the road. I was worried we would be caught and entombed in Mental. Or worse—that we would be committed to asylums. Or even worse—that we would all be sent home to our parents. Corin's plan had to work, because if it didn't, we were screwed.

There were lights aimed up at the rainbow arch, illuminating the engraved letters of the camp's signage. We stopped outside the gate. Corin placed her crate at our feet and started to dig through her backpack.

She pulled out her stolen keycard, marched over to the scanner, and waved it across the magnetic reader. The scanner beeped, and the red light blinked red. The motorized gate didn't budge.

"Shit," Corin said.

My heart stopped, again.

"*Shit?* What does *shit* mean?" My voice cracked.

"Nikki must have finally reported her keycard as missing. Hand me Asshole Jim's, quick."

I did. She swiped it, and it blinked red, too.

"Fuck. They must have deactivated *all* the keycards," Corin said.

We were totally screwed.

My lungs felt like they were superglued together. I froze. Like an idiot, I just stood there, waiting to get caught—waiting for the counselors to take me to Mental for the rest of my life.

Corin tossed the keycard to the side and began to sift through the contents of her crate. "Time for our backup plan."

As soon as she finished her sentence, the floodlights around the perimeter fence of the camp suddenly blinded us in bright white light. We stopped as though posing for a portrait, then looked at each other as if to ask, *Who did it?*

The purr of an engine echoed in the distance. I turned to glance up the road and noticed that there were headlights barreling toward us.

"Hunter, what do we do?" Quint asked, panicked.

I didn't have a response. I panicked, too. I was drowning in my thoughts. I was a deer caught in *literal* headlights.

Corin pulled a pair of metal cutters out of her crate. She began to cut the links of the gate to form a hole.

"Hurry!" Quint urged.

Corin responded as she cut the wires, "You all need to chill. I'm going as fast as I can."

An alarm started to blare through these megaphones that were attached to the floodlights.

"There, see if you can fit through, quick!"

Corin forced the hole in the fence open. Quint, Finley, and Paisley quickly stepped through, immediately sprinting up the road on the other side. The headlights were close now—like, really close.

Corin slung her backpack over her shoulder and said, "Shit! Hunter, we have to go! Now! Stop standing there like an idiot and move!"

I watched as if I were outside of my body.

She grabbed my arm and forced me through the hole in the gate. The sharp wire tore holes in my pants and cut the skin on my arms. Everything was a blur. It was as if the bright floodlights had wiped my brain. The headlights behind us were close enough that our elongated shadows danced up the road in front of us.

Corin sprinted so fast that I could barely keep up. She yanked me to the side. I felt my shoulder pop.

"Off the road! Quick!" she ordered.

We dived off the road and lost our footing as the level forest sank down a small hill. Our knees abandoned us. We fell to the forest floor. I remember rolling, and rolling. I lost my crate and heard my backpack rip. I didn't stop tumbling until my torso collided with a tree.

I tried to breathe, but I couldn't inhale.

I tried to cough, but I couldn't exhale.

I peered up through the darkness, trying to grasp my focus enough so that I could see the road. I could hear an engine roaring. I saw a Jeep speed down the road. I gave whoever was in the Jeep the finger—even though I knew they couldn't see.

I was finally free of all the rules, of the counselors' manipulation, of therapy, of all that nauseating happiness.

My lungs suddenly inflated.

We had escaped with our lives.

I sat up. My backpack felt light.

I remembered the file—I rotated the backpack to my front.

I peered into a gaping hole to see that the file was gone.

THIRTY-NINE

CORIN PLACED her hand on my shoulder, and the agony from my tumble vanished.

All I could focus on was the missing file. I hoped that she wouldn't find it before I did.

Shit.

"You okay?" Corin asked.

My ribs were screaming at me as I nervously scanned the ground for the file, praying that she hadn't already spotted it. The noose fastened, causing my stomach to cramp.

"Something cracked when I hit that tree," I groaned. "And I lost all my stuff."

"Well, you have to see if you can get up. It won't be long before they circle back. The rest of the group is waiting for us at the bottom of the hill."

In that moment, I wished that she had more sympathy for me, but I understood where she was coming from—she didn't want to end up back in prison after we'd just gotten out.

I nodded, and then cringed as I tried to rise. My ribs throbbed like I'd been hit in the side by a wrecking ball. I let out a bit of a loud grunt, and Corin immediately put her hand over my mouth to silence me.

"Quiet," she ordered. "Stop acting like a baby."

I was starting to get a little pissed by her lack of sympathy. Was she going to clock me over the head like she did to Asshole Jim? I hated thinking it, but I couldn't help it.

"I'm trying to be quiet. I think my ribs are broken," I self-diagnosed.

Corin started to pick up supplies strewn throughout the area. My heartbeat staggered as she literally stepped over her massive green file to collect my crate. The noose choked my stomach as I stumbled over to the file while Corin gathered up the cans of food.

I sighed with relief as I stuffed the file back into my torn pack and quickly zipped it shut.

Corin filled the crate back up, although I'm positive she forgot a few things that she couldn't see. She put the crate at our feet and stared at me for a second as I clenched the ripped fabric of the pack together in my hands.

"What?" I asked.

She suspiciously stared into my eyes. I gulped.

"Why are you holding your backpack like that?"

"It ripped."

Corin seemed distrustful as she looked into my eyes.

Had she seen her file? Was she waiting for me to fess up?

She pulled out a roll of duct tape. The tape squeaked as she ripped off a piece and handed it to me.

"Tape up your pack. You don't want your clothes to leave a bread crumb trail."

Phew.

I carefully continued to hold the fabric together as we mended the hole in my backpack. I was so glad that she hadn't seen the file.

That was too close.

I let out a huge sigh and the noose loosened its grip around my stomach. I slung the pack over my shoulders, and Corin handed me my crate. Then she picked up her own crate and pack.

"You seem fine now," Corin said.

But I wasn't fine. The agony returned. My ribs felt like they were in flames, like they were roasting in an oven. The only reason I'd been able to ignore the pain was because I was so worried about Corin finding her file. I didn't want her to know that I had betrayed her by stealing it. I grimaced.

Corin turned away from me. She began to descend the hill, and I was left with no choice but to follow her.

My ribs exploded as I hiked down. They pulsated with a constant twinge of torture, but the misery was nothing compared to the way I felt about how Corin was treating me. I thought she cared about me, but I was starting to think that she didn't. She didn't care that I was hurt—at all.

We joined Quint, Finley, and Paisley at the bottom of the hill. Our eyes were slowly adjusting to the darkness. But it was dark—like, really dark. The trees were like ominous shadows in the night, and clouds had completely covered the sky. We were living in a self-inflicted horror movie.

Quint approached me. "You okay?"

"No," I quickly responded. "I'm not."

"Stop acting like a girl. He's fine," Corin interjected. "We have to keep going. Follow me."

Quint tried to protest, "Don't you think we should make sure he's—"

Corin cut him off. "Quiet. You either listen to me, or you'll end up in a place far worse than Mental," she threatened. "I've been to that place—that's how I know that we have to get away. Eventually, we all end up in that place, because they don't understand people like us—they never will."

Corin's leadership abilities had gone from sexy to scary.

I think at that point we realized that Corin would have done anything to get away. She admitted that she'd experienced places far worse than Camp Suicide—which only worried me more. Corin was acting fanatical—like our stupid miscalculations would suddenly disappear once we got to wherever we were going. But our stupid miscalculations were permanently on paper.

Hers were in my backpack.

Quint placed a hand on my shoulder to assure me that everything would be okay, but I was starting to think that it wasn't going to be okay.

Maybe she wasn't going to make me happy.

The forest floor crunched under our feet as we dodged around the shadows. My legs were really starting to itch as we walked through the plants. I couldn't see more than a few feet in front of me. I knew that Quint was leading me, and that Finley was at my back. No one said a word for at least twenty minutes. We were all too worried about being silenced by Controlling Corin.

And then Quint smashed face-first into a tree. "*Ow*—tree. I found a tree, guys."

Everyone except for Corin burst into a fit of quiet laughter. It felt good to break the tension—even though my ribs exploded with pain.

Finley added to the humor. "There are limbs coming at me from every which way!"

My ribs throbbed as I laughed again.

Ouch.

Corin stopped and turned to stare at us with her hands placed on her hips like she was a disappointed parent. "Do you guys want to get caught?" she asked.

Quint defended us. "Corin, I don't think any of us actually want to get caught; that's a crazy accusation. We are far enough away from the road that a little talking will be fine. Okay?"

Corin glared at Quint as if he had just challenged the queen of England. She slammed her crate into the ground and pulled out a flashlight for each of us.

"Fine, you want to get caught, get caught," Controlling Corin snapped.

We all felt slightly guilty as we received our lights.

"Corin, like Quint said, it will all be fine," I said. "You know where to go from here, right?"

Corin ignited her flashlight so that I could see the disgusted look on her face. "You trust me, don't you?"

I frowned. I could tell she was actually upset that we were challenging her. But where was she taking us? I wanted her to tell us the rest of the plan.

"It's not that I don't trust you," I reassured her. "It's just that we don't need any more broken bones."

Quint tried to lighten the mood. "Quint appreciates Hunter's worries and doesn't want to break any bones, either."

"Okay, Ash the Loudmouth," Corin snapped. "Stop talking about yourself in the third person. Now you have lights."

Quint diverted his eyes to the ground.

Corin rounded away from us and began to stomp through the trees. We all exchanged looks of doubt. I continued to wonder if we were in over our heads. What if Controlling Corin was acting this way because she had spotted the file before I was able to get it back into my pack? My stomach was in shambles, twisting up against a relentless noose.

Even Ominous Paisley seemed silently worried.

"At least she brought flashlights," Quint muttered to me under his breath.

The sky cracked, and suddenly, it began to pour. The rain came down in sheets over our heads. Lightning ignited the hills with the power of Zeus. And the wind gusted through the trees like a wailing infant.

We were soaking wet. We were covered in mud. We were cold. We were moody. We were sick of Corin not divulging details. We were worried. And we were starting to regret escaping at all. But there was no turning back.

Not with Controlling Corin dictating our every move.

FORTY

THE GRAY LIGHT slowly started to illuminate the glistening forest.

I was so cold that I'd completely forgotten about the pain in my ribs. My legs were still itching a butt load, and now I could see why—the forest was full of poison ivy. My skin was red and it was starting to swell. With each squishy step, I started to regret more and more my decision to blindly follow Corin.

Where were we going?

I hadn't thought we'd make it this far, and I had no clue how far we'd get. The rain continued to pound our backs. It covered my face like a curtain. My clothes were so wet that I may as well have been dunked in a dunk tank.

Corin was acting more and more controlling. My doubt was growing that she'd ever tell me about her history on her own. I hoped that the file in my backpack would still be legible by the time we got to our destination—it must have been soaking wet. I was eager to read it, to know why she needed to be in complete power over every situation. The noose around my stomach suddenly felt like it was desperately trying to kill me.

I noticed the misery on everyone's faces. Corin was at least thirty feet ahead of us, and we were growing weary of her brisk pace.

Quint obviously felt like Corin was at a safe enough distance to discuss the situation. "Dude, it feels like we've been walking forever. She knows where we're going, right?"

The truth was that I knew as little about where we were headed as Quint did. We had to be at least ten miles from Camp Suicide.

How far did she expect us to walk?

I sighed. "I hope so."

Quint glanced down at his legs. "My legs are itching like crazy."

"That's because we've been walking through poison ivy all night."

Flinching Finley was flinching like crazy as he scratched his legs raw.

"Finley, stop! You're making it worse," I urged.

"Itch-itch it-it itches!"

I glanced at Quint and frowned.

This suuuuuuucked.

He stared into my eyes as if I had betrayed him. I guess in some ways, I had. My lies were beginning to catch up with me. That's the thing about lying. No matter how small of a lie a person tells, it always comes back to bite the person in the ass.

"How long are we supposed to put up with this shit?" Quint sounded disgusted.

Finley was exasperated. "I feel like I'm in *Lord of the Rings*, on the journey to Mordor."

Quint mocked Finley, "And what character does that make you, Finley? Gollum?"

Flinching Finley flinched and scratched his legs some more.

I had to do something before the group decided to unite in a mutiny. Corin was still the girl who stopped my bladder. I had to trust her. I had to have faith in her.

She might be my key to a happier life.

"I'm thirsty," I said. I raised my voice so that Corin could hear. "We should stop for some water."

Controlling Corin called back, "We aren't stopping. Annnnnd I can hear everything you're saying, by the way."

I cringed. I didn't want Corin to think that I was the type of person who would talk trash behind my significant other's back.

Especially when I had an entire file about my significant other literally in my backpack.

"We've been walking forever," Quint complained. "And in case your legs haven't started to itch yet, we've been walking through poison ivy."

"Forever is relative," Controlling Corin rebutted. "Plus, you three are in pants. Paisley and I are in dresses—I assure you that we are receiving the brunt of the poison punishment. Stop complaining. It's just a few more miles."

"Miles?" Quint said in exasperation. He stared at me. "Did she say miles?"

Flinching Finley flinched. "I thought you said this place was close."

Thunder shook the hills. We all jumped. I thought Finley was going to piss himself, he looked so scared.

I was sick of the rain, my ribs ached, my legs itched, and I was tired of hiking. "Seriously, Corin."

"What?" Corin turned back so that she could glare at us. "I thought you were supposed to be big, strong men. You don't hear Paisley whining about any of this, do you?"

Finley was very frustrated. "Paisley doesn't talk!"

"Precisely," Corin pointed out. "Maybe all of you should talk less."

Controlling Corin picked up her pace, and we had no choice but to try to keep up.

Every so often, we slipped through the mud as we went. We walked for what must have been three more hours. The sun rose up behind the clouds, and the rain weakened to a light drizzle. The trees sparkled in the diffused light, and what should have been the happiest moment of our lives began to feel like misery.

I started to worry that we were better off enslaved in Camp Suicide. That following Corin along this escapade was a stupid miscalculation. And just when I was about to abandon all hope, it stopped raining.

We stepped through a wall of thick trees. The sun broke through the clouds, and the dense forest thinned into a flat meadow. In the distance in front of us, we could see an old, abandoned half-burnt farmhouse perched on top of the plains.

A dirt road extended into the forest from the entrance of the scorched house. The intact wood panels covering the outer walls were rotting or charred. The blue paint was peeling. Dead vines covered every inch of the surface of the exterior. The house had a porch. Square tile windows. A peaked shingled roof. It was the most picturesque site.

I was relieved that we had finally arrived. Thankful that Corin hadn't actually led us astray. I knew that I had to confront her about the way she'd been acting. I didn't like how controlling she'd gotten—and I especially didn't like all the name-calling. I hoped that she would tell me the truth about everything, and that if she didn't, her sopping wet file would still be clear enough to read.

Corin held out her arms as if they were wings—like she did in my fantasy back on Happy Lake.

Suddenly, I trusted her all over again.

"This is it. We're home," she promised with a grin.

FORTY-ONE

"OH, THANK GOD. I could kiss you right now!" Quint exclaimed as he ran toward the porch.

Corin called after him, "Something tells me that Mr. Thompson would have a little bit of an issue with that!"

Flinching Finley flinched with excitement. "I feel like I'm about to combust."

Corin raised an eyebrow. "This house is already burnt enough."

I laughed and my ribs throbbed.

"We should get into some drier clothes to warm up," Corin directed.

"Good idea," I agreed. "Although I'm pretty sure all our stuff is at least damp."

All my worries started to fade away—kind of. We trekked through the tall grass to join Quint. Corin hadn't led us astray—she knew exactly where she was going, which was a huge relief. This place looked amazing. The four stairs leading up to the porch creaked as we stepped up them. Quint peered through the dusty windows, trying to make out what was inside.

I joined him, wiping away some of the grime, before pressing my forehead up to the glass. The interior of the house had been ransacked. The moldy furniture was tipped on its side. The walls were covered in neon graffiti. And there were thousands of papers scattered across the floor. It wasn't exactly paradise, but it would do.

"Looks like they left in a hurry," Quint noted.

"They left during a fire," Corin pointed out.

Quint laughed. "Yeah, I guess you can't exactly take your time doing that. What do you think happened?"

Corin shrugged. "Probably an oven fire, or something like that."

"Who would live way out here in the middle of nowhere?" I asked.

Corin shrugged. "Cannibals."

We all chuckled.

I started to wonder if Corin had been to this place before. Even with satellite mapping, this place wouldn't exactly be easy to find, but she knew exactly where it was—had she found it in her previous sessions? Or was she telling the truth about image-mapping it out?

I turned to her. "How do we get in?"

Corin opened the door. "Through the front door."

"I probably should have tried that first," I joked.

How did she know the door would be open?

If she had been here before, who had she brought with her?

Everything about her was still so freaking mysterious, but I knew that eventually I would know the truth.

The entry to the house was massive. There was a grand staircase on the right side leading up to the second-story balcony and rooms. We walked inside and put our crates on the floor. There was a huge gaping hole in the ceiling where the fire had burnt through the roof. The house smelled like a combination of burned firewood, mildew, and spray paint. I was already starting to get a headache from the fumes.

"Isn't it great?" Corin asked.

Quint frowned. He clearly wasn't impressed with our new abode. "It's fine. You didn't happen to bring any calamine lotion with you, did you?"

"Yeah, it's right next to the bath salts and moisturizer," Corin deadpanned.

I glanced down at her legs, which were swollen and red all the way up to her calves. If the welts weren't driving her nuts already, they would be soon.

Finley added his two cents—he wasn't impressed with the house, either. "It smells terrible."

Corin didn't want to hear any more negative commentary. "You're coming with me," she said as she grabbed hold of my arm.

Corin yanked me away before I could say a word. We bounded up the creaky wooden stairs with so much force that I thought they might break under our feet.

"What are we supposed to do?" Quint asked

"Make yourselves at home!" Corin shouted back.

My ribs throbbed as Corin tugged me through the entry into the master bedroom. She slammed the door behind us and stared at me through her sopping hair.

"This will be our room," she told me.

I let my taped backpack fall to the scratched wooden floor of the massive empty room. I heard the file thud as it loudly hit the ground. I grew nervous at the sound, wondering if she thought it was suspicious—the guilt returned and the noose tightened its hold around my stomach. Corin would never want to be in the same room as me if she knew what had caused that noise. I had to divert attention away from it.

I pinched my nose shut. "What's that smell?"

"Old plumbing, I assume," Corin explained as she moved to seal the door to the master bathroom.

I didn't care for more of an explanation as to why the bathrooms in the house smelled so rank.

Corin dropped her knapsack and lurched in for a kiss.

I recoiled as her chest collided with mine. "*Ow!*"

Corin backed away. "What?"

"Sorry, it's just, my ribs."

Corin tenderly moved in to put her hands under the bottom of my shirt. My heart began to race. I could feel her hard nipples pressing against me through our clothes. This was the moment I had been eagerly awaiting. Corin and I were finally alone. I was supposed to be excited, but I just felt worried, awkward, and guilty about the entire situation. It felt like the file in my backpack was watching us from the floor.

She started to unbutton my shirt—I quickly stopped her.

"Wait," I said.

Corin frowned. "What?"

"I dunno, just . . . I hate taking my shirt off. I—"

Corin put her finger up to my mouth. "You're sexy, so quit making excuses."

"I don't feel sexy."

"Just relax," Corin urged.

I reluctantly submitted, and Corin unbuttoned my shirt a bit and then lifted it up over my head to reveal a massive, nauseating bright-purple bruise on my ribs. I cringed at the sight of it.

Corin gazed up at me. "Looks like it hurts."

"It does."

As I stared into her eyes, I realized that I was staring into an ocean of lies—we were both indirectly lying to each other by not exposing the truths about our pasts.

Was she lying to me about thinking I was sexy? Or was she actually attracted to hobbits?

"I'll make it feel better," she whispered as she got down on her knees.

Corin began to lightly kiss each of my ribs. I closed my eyes as I tried to enjoy it, but I couldn't stop thinking about asking her *the question*. I couldn't stop thinking about her green file. I didn't know her. She didn't know me. It was all happening so fast. She unbuttoned my pants and pulled them down to my ankles. She could see my extremely hairy thighs, but she didn't comment on them. She kissed my abdomen and began to gently massage my *extremely* limp dick.

"Something wrong?"

"It's just my medication," I lied.

I closed my eyes and forced myself to try to push my worries to the back of my mind. This was the moment I had imagined. Everything was perfect. We were alone. Away from Camp Suicide. Away from all the rules. I pulled her up and began to kiss her.

I started to think about our first encounter—how Corin claimed that she wanted me to get to know her. I had to prove that I wasn't just like every other guy. I *did* want to get to know her. It wasn't just physical for me. Everything was happening so quickly, before we really knew the truth about each other. Being with her was supposed to make me feel happy. But kissing her was making me feel even more depressed.

The noose cinched so tightly that my stomach throbbed in agony. Then, without warning, I started to cry. I felt terrible—both physically and mentally.

Corin gazed into my eyes. "It's okay. The side effects of the meds will wear off soon. We're alone; that's what's important."

She hugged me, causing me to cry even more. I felt so guilty for stealing her file. I also felt so frustrated. Frustrated with Corin for knocking Asshole Jim unconscious. Frustrated with her for dragging me along on this crazy expedition. Frustrated that she acted so controlling. Frustrated that I still felt like I didn't know her at all.

"Hunter, I want you to know that I *actually*, genuinely like you," Corin whispered into my ear. "Everything will be okay."

But she didn't really know me.

And I didn't really know her.

FORTY-TWO

QUINT, FINLEY, AND PAISLEY were lying on the floor as I stepped down the stairs.

Quint sat up. I think he could tell that something had happened from the tears in my eyes. "Hunter, dude, what's wrong?"

I wiped my eyes. "Nothing."

"Doesn't look like nothing," Quint said.

"Hey, Paisley." My voice cracked.

She inquisitively looked up.

"Do you mind if I talk to the guys alone?"

She nodded and silently collected her things. She headed upstairs to join Corin in the master bedroom.

Quint waited until she was gone to inquire, "What happened? You look like you just saw your mother naked for the first time."

I glared at Quint. I didn't find his joke funny.

At all.

"Hunter, seriously, though, you okay?"

I shook my head. "I'll explain in a second. Let's find another room to change in."

Quint and Finley gathered up their knapsacks and we began to explore the abandoned farmhouse.

We entered a hallway where the pictures were scorched on one side of the wall, but the dusty frames on the opposite wall were completely untouched. The whole place reminded me of the kind of house you'd see in an apocalyptic movie.

I stopped outside of a weathered door. The knob jerked as I twisted it open. We stood, staring inside. The room must have once belonged to a young boy. There were a few basketball posters under the graffiti on the wall. A small bathroom connected to the room. But it didn't smell as bad as the one in the master bedroom.

We entered and I closed the door behind us. We all dropped our packs on the floor. Quint and Finley began to sift through their gear to find some semi-dry clothes.

I unzipped my pack and stared down at the sopping wet, thick green folder—my stomach was in shambles. The edges of the folder were caked in mud. I prayed that it would still be readable. I wondered if it held all the answers as to why Corin had acted so controlling in the woods. And why she'd acted like nothing had happened as soon as we were alone upstairs. I forced my curiosity to the back of my mind—my stomach needed a break. Plus, I wanted to give her the chance to explain herself before I opened the file, because after I read it, I would know everything about her. And I wasn't sure if I was ready to.

I needed to allow her to tell her side of the story. That was important to me. On a piece of paper, it would seem like I was a horrible person. And that wasn't the whole truth.

I pulled out a damp pair of jeans, a shirt, and boxers. We began to strip out of our wet dress clothes.

Quint noticed my bruise when I took off my shirt. "Holy shit. Hunter, your chest. Is that why you were crying?"

I maneuvered into my damp shirt as quickly as I could. "No. It's okay."

"You're ribs are b-broken," said Finley.

"I'm fine."

We were silent for a moment as we continued dressing. As soon as Finley had his pants off, he started scratching his legs again.

"Finley, stop. Seriously, you're going to make it worse," I said.

"C-can't stop. Won't stop."

I gave up.

Quint brought the conversation back to Corin. "So what's the word? What happened with Corin?"

I racked my brain for a simple answer. "I dunno how to explain it," I said.

I really didn't. Under all of Corin's mystery was even more mystery. I felt like I had no idea who she really was behind the layer of confidence. I also felt so guilty for stealing her file—but I couldn't tell the guys about that. They wouldn't understand.

Flinching Finley flinched. "Try."

"I mean, she was all over me. It all happened so fast," I elaborated. "I just felt weird about it. And I couldn't get a boner."

Quint stopped dressing and Finley stopped itching. They both stared at me with their mouths hanging open. I realized suddenly after saying it out loud that the scenario I'd described was exactly what every guy dreams of happening with a girl—I had been dreaming about that moment, too.

"So what's the problem?" Quint asked. "Are your meds messing with your junk? Mine do that shit sometimes, too. It'll wear off."

"Maybe," I said.

I knew that it wasn't the meds, though. The noose around my stomach was messing with my junk—my worries and regrets were messing with my junk.

"Dude, I promise it will. One time, after they switched my dose, I couldn't get it up for a week. No matter how much porn I watched, no matter how much lotion I used, it just wouldn't get hard," Quint assured me. "So that's what the tears were all about?"

I wanted to tell them that it wasn't my happy pill—it was the fact that I felt so horrible for stealing Corin's file, the fact that Corin was acting like a literal roller coaster. But I had convinced them to break out of Camp Suicide with me so that I could be with the girl in question.

"I dunno. My ribs hurt, and back in the woods, she didn't care. She cared as much about my ribs as she did about knocking out Asshole Jim. She wasn't seeing me as a person. Then, up there, she started kissing me to make me feel better." I took a deep breath. "It's just weird. I can't stop thinking about all the crazy things she's been doing. She doesn't really know me, so how could she possibly care about my well-being? Plus, I don't really know her. If she *actually* liked me, then she would have sympathized about my ribs after it happened—even if it caused us to get caught. It's all throwing me off."

"You need to get out of your head. If it's your meds, it's one thing, but if you're telling me that we went to these extremes to escape with a girl you like, and now you don't like—"

"I do like her," I interjected. "She's just acting weird."

I just wanted to get to know her. Originally, she had claimed that she wanted me to get to know her, too. Being with Corin made me happy. And I didn't want to ruin that by forcing myself to have sex with her before it felt right.

Sex was supposed to be the ultimate cure for my depression.

"Plus, I didn't make either of you come with me. You chose to come with me."

"Keep telling yourself that," Quint said. "But we wouldn't be here if you weren't thinking with your dick to begin with."

"It just didn't feel right, okay? I want her to actually get to know me before we take that step."

I kicked off my nice pair of sneakers, and noticed, for the first time, that they were caked in mud. "Ugh, my sneakers are ruined."

"They're fine," Quint said. "So are you going to bone her? I mean, maybe if you both get naked, your dick will start working again. What do you think, Finley? Maybe we should just have an orgy. Then we can all lose our virginities at once."

Flinching Finley flinched, unable to respond.

"He's so excited, he's speechless," Quint joked.

"We're not having an orgy," I responded. "It's not just about sex for me."

Quint raised his eyebrows. "Sure it's not. You just wanted to get away from therapeutic hell so that you could talk about your feelings more. You're not fooling anyone, dude. It was always about sex."

"Okay, at first, maybe it was, but I actually want to get to know her better now."

"You can do that after you have sex. Isn't that what pillow talk is for?" Quint asked.

That's the problem with guys. They all claim that they just want sex, but most guys want an emotional connection, too. You can't make love to a blow-up doll. I knew that if I didn't get to know the real Corin, then sex would feel awful. I wanted an emotional connection with her—that was the therapy I needed.

I was starting to get annoyed. "Seriously, Optimist Quint, stop. I don't feel like I lost anything."

And the jabs just kept on coming. "Exactly, Horny Hunter, you didn't lose anything."

I punched Quint in the shoulder to get him to shut up.

Quint shook his arm. "*Ow*, Jesus, that was the last one."

I cringed from the sharp pain in my ribs. "It better be."

"I think that hurt you more than it hurt me. Don't start crying again. I promise, I'll play nice." Quint gently patted me on the back to try to make it all better. "You're a good dude. Whether it's your meds, or your thoughts, you can overcome any demon."

I knew that statement didn't hold a single shred of truth. Quint had no idea who I actually was, either. He didn't know about The Incident. I couldn't overcome that demon—some demons are just too evil to conquer. I wondered if I would ever tell him about my past, or if I would just leave him in the dark forever.

"I'm not," I responded. "If you knew me, you probably wouldn't like me, either."

Quint didn't believe me. "Doubt that. I'm—"

"Right, I know. Nothing matters."

"Actually, I was going to say, I'm sure it's fine, whatever you're talking about," Optimist Quint said.

We finished changing and draped our wet clothes out on the floor to dry. I sighed as sleep deprivation began to run its course. We hadn't slept at all the night before, and we were all exhausted.

Quint yawned. "I feel like I'll fall asleep if I close my eyes."

We fell to the floor to lie on our backs with our heads in a circle. Our bodies spanned out in the shape of a star.

"Agreed," I said.

Quint and Finley both closed their eyes, but I kept staring at my duct-taped backpack. The noose around my stomach was getting tighter and tighter. I knew that the soaking-wet green folder was inside. I wanted to know the truth about Corin's identity.

I closed my eyes to try to sleep. The wooden floor was cool under my back, but it was hard and extremely uncomfortable.

"This floor sucks."

But I didn't get a response. They had already passed out, leaving me with my thoughts.

I closed my eyes, and in my dreams, I knew everything about Corin, and she knew everything about me.

In my dreams, we accepted each other's truths, and it just made us closer—everything felt right.

FORTY-THREE

CONTROLLING CORIN opened a can of corn with the pocket-knife Surgeon Dick had given me.

The sound ground on my nerves—I'd almost completely forgotten that Corin had the knife at all. I don't know why it put me on edge so much. It was just a knife—but a knife can easily cut through skin.

Corin slid the pocketknife back into the pocket of her extremely tight jeans and handed me the corn. Quint was already shoving a can of green beans into his mouth, while Finley chomped on some beef jerky, and Paisley slurped up some canned peaches.

I stared into the can at the yellow kernels. I'd never had cold canned corn before, but it had to be better than green beans. I hesitated, glancing around the massive entryway.

I wondered how much an enormous farmhouse out in the middle of nowhere would cost. There was this really cool, dusty crystal chandelier hanging from the ceiling over our heads. And the banisters were carved like vines. I'm sure that this house was pretty neat before it caught fire.

I put the can of corn up to my mouth and sucked in some of the slimy kernels. I chewed on the cold canned corn and gagged. "This is awful. I didn't think canned food could possibly taste any worse."

Corin took a bite out of a block of processed meat and made a horrendous face. "At least you got corn. Corn at least tastes good."

She forced herself to swallow the mouthful of disgustingness. We all laughed at her expression.

I handed the corn to Corin, deciding that I had lost my appetite. I'd rather go hungry than eat nasty, cold canned food. "I'll have some jerky when Finley's finished."

Corin took the corn and batted her eyes. "How chivalrous."

Quint joked, "Get a room."

Corin explained to Quint in a very matter-of-fact way, "We plan to, Quint. Hunter and I are made for each other."

The guilt returned and I lost my appetite completely.

What if I couldn't ever get a boner again?

I wondered if guilt and insecurities were what caused all erectile dysfunction. I had to ask her *the question* before we ended up alone together, because if I didn't, I knew that I would only disappoint her again. This charade could only go on for so long before she realized that my limp dick wasn't a side effect of my happy pill.

Thankfully, Finley changed the subject. "I-I'm itching so freaking mu-uch."

Finley was clawing at his leg like he wanted to cut it off.

"Stop scratching," I said.

"I can't!" Finley shouted back.

We all exchanged concerned glances.

Quint tried to diffuse the tension. "What do you think is going on back at camp?"

"Probably something colorful like a rainbow, or shiny like the sun," Corin mocked.

"C. Dermont is about to explode with joy," Quint added.

"And Counselor Kylie's shooting up with steroids before sailing," Finley joked—he'd finally stopped scratching.

I glanced at Corin, and she returned my gaze.

Behind a thin layer of confidence I could distinguish insecurity lurking in her eyes.

FORTY-FOUR

I WAS GOING to confront Corin—I *had* to confront Corin.

I'd become obsessed. I could feel our relationship slowly falling out of my grasp. If I didn't find out the truth about her past, and soon, I knew that I would never be able to truly love her—I wouldn't find out if sex could cure my depression. But I also realized that if I wanted to know her truth, I would have to expose the truth about The Incident.

That afternoon, we were all knee-deep in a stream building a dam. The water felt good against our poison ivy rashes—even Finley had finally stopped scratching. Ironically, the activities we found to keep ourselves occupied outside of Camp Suicide were just as lame as the ones at Camp Suicide. I think we all realized that we were just biding time until we got caught or had to turn ourselves in. We thought that we should at least try to have some fun before that moment overtook us.

All of us realized that—except for Corin.

The massive trees with gray trunks and thick green leaves surrounded us. The shore was covered in rocks shrouded under moss, and thick, tall grass sprouted out of the shallows in the water. It was a pretty neat spot. I could see the peaked roof of our new abode peeking out above the tree line.

We were all quietly stacking logs on the dam, when, without warning, Quint intentionally dropped a rock, splashing Finley in the face. The water erupted up into the air, drenching not only Finley, but Corin and Paisley as well. When the turmoil subsided, Corin was standing with one hand perched on her hip, Paisley was staring at Quint in disgust, and Flinching Finley was flinching.

"Seriously?" Corin said.

Quint laughed. "It's fine, Corin. You can thank me for cooling you down. It's hot and humid out here."

"Quint the Optimist, you will meet your end," Corin threatened.

I decided to join in on the fun. My ribs exploded as I picked up the biggest rock I could find. I lugged it closer to them, into the knee-deep water. Corin, Quint, Finley, and Paisley all stopped to look at me. I held the rock up over my head as they watched in horror.

"Hunter, you're going to hurt yourself even more. I seriously will kill you if you splash me with that rock," Corin said.

So, of course, I let the rock fall into the water. The liquid exploded up into our faces. Corin stared at me with this disappointed expression when the turmoil subsided.

I shrugged. "Sorry. That rock was super heavy, and my ribs are super broken."

Corin responded by kicking water up into my face. Chaos ensued. The dam-building activity erupted into an all-out splash war. It wasn't guys against girls or girls against guys—it was everybody for themselves. We soaked each other, and then we soaked each other some more. We tried as hard as we could to empty the water out of the stream and into one another's faces.

Eventually, we were so drenched that we couldn't possibly drench each other any more, and the war came to a cease-fire. We were all laughing and my ribs burned. Corin's wet skin glistened in the sunlight. Her expression glowed with a light that overshadowed the darkness behind her eyes. I knew that her happiness was a lie. I couldn't stand it anymore. I wanted to love her, to know the truth about her, to feel comfortable around her. Now was as good a time as any. I had to get her away from the group to confront her before I lost my nerve.

"Can I talk to you for a second? Maybe we could go for a walk or something," I asked.

Corin batted her eyes. "Hunter the Mysterious. Of course we can talk." She scanned the faces of Quint, Finley, and Paisley. "We'll be right back. Keep up the good work."

Corin splashed through the water over to me and stepped out onto the shore. She took my hand and led me into the woods. We dodged bushes and shrubbery as we escaped into the trees. When we were far enough out of sight, Corin turned to me and wrapped her arms around my neck. She looked me in the eyes. I could see the white flecks of her iris dancing in the sunrays. She went in for a kiss.

My heartbeat raced so fast that I almost lost focus. I pushed her back. "Wait."

Corin backed away, completely defeated. "I'm being careful of your ribs."

I couldn't control my worries around her. The noose wrapped around my stomach again and again. I could feel it choking my insides. I wanted to want her—to love her. But I didn't know her. I had to ask—

"Why were you sent to Camp Sunshine?"

Corin froze. Her eyes turned to hate. She glared at me like I'd been sent up from hell by the devil to ruin her. She shook her head. "You can't just ask that."

I explained myself. "But what if it's the one question that we all need to answer for ourselves?"

Corin disagreed. "You don't need to know about my past to know me."

"But I do. Corin, I don't feel like I know you at all. You were the one who told me to get to know you. You told me that I had to prove that I wasn't just like every other guy. Well, I'm trying to get to know you. And honestly, you've been acting a bit controlling ever since we left camp," I pointed out.

Corin got defensive. "I haven't been acting controlling, Hunter. I'm just trying to be a leader. I'm obviously the only one willing to step up."

I subdued the urge to get into a heated screaming match with Corin over that statement. She kept questioning my manhood, and I hated it, but this conversation wasn't supposed to be about me, or Corin. This conversation was supposed to be about us, and our future together.

"Corin, I see a future with you."

"I see a future with you, too."

"Okay, good." I paused to stare at her beautiful, flawless skin. "Corin, you're the most striking girl on the outside. But for us to have a future together, I need to get to know you better on the inside."

"Well, it goes both ways, Mr. Thompson."

"Stop calling me that. It feels like you're belittling me."

We were at a standstill. The conversation was going nowhere.

"Well, if it's so easy to talk about our pasts, why don't you tell me about yours? How about you go first? Why are you here?"

My mind flashed back to The Incident. I could feel the noose around my stomach burning, trying to convince me not to talk about my stupid miscalculations. My throat got dry, like I had been eating chalk. But even though I was nervous as all hell, and I knew that my truth might change everything, this time I didn't freeze up. This time I talked about everything out loud: "Okay. I'll tell you."

I took a deep breath. "On the worst day of my life, I was sitting in my room, playing video games, and eating Cheetos. Harpy Patricia was supposed to be home already, but naturally she wasn't. She was always running late. My little brother—Levi—had been acting like a total pain in the ass all day. I honestly just needed a break, so I locked him out of my room. He was banging on the door, throwing a tantrum, and screaming bloody murder. That's when I decided to take a few rips from Lola."

Corin stared at me with this blank face.

"Lola was my bong," I said.

She understood.

"The next thing I knew, I woke up—I guess I'd passed out from the bong rips I'd taken. I was on this new dose, and the combination had done me in. I wasn't sure how long I was out for, but I had finished my bag of snacks, so I called out to Levi, 'Bring me some more

Cheetos and I'll let you hang out in here with me.' But Levi didn't answer. I shouted this time. 'Levi! Did you hear me? I said bring me more Cheetos.' No response.

"I was starting to get really annoyed with him because I had to pause my game. And my parents still weren't home."

Corin interrupted, "What does sharing our pasts have to do with us?"

"Just hold on. You'll see. Eventually, you'll hate me," I explained.

She shook her head. "I could never hate you."

"You will," I assured her. I continued, "I wasn't supposed to be watching him in the first place. I figured he was probably hiding from me, waiting for me to find him. We played that game sometimes, but at this point I was still so high that I wasn't in the mood for games or anything besides Cheetos. I called out to him again. Nothing.

"Finally, I got up to go look for him. I took Lola with me and took another rip from her as I made my way through the halls of our massive house. I searched for him everywhere, but Levi was nowhere to be found. He wasn't answering my calls. Then something outside the sliding doors near the kitchen caught my eye.

"A pair of small light-up sneakers had been carefully placed on the pool deck. They were Levi's shoes.

"I went outside, and that's when I saw his teddy bear bobbing on the surface of the water. And you know what was floating next to his teddy bear?"

"Hunter, don't," Corin urged.

"Levi was floating facedown in the pool.

"Lola slipped from my grasp and shattered against the ground.

"But even that didn't snap me out of it. I just stood there. Corin, I just stood there and didn't jump into the water to try to revive him. I didn't do anything because it honestly felt like I was living in a horrible dream. I sat down with my feet in the water and watched his body bounce up and down, up and down. I couldn't move.

"And that's when I heard her voice. 'Hunter, how about a little help?' The front door slammed.

"After that, everything happened in slow motion. Patricia stepped outside and saw me staring at Levi's body. She jumped into the pool and cradled him in her arms. She told me to call an ambulance. But I just sat there the whole time. Patricia laid Levi's body on the deck and ran inside to call for help. His skin was so blue.

"The police and paramedics came, but they couldn't revive him. This cop led me outside to take a statement. Surgeon Dick arrived home to the commotion. And the last thing I remember from that day was watching as they carted my little brother away under a sheet."

I exhaled and peered into Corin's eyes. The noose loosened its grip. I felt a little better—like some of the weight had been lifted. "I'm a murderer, but it wasn't entirely my fault. I couldn't have possibly known that the combo of weed with my new dose would make me pass out. Harpy Patricia was supposed to be watching him. I was supposed to be with Stoner Claire. Surgeon Dick was the one who decided to open the pool early. If he'd just waited another week, if my parents hadn't been so neglectful, Levi would still be here, and I wouldn't have ever ended up in this place."

Corin started to cry, but my eyes were as dry as a desert. As I watched the tears stream down her cheeks, my spirit crumbled.

"You hate me now, don't you?"

She stared at me as her face melted. "I don't hate you, but you're lying to yourself if you think that you wouldn't have ended up here."

"What are you talking about?"

Corin's voice cracked. "If you named your bong, then you were obviously addicted to weed. Something like that was bound to happen eventually. And, Hunter, I gotta be honest, you're also lying to yourself if you think it wasn't your fault."

How dare she!

I glared at her. My blood boiled. I couldn't believe that she was trying to play therapist. I was so frustrated. So annoyed that she thought she knew everything about me now, and I still felt like I didn't know the first thing about her.

"Weed isn't addictive." I shook my head. "It wasn't completely my fault."

"It's psychologically addictive, Hunter. Especially for people like us." Corin wiped away the tears. I could tell that my story had really affected her. "Okay."

I waited for her to say something else. "Okay?"

"I'm glad you told me that story. It must have been hard for you. But I still love you. I don't see you as a murderer, and I definitely don't hate you. I'm glad I know you. But I hope you know that I can't fix you. Only you can fix yourself."

"I'm not asking you to fix me. I'm asking you to tell me about yourself. Corin, I told you why I'm here; now it's your turn."

She stared at me with sincerity. "That story doesn't define who you are unless you let it. But I don't have a story like that. I'm just depressed. There's no magical reason or explanation as to why I'm here. I just am."

"At Campfire Confession you acted like it was something more. Corin, you're lying to me."

"I'm not." She moved in to kiss me on the cheek. "Take some time to cool off. I'll see you back at the stream."

And with that, Corin deserted me. I had opened my heart to her, and she left me with my chest wide open. She had basically responded by placing the blame entirely back on me. People who are *just depressed* don't have thick green folders filled with notes about their past. Something else had happened to Corin that she didn't want to talk about—ever.

The noose retightened its grip—I clenched my jaw. I was so frustrated with her. I had given her the perfect opportunity to come clean. I had told her everything about myself.

She returned my openness by walking away.

FORTY-FIVE

THE ECHO of a helicopter thundered with the sound of reality.

I squinted up to see what was flying overhead, but I couldn't see anything through the branches. I had to get back to the stream—fast. I sprinted as quickly as my short, hairy legs would carry me toward the dam.

When I got back to the stream, Corin, Quint, Finley, and Paisley were all staring up at the sky with their mouths hanging open. My eyes drifted up, and my stomach sank down against the noose when I saw the search helicopter. Its orange paint glinted in the sunlight. I could see a man hanging out the side door. People were searching for us. And they were going to spot us if we weren't careful.

"We better head back to the hideout," Corin directed.

"Whatever, it's fine. We had our fun." Optimist Quint sighed.

"It's not *fine*; we've only been gone a day. I need more time." Controlling Corin's voice cracked, like her world was crumbling. "Let's go!"

She began to stomp back into the trees in the direction of our sanctuary. The mood took on a somber tone as the rest of us followed her through the woods. Suddenly, we were forced to come to terms with the fact that we might actually have to face the repercussions of escaping from prison camp. None of us wanted to get caught, but we also realized that eventually we would have to go back.

Once they detained us, who knew if I'd ever get the chance to find out Corin's truth, or if we'd even be able to stay together? They'd probably make sure we never saw each other again.

We walked between the trunks of the trees and created our own path. There was no way that the team in the search helicopter was going to see us walking in the forest, but eventually, they were going to spot— and search—the gigantic abandoned farmhouse out in the middle of nowhere.

Corin slowed down so Quint could take the lead. She approached me and said, "I feel like we need to talk." She waved Finley and Paisley ahead. When they were finally out of earshot, Corin explained, "Listen, I'm sorry about before."

The sound of the helicopter boomed in my ears as it zoomed through the clouds.

"Okay," I responded.

Corin looked like she was waiting for me to say something. She sighed. "You're not going to apologize, too?"

"I don't think I have anything to apologize for. You don't want to tell me the truth about your past, that's fine. But I'm not going to pretend like I'm your boyfriend anymore."

"I never asked you to be my boyfriend."

Seriously?

"But you told me you were falling in love with me. You see how that would be confusing to me, don't you?"

"You've been pretty mean to me when all I've been is support-ive," Corin said. "I feel like your problem is that you never accept responsibility for your actions."

I got really annoyed by that statement. Who was she to tell me what *my* problem was? The noose was cinching my stomach with so much pressure that I couldn't control my frustration.

"Corin, you've been sneaking around Camp Suicide and stealing supplies for an escape since the day we arrived. You recruited me to participate in that escape plan. You knocked Asshole Jim uncon-scious. You refuse to sympathize with me about my rib injury. And you're telling me that I'm not supportive, that I'm mean, and that

I need to accept responsibility for my actions? What do I need to accept responsibility for? Tell me."

Corin didn't respond.

"You have this unexplainable need to be in control of every situation. You won't tell me why you're here. I feel like we don't know each other at all."

The helicopter made another pass. It was so loud that my ears started to ring.

Corin seemed taken aback by my candor. But she didn't react in anger, or haste, even though I was basically yelling in her face at that point.

"I know. That's *my* problem, and I promise, I'm working on it. Telling you about my history won't change the fact that I need to deal with what happened to me on my own. I just need to feel like you still want me," Corin justified. "I still want you."

I tried to swallow but I couldn't. I just wanted something in my life to go the way it was supposed to go. Corin was the girl who stopped my bladder—I wanted a perfect fairy-tale relationship with her. But fairy tales aren't real. I was starting to realize that reality was always going to suck, that Corin might never let me know her truth. She might never feel comfortable enough to let me in.

"I do want you," I responded.

"Then I'll give you the chance to prove it, Hunter S. Thompson. Tonight, after everyone else is asleep."

The helicopter made another pass as she turned and started hiking away from me.

I was so taken aback by our conversation that I needed a minute to absorb what she'd disclosed. She'd admitted that she had a problem, but she didn't think that it would help our situation to expose the details of her past. And yet, she had the nerve to tell me that I needed to take accountability for my actions.

Our fairy tale in the forest was suffocating in reality. I was out in the middle of nowhere, taking sanctuary in an abandoned half-burnt house because I thought that I loved her. But now I was having doubts—love at first sight might not exist. Of course I was going to fall for the only girl who had ever taken a real interest me.

I was beginning to think Camp Suicide had been the glue to our relationship. I was starting to think I had been wrong about Corin. She wasn't this special creature who was immune to all the bullshit in life.

She was just as depressed as I was.

I wouldn't be able to give her what she wanted until she let me inside her head.

FORTY-SIX

THE SEARCHLIGHT IGNITED the fear on our faces.

Every time the helicopter made a pass, it illuminated the entire house with a bright white light that pooled in through the windows and the holes made by the fire. We were about to be in serious trouble.

We were in a circle on the floor in the entryway, sitting in complete silence. We had opened a few cans of corn, green beans, and a bag of beef jerky, but no one was eating. I could hear the helicopter chopping across the hills—an echoing reminder that we were doomed.

Flinching Finley flinched when the bright light passed through the house. "What happens when we finally turn up?" He'd asked the question we all wanted to know the answer to.

Corin tried to act like we weren't defeated, but I could tell she was a nervous wreck. "We can't give up now, not after we've worked so hard to get here," she protested.

Finley stated the obvious: "We can't stay here for-forever."

"He's right," Quint said.

Ominous Paisley nodded in agreement.

Corin shot her a death glare. "You're taking their side?" She turned to Quint. "I thought you said nothing mattered."

Quint made eye contact with me like I should say something, but I was trying to stay out of it. No reason to add fuel to the fire. I couldn't stop thinking about Corin's file. I had to wait for the right private moment to read it. I felt like it was calling my name.

"This might actually matter," Quint explained. "I don't want to end up in juvie, prison, or an asylum for the rest of my life."

"I can't believe what I'm hearing. You two are supposed to be men. Man up!" Corin exclaimed.

"How does acknowledging the reality of this situation make me less of a man?" Quint looked at me again. "Hunter, could you weigh in?"

I really didn't want to get involved. Corin gave me this look of desperation. I was frustrated with her, but I didn't want to gang up on her. I still cared about her. "I . . ."

Quint grew impatient. "Do you realize how much trouble we're going to get in?"

I shook my head. I tried to silently communicate that I didn't want to take anyone's side. "Optimist Quint, lay off," I ordered.

Quint could see that something was bothering me, so he dropped the subject altogether.

"Everything's going to be fine," Corin assured herself. "I haven't led you astray so far, have I?"

We all exchanged worried looks, but no one answered. She had *definitely* led me astray. This place was supposed to be the greatest place on earth. And it was far from perfect. It was clear to me that Corin was never going to allow us to turn ourselves in. She clearly thought we were going to be able to live out the rest of our days eating cold canned food in the burnt farmhouse.

"Let's clean up," Corin said.

We started to gather the trash, and we piled it in a corner of the room. Corin grabbed my hand as I started to follow Quint and Finley back to the boys' room. My heart started racing. Her touch was still intoxicating, even if my brain was all jumbled about the issue of me and her.

"You ready for tonight?" Corin asked. "The side effects might have worn off by now."

I wanted to be ready—I really did. But I wasn't even remotely aroused. It was like my dick had disconnected itself from my heart and attached itself to my brain. I was finally thinking with my head instead of my emotions. I knew that I wasn't going to be able to make love to Corin until I knew about her past. But as much as I wanted to turn her down, I just couldn't. Ever since I got diagnosed with depression, I thought sex would be the cure-all for everything. I had to read her file so I could go through with the deed.

I still needed to find out if sex could cure my illness.

"I guess we'll find out," I responded, knowing it was time to expose her truth.

FORTY-SEVEN

WE WERE ALL sleeping on the floor, back in the boys' room.

The smell in the master bedroom was too rank for anyone to handle.

Corin was snuggled up against me, with her arm wrapped around my bruised chest. Quint, Finley, and Paisley slept soundly a few feet away. The search helicopter continued to whirl overhead, and every time it passed over the house, the searchlight ignited the room in a flash of white. My eyes were wide open, staring at my backpack against the wall.

The file was watching me.

I could feel Corin's breath wrapping around the sides of my neck like it was choking me. My stomach was throbbing against the noose. Sex still could be the hidden cure for my depression, but I was starting to understand how complicated relationships were. Relationships were full of lies. And I had become something I hated.

I had become a liar.

I was lying to Corin. Our entire relationship had been built on a lie. We didn't trust each other. We didn't love each other. We didn't know anything about each other.

I had to get up to see what was in that file. I tried to lift Corin's arm off me without waking her, but she wasn't actually asleep, either.

"It's time," she whispered in my ear. "I love you, Hunter. I really do."

I felt her hand glide under my T-shirt, down my stomach, and into my boxers. She started to massage my dick as I fought the urge to run away. I literally didn't know what do. My dick was so freaking limp—the most limp it had ever been. My heart started to race, trying to regain control over my emotions. But my brain wasn't going to release its power.

Should I ask her the question again? Or should I just show her the file so she could explain?

"Feel good?" she asked.

It wasn't ever going to feel good, not until I knew her truth.

Corin started to kiss me. My heart started beating even faster. Everything felt warm all of a sudden. Then she started to jerk me off, desperately trying to get me hard. She pulled up faster and faster—so fast that it was starting to hurt. I tried to enjoy it. I wanted to love her. But I just couldn't. It didn't feel good at all. It felt like she was going to rub my skin raw.

Nothing about this felt right. And no matter how much I wanted to know what sex felt like, I knew our relationship was drowning in a sea of lies. I hated myself for lying to her, and I still felt like she was lying to me.

I pulled her hand out of my underwear and explained, "My breath is terrible."

I didn't know what else to say. I didn't know how to tell her the truth. The truth was confusing—even to me. This was what I had always wanted. But my brain was screaming at me, and I couldn't turn the volume down.

Corin put her hand up to my lips to signal for me to be quiet. She didn't want me to wake Quint, Finley, or Paisley. Corin kissed me again, but not in the gentle sort of way. She gripped the back of my neck and opened her mouth wide. She shoved her tongue to the back of my throat and got on top of me. My ribs exploded in pain as she began to grind on me. That was all I could take. I pushed her away—hard.

"*Ow!*" I rose to my feet and shouted, "Stop! Seriously, just stop!"

Quint, Finley, and Paisley jolted awake.

"What's going on?" Quint asked.

My stomach was hanging from the noose as I continued on my tirade. "I've said no nicely, and you just won't stop! I don't know how else to say it!"

Finley backed into the corner of the room. He covered his ears and began to rock back and forth.

Paisley froze up as if she had seen a ghost.

Quint tried to calm us down. "Corin, Hunter, maybe—"

"You can't be serious?" She looked at me like I was a monster for not wanting to have sex with her without getting to know her first. "What the hell is wrong with you? I thought this was what you wanted—this is what men want."

I couldn't believe that she would have the nerve to deflect what was happening back onto me.

"What the hell is wrong with *me*?" I was really angry now, so angry that I couldn't stop myself. "Ever since we got to this house, you've turned into some sort of . . ."

I stopped.

Corin finished the sentence: "Rapist? That's what you were going to say, isn't it? You think I'm a rapist."

This couldn't be happening; this wasn't real. This was some sort of upside-down fairy tale. I wanted to take it all back. I watched as Corin's soul shattered. I thought about her file. I had to come clean.

"Corin, I didn't mean . . . I . . . Corin . . ."

I couldn't find the right words to explain myself. My stomach hurt so bad that I was starting to feel nauseous.

"Hunter, why don't you want me?"

I felt so guilty for stealing her file. But I still didn't know anything about her past.

I wanted her to know that she could tell me anything—that she didn't have to hide.

I briskly walked over to my backpack, unzipped it, and pulled out the soggy massive green file.

"What the hell is that?" Quint interrogated.

"No," Corin said. "Please, no."

"Hunter, if that's what I think it is, you shouldn't open it," Quint protested. "That's just one side of the story. Think about how you'd feel if I read your file.

"Tell me what's inside of it."

She shook her head, unable to respond.

"Hunter—"

I interrupted Quint. "Stay out of this!" I said again, "Corin, please. Tell me your side of the story. I need to get to know you—otherwise, I can't be with you. Please. I want to make love to you, but I just can't, not until I know you."

Tears started to leak from Corin's eyes. "No. No. No. No. No," she kept repeating herself.

"Fine," I said.

I opened the file.

Corin screamed, "No!"

She ran at me and grabbed the file from my hands. It flew up into the air, and the papers spilled everywhere. She began to frantically snatch them up, ripping them apart. I quickly fell to my knees to gather some of the file's contents. When she saw me collecting the notes, she screamed at the top of her lungs, and then she collapsed to the floor—defeated.

"Hunter, please, stop," Quint said.

"No," I snapped.

I stomped over to my backpack and grabbed my flashlight so that I could read. My thoughts were poisonous. I had become obsessed with knowing about Corin's past, obsessed with falling in love, obsessed with the idea that sex could cure my depression. I couldn't stop myself—even though I should have. The noose around my stomach was on fire, but Corin had forced my hand. The confident girl who stopped my bladder was just a fantasy. I was finally going to know the truth.

They all watched in horror as I began to peel a few of the notes apart. Corin quietly cried on the floor. Finley rocked back and forth while Paisley rubbed his back. And Quint kept shaking his head while he watched me scan the smeared papers.

I didn't stop until I'd glanced at most of them.

As it turns out, it was no coincidence that Corin had picked me as an accomplice. She had attempted to escape from Camp Sunshine with two different guys in both of her previous sessions.

I stared at their pictures. Both of the guys were stocky. Both of the guys could never have hoped to talk to a girl like Corin. Both of the guys were exactly like me. But unlike in my situation, both of Corin's previous escape attempts had failed. One of the guys had turned her over to the counselors. The other had tried to drown himself in Happy Lake because he was so confused about how she felt about him—that's why they installed the fence.

I held up the photos for Corin to see. "What are these? Who are they?"

Corin continued to cry, staring at me with this petrified look on her face.

Chills ran down my spine. I realized that the counselors were right—Corin had been manipulating me the entire time. I found myself getting even more depressed and angry. Corin had picked me because she knew that she could influence me into doing whatever she asked. Corin had chosen me because she knew that I would help her.

"Hunter, stop," Quint said. "You're hurting her."

Her truth was hurting me.

I ignored his pleas. The saga went on. There were tons of different notes explaining Corin's diagnosis. Her father had been the mayor of some Podunk city that I'd never heard of. At fundraisers he would sell her to big-time donors. By *sell her*, I mean that these big-time donors were literally paying to have sex with a minor. They were paying to have sex with Corin.

I froze—I suddenly realized that I was making a hugely stupid miscalculation. I looked up into Corin's eyes, and I could see her spirit splintering.

I wanted to stop. But I forced myself to read to the end. I had to know the whole truth. I thought it might help me understand her better, but it was only making me feel like an asshole. I had treated her like a rapist, and she was far from that. Even though she didn't act like it at all, Corin was a victim.

Both her mother and father were arrested in the case. I guess her mother knew where all the money was coming from, but she just looked the other way. All the donors were eventually arrested, too. Corin had to testify on fourteen different occasions. Corin had to testify about fourteen different rapes.

The state put her under the custody of her aunt, but the damage was already done. Corin tried to kill herself over and over again. Her aunt tried everything—group homes, boarding schools, and institutions.

I guess Camp Sunshine was supposed to be a break from all of that—a place for her to escape from her history. A place where she could get the help she needed, away from the trauma of her past.

That's where I stopped reading. I realized that the counselors were right about everything. We couldn't treat ourselves on our own. We needed them. We needed therapy. And we needed structure. Corin had manipulated me into believing that she was okay. That she didn't have any problems. That Camp Sunshine was the problem.

But as it turns out, that was the stupidest miscalculation of my life.

Suddenly, I had the saddest realization. In a way, we both had the same problem: I was desperate to find out if sex could cure my depression—Corin was desperate to find out if sex could still make her feel loved.

"You only chose me because you knew that you could manipulate me," I accused.

The tears glistened on the sides of Corin's cheeks. She stared into my eyes. "It's different with you. I *actually* like you. I love you. I promise, you aren't like the others."

"But how can I believe you?" It felt like the noose around my stomach was cinching itself around my other organs. My entire body hurt—my heart felt like it had been flipped upside down. "You should have told me the truth when I asked you why you were here. You should have—"

"I get it. You don't want me because I'm used up."

That wasn't it—*at all*.

I was furious with Corin for manipulating me. But she was so confused about what love is, how could she possibly know that she loved me? I knew in my heart that I was right—a girl as pretty as Corin could never truly fall in love with a guy like me.

"It's okay," I said. "I get it now."

Corin was really crying now. She screamed, "I'm the worst! I am seriously the worst person on the planet! I just want to be with you! Don't you get that?"

She was telling me the truth. In her mind I really was different from the other guys. Maybe she had finally found love with me. Maybe she wasn't confused anymore. Maybe Corin and I were *actually* meant to be.

Corin screamed at the top of her lungs and stormed over to the nearby bathroom. She slammed and locked the door.

Finley began to scream at the top of his lungs as well. Quint joined Paisley and tried to comfort him.

I ran to the bathroom door. I could hear Corin screaming on the other side. I heard the mirror shatter.

Oh no.

I banged my fist on the door. "Corin! Please! Let's talk this out. I'm sorry for stealing your file. I just wanted to know why a girl so confident and sexy would fall for a guy like me. I wanted to know the truth about your past!"

Corin kept screaming and throwing things. "I'm not your confident, sexy little princess. I'm ruined. He ruined me."

I realized that she wasn't listening to any of the words coming out of my mouth. She *actually* did love me. She wasn't confused about me. She was positive. And by rejecting her, by stealing her file, by lying, I had triggered something in her.

Something bad.

Quint finally had the courage to weigh in again. "Dude, I can't get Finley to stop screaming. What the hell do we do?"

Corin continued to shout, "I'm just a used-up, manipulative slut who will always be alone. He hates me. Everyone hates me. I deserve it! 'Sluts deserve everything they get.' That's what he would always say. I deserved all of it!"

The searchlight ignited the room in a flash of light. I heard the helicopter zoom overhead. We needed help—fast.

I spun around to see Paisley in the shadows. "Paisley, you and Quint take all the lights, go outside, and flag down that chopper. We need help—now!"

"I'm staying here. I'm not leaving you alone," Quint protested.

I agreed. I didn't want to be alone.

"I got this," Paisley said.

Quint and I watched her go over to Finley. We were speechless—she was talking.

She got down on her knees and spoke in this soothing tone, "Finley, you're fine. We're fine. I need you to have courage. We need your help."

Finley stopped screaming and stared into her eyes—shocked.

"Good, you're good. I need you to come with me; can you do that?" Paisley asked. "We need to go get help, now."

And to our amazement, Paisley got Finley up on his feet. But we didn't have time to talk about what had just happened.

They both quickly slipped into their shoes—Finley was still in his boxers—grabbed flashlights from their bags, and ran out of the room. I just hoped that they would be able to flag the chopper down before it was too late—before Corin did something rash.

The commotion on the other side of the bathroom door stopped—Corin went quiet. Chills took over every inch of skin on my body.

Quint's eyes met mine. "What do we do?"

I didn't know what to do.

We were helpless.

I put my back up against the door. I slid down to the floor with my knees to my chest. I prayed that Corin was listening to me. "Corin, please. Open this door. I swear, when I first saw you, I had no idea what you were even doing at Camp Sunshine. You're the most beautiful girl I've ever seen. That's why I felt like I couldn't trust the situation. You're confident, kind, generous, smart, and witty. I have no idea what you're even doing with a guy like me."

"Don't you get it? He used to say all of those things, too." Corin's voice sounded weak. "He used to tell me all of those things, and . . ." Her voice trailed off.

My heart stopped beating for a second. I forced my voice out of my throat. "I'm broken, Corin—you're not. No matter how many times they tried to break you, you've still stayed strong. You can still see the good in people like me. You still have the ability to love, even after everything they put you through. You're amazing, and you're a better person than me. You're not the problem with our relationship—I am. I hope you still love me. I know I made a mistake tonight. I know I shouldn't have read those notes. You matter to me. You matter, period."

And then it hit me. It hit me all at once. Corin was going to die in that bathroom—I was going to be responsible for her death. The tears started to flow down my cheeks. I wanted to die. I ruined every relationship. I had hurt Corin just like I had hurt my family.

I wanted to be with her. I loved her. I had to stop her.

"I'm sorry, Corin. I swear, I'm so sorry. Please, don't do something stupid. Please, open this door so we can talk about this."

But I didn't get a response.

I stood up and stared into Quint's eyes. I flashed back to that moment—on the pool deck—when Patricia was shouting at me to call an ambulance, but all I could do was just sit there.

I wasn't about to let that happen again.

I slammed my shoulder into the door.

"We have to break it down!" I shouted.

Quint joined in. We both simultaneously slammed our shoulders into the door. It cracked.

"Again!" I ordered.

We slammed into the door and it splintered against the frame—I stumbled into the bathroom. The floor was covered in broken glass from the mirror over the sink. Then I saw her in the tub. I realized that I had made the same mistake that Counselor Kirk had made with his sister. Corin's limp, bloody hand was clenched around the pocketknife Surgeon Dick had given to me.

There was so much blood leaking from her wrists. I froze for a second as I stared at her pale, lifeless skin. Her lips had lost some of their rosiness, and her eyes were open but unseeing. She was dead. My entire body started to go numb.

"Hunter." Quint's voice was muted under the ringing in my ears.

I kept staring into her eyes, and then she blinked, snapping me out of my trance. I quickly slipped out of my T-shirt, ripped it in half, and began to wrap it around the deep cuts in her wrists.

"Corin, stay with me," I said. "Stay with me!"

Her eyes rolled to the back of her head. The wrappings were already soaked in blood as I desperately tried to close the gaping slashes. I got into the tub with her—I thought that I might be able to hold the bandages tighter. There was at least an inch of blood surrounding her body at my knees.

"There's too much blood. . . . I . . . There's too much blood," I said.

I turned to Quint. He stared at me with this horrified look on his face. He was frozen.

"Quint, what do I do?"

But Quint didn't have an answer.

The helicopter was directly overhead, and suddenly, the searchlight continuously lit up the room.

"We have to get her outside."

Quint didn't budge.

"Grab her legs!"

He was still motionless.

"Grab her legs! Please!"

Thankfully, Quint snapped out of his trance. He quickly moved to her legs and grabbed her ankles. I put my forearms under her armpits and hoisted her up.

"We have to hurry," I said. "Ready?"

We lifted her, and blood dripped everywhere. The world blurred around us as we swiftly carried her through the house and out the front door. The spotlight blinded us as we stepped down the porch. Quint lowered her legs to the ground and ran into the field, joining Finley and Paisley as they desperately waved for help.

"Hey! Over here! Hey!" Quint shouted.

I cradled Corin in my arms. Her skin was cold to the touch. "Please don't die on me, too. Please don't die. Please don't die. Please don't die."

I kissed the top of Corin's head as three forest rangers rushed toward me.

She was so limp—so lifeless—I realized that she might already be gone.

And as they pulled me away from her, I saw my pocketknife fall from Corin's bloody hand.

FORTY-EIGHT

"AND THAT'S EXACTLY what happened," I say.

The hospital lobby is dark and smells of ammonia. The police officer—Lew—stares into my eyes before he finishes jotting down the last of his notes.

It's been a long story. He shakes the cramp out of his hand.

Officer Lew removes his hat and places it on his knee. I can tell he's thinking about something. Maybe retirement.

I'm still shirtless, with an itchy blanket wrapped around me and Corin's dried blood all over my skin. I glance back at Quint, who's sitting in a blue chair, explaining the situation to another police officer. Over in the corner of the room, another police officer is hounding Ominous Paisley to talk, but she won't. And in the hallway next to the emergency room entrance, a nurse and a police officer comfort Finley.

I want to see Corin.

Please don't be dead. Please don't be dead.

I can't bear the thought. My stomach has become the noose itself, and it's killing my body.

I want to hold Corin's hand, to assure her that everything will be okay. I want to tell her I'm sorry a billion times, that I will never betray her trust again. I know from her extreme reaction to my rejection that she wasn't manipulating me. Now that we know each other's truths, I finally trust that she does love me.

I love her back.

I turn to Officer Lew. "I want to see her."

"I know, son," says Officer Lew. "But I can't do that. We have to put you back under the custody of Camp Sunshine. They'll decide how to handle the situation from here."

My stomach sinks. I can't believe they're sending us back to Camp Suicide.

"I have to tell her something. She has to know that I still love her—that I'm sorry. I need her to know," I beg.

I try to force my way past Officer Lew, but he gently pushes me backward. I groan as the pain surges in my ribs.

"I have to see her," I say.

"We need to get those ribs looked at."

My voice cracks. "I need her to know. I need to make sure she's okay."

He sighs. "Look, I'll take you to see her, but it has to be quick, and I warn you, she's still unconscious. After that, you need to let me get those ribs of yours looked at, and you need to cooperate. Deal?"

She's not dead.

"Deal."

He leads me through the emergency room doors, back to the overnight rooms. I bite my lip and clench my fists. I can feel the sweat on my brow.

Officer Lew stops and points at a window. "Just have yourself a look, son, but don't go in."

He stands back, giving me some privacy. He hasn't put his hat back on.

I slowly approach the glass and close my eyes as I stop in front of the window. I'm not sure if I'm ready to see her like this.

I have to see her.

I open my eyes.

Corin is attached to a number of devices, including a heart monitor—I can hear it beeping with her pulse. Her skin is still extremely pale and lifeless. And there is a pint of blood flowing through a clear tube into her arm.

She doesn't look good.

I fight the urge to run into the room. I want to hold her. To tell her that I love her. To kiss her. But I know that she can't kiss me back. And she won't hear me.

My heart sinks.

I realize that she's still not out of the woods yet.

I'm not sure if she'll make it or not.

FORTY-NINE

ASSHOLE JIM rides shotgun while Counselor Winter drives us back to camp.

A little over twenty-four hours have passed since our escape. Asshole Jim has this massive bruise and stitches on the brow of his head where Corin struck him. He wears dark aviator sunglasses, which make him look like an even bigger asshole—as if that were even possible. Counselor Witchy Winter's warm fake smile has finally frosted over.

We're in this long yellow van—you know, the kind of vehicle that looks like a kidnapper's van. Quint and I have taken the seats in the way back. Finley and Paisley have taken seats in the middle.

The nurses made us take showers at the hospital to get the blood off our skin. Then they lathered us up in calamine lotion to help with the poison ivy rashes and gave us each a pair of scrubs to change into before they sent us on our way. I can barely move my upper body because of the tape they wrapped around my ribs—I cracked two of them. Luckily, they gave me some medicine to numb the throbbing pain.

We're all silent.

I watch the small hills roll by outside the window as the sun mounts the horizon. In this moment, it feels like those hills go on forever. I can't stop thinking about Corin. I regret allowing her to keep the pocketknife. I regret stealing her file. But I don't regret that

I finally *really* got to know the girl who stopped my bladder. And my heart.

Counselor Winter breaks the silence, "Your parents will be here to pick you up this afternoon."

None of us say a word in response.

"Do any of you have anything to say for yourselves?" she interrogates. "Hunter?"

I can see her eyes glaring at me in the rearview mirror. I shake my head.

"Of course not. I suppose *this* isn't your fault, either," she jabs.

I let my body slide down in my seat so that she can't see me anymore.

When we get back to camp, Asshole Jim leads Quint, Finley, and Paisley to Ray and Solas so that they can collect their belongings. Counselor Winter escorts me to the Shrinker. Therapist Jess is waiting for me in the Sunshine Room when I arrive. She and Counselor Winter take the two squeaky chairs, and I sit on the chaise longue.

We stare at each other for a moment.

Therapist Jess starts, "We know you stole Corin's file. We don't care why, but we want to talk to you before your parent arrives."

Counselor Winter continues, "We aren't shocked this happened, because as you probably know by now, she's tried this before. I'm not telling you this to make you feel bad, but Corin has attempted to pull this stunt for the past two summers. We should have banned her after the last one, but we just feel so bad for her. She is extremely manipulative. We keep giving her these extra chances—maybe she's been manipulating us, too." Then she glares into my eyes. "I warned you, Hunter, but you ignored me."

I feel the need to defend my actions. "But this time it's different. She *actually* likes me. She wasn't manipulating me. I like her, too."

Counselor Winter raises her eyebrows like I'm an idiot. "Is that what she told you?"

"It's the truth," I say.

I really do believe it is the truth.

Counselor Winter goes into detail. "Corin has no idea what love is. She was drawn to you because you aren't intimidating. She doesn't actually like you—she was just using you to validate her own existence, to make herself feel like she could be loved after everything that happened to her. Hunter, she was using you to deflect her focus away from a very traumatic past."

Corin realized that I would never reject her. She manipulated me because she needs to feel like she isn't broken, like she matters to someone, like someone can *actually* love her after she's been through so much. That's *her* problem.

Therapist Jess intervenes. "The truth is we should have been more vigilant about her condition and her treatment. We accept responsibility for what happened here. This should have never happened in the first place. We're recommending that Corin get the serious help she needs."

"You mean you're recommending she be institutionalized again?"

"After she recovers."

My entire body goes numb. My depression hits me with its full force. The noose permanently cinches my stomach. I realize that I'll probably never see her again.

Counselor Winter elaborates. "The problems you kids are facing aren't problems you can deal with on your own."

Therapist Jess sounds sincere. "We can't help you here. Not after what's happened. But we are recommending a therapist in your hometown that we insist you see at least two times a week."

They stare at me like all of it is my fault.

And it sinks in that they're right—I'm entirely to blame.

FIFTY

SURGEON DICK is the first parent to arrive.

He stands in Ray's doorway—holding his cell phone up toward the sky, trying to get a signal—as I pack up all my stuff.

Quint, Finley, and I exchange numbers so we can stay in touch. We promise one another that we will hang out as often as possible, even though none of us live in the same city. Counselor Kirk gives me the biggest hug ever. He gives me his e-mail address and assures me that I can write to him anytime I need to talk. C. Dermont laughs at a few of his own jokes, and promises me that he holds no ill will toward me. Ash, Blaze, and Wyatt say they'll connect with me on social media after they get home. I promise to reactivate my accounts so that they can find me online.

The sunlight pools into the room as I take one last look at Ray. I thought I hated Camp Suicide. From the moment I arrived, all I wanted to do was escape. But as I look at all my friends' faces, I realize that I feel grateful for my experience.

I wave good-bye one last time, and we're on our way.

But before I can leave, Asshole Jim is standing in the parking lot between me and Surgeon Dick's BMW. Without the aviators, Asshole Jim's eyes are totally bloodshot. He places a hand on my shoulder.

I wince, feeling like he's about to take me to Mental for the rest of my life.

"She's strong. She'll be fine. She's never fought this hard for anyone. I thought you should know that," he says. "Hold on to her. Don't let her get away."

Asshole Jim tries to smile but decides to spit a mouthful of tobacco onto the dirt instead.

I'm so shocked that I can't respond.

He nods at me, ever so slightly, before he goes marching off.

The car ride home is spent in excruciating silence. Surgeon Dick's cell phone can't get a signal. He checks the screen every five minutes, and I almost wish it would ring. The noose is one with my stomach—between it and the wrap around my rib cage, my upper body is a firestorm of suffering.

After about three hours of driving, we pull off the road to get some gas at this really old-fashioned gas station in the middle of nowhere. I get out to stretch my legs while Surgeon Dick fills up the tank. The sun is sinking under the vibrant plains. And as I stare out at the horizon, I notice that the blue of the sky eventually blends with the greens of the grass.

I suddenly realize that Corin is right—forever *is* relative. It's all about perspective.

Every forever ends.

I hope that my forever with her isn't over.

The gas pump clicks, and Surgeon Dick places the nozzle back into the holder. He turns back to me and stops. I can see the deep bags under his eyes—he looks exhausted. After staring at me for a relative forever, he asks, "What?"

"I didn't say anything."

"Oh, you still don't have anything to say?"

And then it finally dawns on me. I remember what Corin said—my problem is that I never accept responsibility for my actions. I'm lying to myself if I think The Incident wasn't my fault. I realize that I've always been something I hate.

I'm a liar.

After the funeral, all those times Surgeon Dick asked me if I had anything to say were opportunities to take accountability for what had happened. Surgeon Dick had been desperately trying to find a way to forgive me because I'm the only son my parents have left.

At that moment, his cell phone rings.

And as he retrieves his phone from his pocket, I turn to my dad and say the words he's been waiting forever for me to say: "I'm sorry."

He just stares at me—his cell phone continues to ring. He looks at me like I've punched him in the gut—like he thought his grief would never come to an end. He exhales a breath that he's been holding in forever and, with one swift motion, he sends the call to voicemail. And then, as he turns to stare out at the horizon, a tear leaks from his eye.

Silence.

In that moment, I burst into tears, and I finally let it all out. I apologize for everything. "I'm sorry for what happened to Levi. I know it was all my fault. I'm sorry for not trying to revive him. I'm sorry for making you pay for that stupid camp. I'm sorry for getting kicked out. I'm seriously sorry for all of it. I'm sorry for everything."

Then my dad does something even more surprising than letting his phone go to voicemail—he *hugs* me, and *he* apologizes. "I'm sorry, too. I'm so sorry."

Guilt is a burden. But the weight can be lifted.

The noose around my stomach slowly begins to loosen its grip.

I should have been more responsible. I shouldn't have been smoking weed while I was supposed to be watching my brother. I shouldn't have locked him out of my room. I should've tried to revive him. I shouldn't have escaped from Camp Sunshine with Corin. I realize the true source of all of my problems, of my depression, and all of my suicide attempts, *is me*. Which means that I also have to be the solution.

I have to be a better person.

Sex isn't going to cure my depression. But my human connection with Corin sure helps. *All* the human connections I've made help with my overall happiness.

I find my mom in the kitchen when I get home, holding a bag of groceries, staring out of the window at the swimming pool that's contributed to all our suffering and pain. I watch her for a moment, and then I give her the first hug I've given her since The Incident.

I whisper, "I'm sorry," into her ear.

My mom lets the bag of groceries fall—some apples roll across the floor.

And even though she doesn't respond, or hug me back, I know I'll get through to her. I can't change the past, but I can right the future by simply admitting that I've made a lot of stupid mistakes.

I understand that forgiveness takes a relative forever. But it can start now.

And as I hug her, I see my reflection in the windowpane. The noose around my stomach finally snaps loose and lets me go. My eyes look different—I feel different, like all the weight has been lifted. My guilt has finally been released.

The lessons I learned at Camp Suicide have followed me home.

Camp Sunshine changed my life . . . *forever.*

FOREVER

CAMP SUNSHINE'S FOREVER came to an end a few weeks later.

The state forced Counselor Winter to close the doors after everything that had happened. But I feel like that's fine—honestly, Camp Sunshine was pretty poorly run.

I still haven't had sex—shocking, I know—but I'm positive that sex isn't a cure for depression.

Therapy is helping me come to terms with all my stupid miscalculations. Instead of spending my sessions in silence—like I did before my experience at Camp Sunshine—I usually talk the entire time. I truly believe that therapy is helping me become a better person. I've stopped using nicknames for everyone and everything. I realize now that it's kind of messed up.

My depression will never completely fade—mental illness is a permanent thing, but thankfully, it's treatable. Our history can't be rewritten. But talking about what happened does help. And taking accountability breeds forgiveness.

I meet with my therapist twice a week after school. His name is Scott. He had me start keeping a journal, which helps, a lot. And every time I meet with Scott to talk about what I've written—I feel like my mind has been cleared. It's a nice checkpoint to my week.

Sometimes my parents join the sessions. We've talked about Levi's death, *a lot*. We've also talked about my suicide attempts, *a lot*.

I think they understand where my mind was after Levi died. I think they're trying to understand my illness better.

They're trying to be better parents.

So I'm trying to be a better son. I help my mom bring in the groceries without her having to ask now. It's a small thing, but I can tell my relationship with her is improving. I don't know if she'll ever completely forgive me, and that's okay. I just hope she finds peace, in whatever way she can.

We visited Levi's grave as a family for the first time since we buried him. It was pretty emotional, but I think it helped us let go. After my parents left for the car, I stayed a little longer and told Levi that I was sorry. He didn't deserve what happened. I should have watched over him—the way he watched over me all those times I tried to kill myself. But I was doing okay now. He didn't have to watch out for his big brother anymore.

I had something for him in my backpack.

His sneakers—the ones he'd left at the edge of the pool that day. I set them down at the foot of his grave. They lit up in the grass.

I told Levi that I'd be back to visit soon. And that I hoped he could forgive me.

I write to Corin every day. Breaking Cloud Center—the institution her aunt checked her into—filters our communication, and even though I know Corin isn't allowed to respond to my letters, I hope she at least gets to read them. I start every note with an apology. I tell her that I want her to feel better about herself. That what happened when she was younger was out of her control. And that she's perfect the way she is now. I assure her that I never meant to hurt her—that I do care about her.

I do want her.

The girl who stopped my bladder changed my reality in so many ways. She helped me identify that I was the true source of my suffering. She taught me how to be honest. And she helped me learn to clarify my truths.

I like to think that I'm helping her, too. She opened up, and I didn't run.

I still love her more than anyone in the world. And I hope she still loves me.

I returned to school and I started senior year. Even though I can tell that everyone knows what I went through, nobody says much about it to me. And that's okay. I understand that it's awkward to talk about someone's stupid miscalculations. It doesn't matter what they think they know about me.

What matters is who I am now—in this moment.

Sometimes my dad lets me have Quint and Finley over to visit for the entire weekend. Finley still flinches a lot. And Quint's as optimistic as ever. But I've got to say, I wouldn't want them to change for anything. We usually stay up all night playing video games and sharing funny stories. We don't ever talk about what happened at Camp Sunshine, but we know that we would never have connected without that place. I'm pretty sure we'll be friends for the rest of our lives.

Yesterday, Corin's aunt—Jane—reached out to my dad and requested that I come for a visit. She asked that I be there when Corin got released from Breaking Cloud Center. It took a lot of convincing, but my dad reluctantly agreed to allow me to take the five-and-a-half-hour drive alone. Aunt Jane assured my father that she would look after me for the night, and that she had a spare room I could sleep in.

A single stupid miscalculation, made in the heat of the moment, could have sent me into oblivion. It could have taken away my ability to experience all the wonderful moments in life, moments like this. . . .

I close my journal and pocket my pen. I'm sitting on this concrete bench in the center of a park in Bettendorf, where Corin's aunt lives.

I kind of have to pee.

The air is crisp in Bettendorf, not like the smoggy air in Minneapolis. There isn't any wind, and there aren't any clouds in the sky. There's just endless bright sunshine.

I see a small red sedan pull up to the curb. There's a girl sitting in the passenger seat. I see her, for the first time in the longest time. I see the girl who stopped my bladder. And right now, she's stopped it all over again. I feel like I'm living in a fairy tale. She looks so much better. Like all her worries have finally been lifted. Like her head is clear. I dunno what I would have done if I'd lost her. If I never got to see that beaming face again.

Aunt Jane waits at the car while Corin walks up to join me at the bench. I stand to greet her, and we hug for the first time in forever. My heartbeat is racing.

I feel like I'm living again.

I stare into her eyes, and she smiles at me with a brightness that I've never seen in her before.

"Hey," she says.

"Hey," I respond. "I'm sorry for everything."

Corin blushes. "I'm sorry, too."

"How are you?"

"Better," she says.

And I can tell that she really is doing a lot better. I can see that she's finally healing.

I smile. "Me too. Thanks to you."

Corin smiles back. "Thanks to you."

We stare into each other's eyes for what feels like forever.

I can't stop grinning, because as it turns out . . .

Sometimes a stupid miscalculation lands you right where you're meant to be.

ACKNOWLEDGMENTS

The first people who need to be thanked are the people who pre-ordered this book on Inkshares—this would not have been possible without you. I really appreciate the support. I was worried that I wouldn't be able to sell a single copy, and here we are. I hope that you'll pick up a copy of my next book—*KARID*—when the time comes.

My mom and dad have always compelled me to push boundaries and take huge risks. I would not be the person I am without their support. Mom, thank you for reading every single draft of this manuscript. You saw it through to the end, and I love you so much for lifting me up every day.

To Petersen Harris, thank you for directing me to Inkshares, and thank you for taking the time out of your busy day to inspire young writers like me. Your willingness to help new authors find an outlet for their work is motivating. I promise I will pay it forward when I can.

Thank you to my editors—Matt Harry, Philip Sciranka, and Pamela McElroy. You all definitely helped make this story stronger.

To Xavier Comas at Cover Kitchen, thank you so much for designing a truly awesome cover. Sometimes depression can make a person feel like the sun is falling from the sky.

There were a lot of people who were instrumental in getting *Sunshine is Forever* to where it is now, and I can't thank them all, but I do want to specifically thank Avalon Marissa Radys, Angela Melamud, Eric Geron, Olivia Croom, Kristen DeVore, Caleb Horst, Paul Goggin, Daniel Chase, Jay Caughren, Scott Little, Kevin Ross, Ryan Levee, Gabriel Chu, Luke Rutz, Slade Pearce, Adam Gomolin, Thad Woodman, and everyone else at Inkshares. I also want to thank Douglas "Grey" Cowan, Elena Stofle, Ginny Bryan, Lisa Opdyke Salem, John Benjamin Hickey, Lew Temple, Jefferson White, Drew Van Acker, Jimmy Bennett, Carissa Mitchell, William Leon, Colton Newman, Jamison Stone, Alastair Luft, Fox Force Five News, the Fanhattans, Sue Smith, Chad Christopher, Jennifer Lovick, Sky Noe, Audrey Knox, Anne Delgado, Drew Van Acker Crew, and the Preacher fans for helping me promote.

I wrote this book for anyone who has ever felt down on life. Depression is as contagious as a virus at times. Maybe this story lifted your spirit, and maybe it didn't, but I hope that it touched you in some way. I ask that you share it with as many people as you can.

Continue to be yourself. Allow the world to be inspired by you.

GRAND PATRONS

Anna M. Fee
Carol S. Cowan
C. Mahlon Fraleigh
Cynthia Williams Adams
William D. Cowan
Dani Castioni
Elena Stofle
Ginny Bryan
Grey (Douglas) Cowan
Heather Jean Knight
In Loving Memory of Walter G. Cowan
James Mather
James Ray Sandison
Keela Johnson
Laura and Pete Hennings
Laure Guillaud Starring
Mark Miranda
Noah Nunnally
Pat A. Cox
Patricia Scott
Shad D. Adair
Victoria Botsford

INKSHARES

INKSHARES is a reader-driven publisher and producer based in Oakland, California. Our books are selected not by a group of editors, but by readers worldwide.

While we've published books by established writers like *Big Fish* author Daniel Wallace and *Star Wars: Rogue One* scribe Gary Whitta, our aim remains surfacing and developing the new author voices of tomorrow.

Previously unknown Inkshares authors have received starred reviews and been featured in *The New York Times*. Their books are on the front tables of Barnes & Noble and hundreds of independents nationwide, and many have been licensed by publishers in other major markets. They are also being adapted by Oscar-winning screenwriters at the biggest studios and networks.

Interested in making your own story a reality? Visit Inkshares.com to start your own project or find other great books.